LONG EYES
and Other Stories

The Complete Collection

by Jeff Carlson

International bestselling author
of *Plague Year* and *The Frozen Sky*

Other Books by
Jeff Carlson

Interrupt

The Europa Series
The Frozen Sky
Betrayed
Blindsided
Battlefront

The Plague Year Trilogy
Plague Year
Plague War
Plague Zone

Movie Scripts
Plague Year: The Screenplay
Shadow Of The Living Dead

Short Story Collection
Long Eyes

Advance Praise For
Long Eyes and Other Stories

"Striking."
—*Locus Online*

"Exciting."
—*SF Revu*

"Chilling and dangerous."
—*HorrorAddicts.net*

"Plenty of old-school sensawunda."
—*Futurismic.com*

"Inventive and always well-observed."
—Nick Mamatas, author of *Sensation*
and *Move Under Ground*

"Wild."
—*Tangent Online*

"Captivating. This collection packs a lot
of adventure and excitement."
—*BookBanter.net*

Praise for
The Frozen Sky

"I'm hooked."
—Larry Niven, *New York Times*
bestselling author of *The Fate of Worlds*

"A first-rate adventure set in one of our solar
system's most fascinating places. Carlson is a fine
storyteller, and this is his best book yet."
—Allen Steele, Hugo Award-winning
author of the *Coyote* series

"Pulse pounding."
—*Publishers Weekly*

"Tense."
—*Locus Magazine*

"Nothing short of amazing."
—David Marusek, Sturgeon Award-winning
author of *The Wedding Album*

"Believable and compelling. This is the perfect eerie
setting for Carlson to flex his creative muscle."
—*Bookworm Blues*

Praise for *Plague Year*

"An epic of apocalyptic fiction: harrowing, heartfelt, and rock-hard realistic."
—James Rollins, *New York Times* bestselling author of *Bloodline*

"Terrifying."
—Scott Sigler, *New York Times* bestselling author of *Nocturnal*

"Chilling and timely."
—*RT Book Reviews*

"Jeff Carlson packs riveting storytelling with a lot of fresh ideas."
—David Brin, *New York Times* bestselling author of *Existence*

"One of the best apocalyptic novels I've read. Part Michael Crichton, a little Stephen King, and a lot of good writing...Carlson makes it all seem plausible and thrilling."
—*Quiet Earth* (www.quietearth.us)

Praise for *Plague War*

Finalist for the Philip K. Dick Award

"Compelling. His novels take readers
to the precipice of disaster."
—*San Francisco Chronicle*

"Intense."
—*SF Reviews*

"Excellent."
—*SF Scope*

"A breakneck ride through one of the deadliest
and thrilling futures imagined in years.
Jeff Carlson has the juice!"
—Sean Williams, *New York Times* bestselling
author of *Star Wars: The Force Unleashed*

Praise for *Plague Zone*

"Gripping. An epic struggle among desperate nations equipped with nano weapons."
—Jack McDevitt, Nebula Award-winning author of *Firebird*

"A high-octane thriller at the core—slick, sharp, and utterly compelling."
—Steven Savile, international bestselling author of *Silver*

"I can't wait for the movie."
—*Sacramento News & Review*

"This installment opens with a jolt. If you love dark SF, you can't go wrong with Carlson's great Plague trilogy."
—*Apex Magazine*

Table of Contents

For John and Ben
who have great vision of their own

INTRODUCTION

THIS IS THE book nobody wanted me to publish — nobody except the fans.

These days, corporate New York has zero interest in short fiction collections except from the most successful authors. I'm merely successful, not a major brand name, so this book has been a long time in the making.

I'm even more excited about it because of the wait.

Not too long ago, short fiction collections were a staple of science fiction and fantasy. Growing up, I tore through 'em like a dingo feeds on human babies. Each collection served up a juicy pile of ideas, never lingering, always moving, banging on your brain like a bell. John Varley. Joe Haldeman. Heinlein. Asimov.

I'm fourth generation sf. My great-grandmother built her library around Frank L. Baum's *Oz* series, the original fantasy epic. She passed those beautiful hardcover editions to her son, my grandfather, who kept them alongside "Doc" E.E. Smith novels such as *Lensmen* and *The Galactic Patrol*, which were the cutting edge in his own time.

Later, when I was a boy, my grandfather introduced me to the world's first media tie-ins like *Han Solo's Revenge* and *Splinter Of The Mind's Eye*. This was not a man who sneered at popular good fun. He hooked me with *Star Wars* books, then fed my new addiction with the classics.

At the same time, my father was bringing home doorstoppers like *The Hobbit* and *Clan Of The Cave Bear*, which, yes, reads very much like alternate history.

This was mind-croggling stuff for a young boy. Obviously it warped me badly. Look at me now!

"Long Eyes" includes all of my short fiction from my earliest sales to several appearances in the top venues in the field.

If a novel is a loaded rifle, a short story is a single bullet. It needs to hit its target perfectly. As a writer, you love 'em and leave 'em. That's a very different experience than sinking fourteen months into a novel, but it's also the sweet taste of freedom. Running from idea to idea is a pleasure.

These stories feature aliens, clones, diseases, and disasters, but you'll also find a bit of the supernatural and the psychotic. Following each story, I've also included an afterword discussing each story's circumstances or inspiration.

It's a tasty stew. I hope it makes your head explode.

NOW ONTO THE title story...

Jeff Carlson

LONG EYES

THE SHIP TURNED to investigate and Clara tried to override, not because she wasn't curious but because she was still *Homo sapiens* in every way that mattered. It frightened her to lose control. But the men and women who'd agreed to invest in her had also invested in the top intelligence designers, and the central computer would not relinquish its orders.

Clara was bound deeply to the ship, so deeply that in one sense she was only another part of it, a human-shaped component in a cradle of gel and splice-wire. The complex nerves of her forearms and vertebrae were joined to plastic, metal, and glassware. She felt and influenced all systems directly — all except this one separate mind.

Their battle was quiet and careful until Clara determined that the central computer was most vulnerable during the corrective burns. The nav program was a doorway between them, and she tried to shut it down. She tried to make it run long. No luck. The cool orange K-star was just too close for the ship to ignore, and even Clara stared in enchantment as they approached the shadows of this system's comet cloud.

Maybe too soon, she stopped fighting and joined her skills with the ship. Dodging their way in through the outer system would be weeks of rapid math. It became a new contest and the adrenaline was good, but Clara still added a dirty word to the ship's reports when it cast a tightbeam back toward home.

THE DARK AND the cold were her friends. More than anything Clara liked to be able to *see*, so light and atmosphere were only complications — light because it blinded her telescopes, air because it distorted. Before her third nameday, she'd also realized that living in one place had limits. She preferred to drift. She was good at it. She was rich for it.

She was a failed experiment, a parentless child of the state, grown *ex utero*, originally gene-crafted to be an asteroid mining dock controller, stacking ore and fuel pods in complex micro orbits, guiding slowboats in and out of the cluster. At first that had been a challenge, then only repetitive.

She'd left home six hundred years ago — six hundred years by herself, jetting away from known space, peering ahead and to all sides with fantastic eyes. The administration had been generous. They regretted what they'd made of her. They gave her the ram ship she wanted. Of course, the vast reach of macroscopes made any explorer almost irrelevant, except that in time she would gain new angles and the chance, here and there, for closer analysis. Her freedom came with a price. They'd programmed the central computer to report on a set list of potentially habitable systems first, all very similar G- and K-class stars. Clara didn't mind. She was doing exactly what she wanted, feeding imagery to her weird brain, as big as everything within range of her long eyes.

She was never lonely. If she needed noise, if she wanted other thoughts, there was always a signal to tap. Almost always. And in those rare zones where communications were sunk or blocked, bent by a sun or degraded by dust, the computer had millions of hours of radio traffic on record.

At a fraction of lightspeed, Clara wouldn't truly be outside the sphere of human activity for centuries to come. So she slept. She slept a lot. The ship went through its self-repairs and it did its work on her as well — and each time she woke, she was met by a new feast of colors and living shapes, the clockwork of stars all pulling on each other, halos of rock and ice. She wanted to go on forever. But she had also come to realize, too late, that she shouldn't have been so trusting.

THEY WERE 17.7 light-years beyond the nearest recorded colony. Clara could not sell information for food or hardware or sex. She could get software patches, however, which could be the keys to reprogram the computer core. Keys to freedom.

She had one more chance to fight as the ship moved inward past a gas super giant, readjusting its course again, but Clara didn't struggle. She put her energy into maps and sims instead. Unfortunately, the remainder of this system was just two inner planets and some groupings of comets falling through and back. There was nothing valuable except the second planet, a brown-and-black rock with a crude atmosphere.

Recalibrating her eyes for close-in analysis was both painful and a delight. Physically painful. Extreme adjustments took sweat and discomfort, but her reward was that she became this world's demigod, aware of every dust mote, able to gauge the poetry of its winds and its lopsided mantle and the hot echoing pockets within its surface.

The oxygen content the ship had locked onto was barely a wisp. Clara didn't wonder that it had been detected at all—her eyes were that powerful — but was it exploitable? Could human beings ever walk on this planet? If she drew down ten thousand comet impacts before she left, slamming more water into the environment, could she kick-start a terraforming effort that might almost become livable before anyone else arrived?

There was a lot of money and clout to be had just in the possibility, and something else she hadn't thought she wanted. Redemption. Clara was happy with the choices she had made, but she was still a woman who'd turned her back on everyone she knew.

This would be a way to reconnect. In a sense, it was almost a way to bring them with her. She hadn't thought that idea would feel so good, and she wasn't sure she liked it. She added a whole string of curse words to the ship's next tightbeam, but she was laughing, too.

"First of all," she said, "you can name it after me."

CLARA RAN A hundred orbits and mostly learned only new questions. The planet's surface was barren. Mold, lichen, and weeds grew here and there, but not enough to explain the fragile, swirling atmosphere or the animal methane.

There was life, but where? Clara sounded the pockets in the mantle but was frustrated by their number. Even the obvious air leaks — the warm storms and bleeds from underground — were little help. All of these were volcanic gases. Twice she isolated vents that also held traces of biological material, but both paths back inward were an impossible maze of fractures and cave-ins.

EVERYWHERE THE MANTLE was breaking. This planet had a weak core and only three-quarters Earth gravity. It had bubbled. Along the equator, in fact, one clump of hollows ran six hundred kilometers wide.

Some of these pockets were self-contained, forever dark and still. Some held or shared small oceans, or had at one time. That seemed promising, but the sulfur content in many was stifling and lethal. Most were empty. Clara's imaging was a busy song of pinpoints and caverns. Each resonated in its own way, holding anything from a few millibars of air to gluey salt sludge.

A huge crater gaped near one edge of the equatorial maze, a fourteen-kilometer bubble that had collapsed eons ago. Clara dubbed it the Kitchen Sink. It had everything thrown in except what she really wanted—positive proof. Dark weeds covered its ragged floor, thriving on outgassing and water vapor. The walls of the pit both protected it from the wind and held the heat of the sun. So she watched. She waited. There were also bugs in the Sink, hardshell creatures no bigger than her fingernail. Some ate leaves. Some ate the others.

The ship wanted to go down.

"No," Clara said, speaking aloud what she only needed to signal.

The muscles in her back rippled as if to turn and run. Would she win a battle for control? The ship's designers had clearly given it more autonomy than they told her.

It cited reasons for landing. Good reasons. They needed samples. They could never know, only by scanning, if the chemical makeup of this ecology held threats too vicious to overcome. For example, there was a viral assembly on Ceti IV that hadn't touched the first colonists but destroyed the second generation, leaving them with eight hundred blind, idiot children. For all its stubbornness, even the central computer knew there was no point wasting more time here if this planet held something just as deadly.

Clara compromised, hoping to placate the machine. She brought them into synchronous orbit above the Sink and began to build a small probe in her nanoforge, using up precious steel and rubber. In the meantime she turned all eyes on the bugs. She ran simulations based on observable metabolic activity. She war-gamed human DNA against incomplete models.

She found another ship.

IT WAS HARDLY even wreckage. It had been stripped down to the hull, and much of that was missing too. What remained was half-buried, separated in a landslide. Clara only spotted it because she was running extremely tight grids.

The broken framework was old — older than her. Alien? The bounty on a find like that would be incredible. Humankind had yet to meet another thinking species. Even bacteria and bugs were rare. More likely it was one of the turn-of-the-millennia seed ships that had gone missing, or a religious group or privateers or just about anybody.

There was heat-warped debris abandoned in the strata around the tail. Had there been an internal explosion? Perhaps they'd impacted with some bit of cosmic junk — but it looked like they'd managed a controlled landing. All dead now. They hadn't even made much of a go of it, or Clara would have seen the evidence weeks before. Even just a few stragglers lost in the caves would have lit up on X-ray or deep red by now, much less a real, thriving outpost.

Clara was mad at herself for feeling relieved. What if she needed rescuing someday? Would she deserve it?

SHE STALLED THE ship with busy work for nineteen days before it got weird. The computer began triple-confirming even routines like meals and exercise and finally Clara gave up, sleepless and uneasy, caught in a rut of doubt. It was awful to distrust her home.

They touched down on the largest slab of rock that she could find, even though it was two kilometers from the wreckage and wet with puddling and ice. They massed only four tons, but Clara was leery of the jags and cracking across the crater floor. She preferred to deal with the slick rime of mud. Even on this plug of granite they might trigger a quake, and Clara wasted more than a minute of fuel letting her jets run, ready to fly again in an instant.

At the same time there was a frenzy among the bugs — a sudden, spiraling frenzy. She'd vaporized most of the pond, and a thick fog swept away from the ship, lifting on the heat of the jets, falling in the cold—and within the fog, the bugs mated and fed. Weeds exploded with spores or slumped apart, revealing strong blossoms like tongues. She should have expected it. Almost any disturbance here was a wealth of energy, and the ecosystem was ravenous. Good. Clara had no intention of venturing outside, and this should convince the ship that she'd already risked enough. She tried to imagine one footstep out there. Motion, noise, the faintest heat of friction — the bugs would swarm. Even the plants might attack with nettles or oils. She couldn't be sure what might damage a pressure suit. The ship was unrelenting in its priorities, but it needed her. It deferred to her, so long as she kept after its goals.

They lobbed their first probe at the wreckage and found nothing conclusive. Meanwhile they shot a dozen self-contained labs into the mud and through the air, busy little boxes full of chem tests. Clara enjoyed the work. Everything here was new and fascinating, and still at a safe distance. Only radio messages came back inside.

The gremlins appeared on the second night, a running, shifting mass of small bodies. Mammals. In infrared they burned hot on her screens, and Clara smiled and flexed. Her hand was exactly the same size as one of the creatures, and she waggled her fingers, mimicking their wire-limbed scramble across the rocky crater.

"There you are," she said. How deep must they live inside the cave systems to have escaped her previous scans? And how many more of them could there be?

They were scavengers, tough and nasty, with a constant jerk of claws-to-mouth. They uprooted weeds and hives in a furious, haphazard path that had its own sense.

With every sunset there was a severe drop in temperature. The plants reacted first. Some curled shut. Some exuded pigment as an insulator. The bugs fled into their burrows and then the air began to stir. Clara found it beautiful, but of course she was immune inside her ship.

A dance of cold swept the crater. On the surface above, the freeze was much worse — ripping winds and knives of dust. Cyclones reached down into the Sink but were countered by thermals and radiant heat, a dynamic in six directions.

The air was not breathable, not outside the mist that formed as the atmosphere separated into layers and tendrils. The fog she'd broiled from the pond had been warm and white. These channels of air were nearly invisible, chill against the ground, and she assumed the gremlins could see in infrared or were at least highly cold sensitive. Occasionally they edged in and out of the globs of breathable air, but in places they had to leave these safe zones. In many places there were gaps.

The gremlins were bipeds, thick in the back and belly. Big lungs. Big stomachs. They either gorged or starved.

They were stalking her.

The realization went through Clara like a seizure. *They're working their way to the ship. They've been doing it from the start.* Edging back and forth through the swirls and dead-ends of the storm, the pack had already closed within two hundred meters. A short dash. Even if the pocket they were following continued to sweep away from her, as it was doing, they could survive that distance. She had seen them go farther.

But then what? Surely they wouldn't risk it unless there was breathable air around her, and even then what could they do? Claws on steel.

There were eighteen of them. They scrabbled too fast for Clara's eyes, but her systems had already detailed and profiled each one. They were smart little hairballs. Organized. Their leader kept scouts to four sides of the group, and these guards constantly ranged out and back again as the pack surged and split apart and re-formed, flowing with and between the available air.

Clara readied a batch of nano tags but didn't fire. Her tracer-recorders would only sting, bonding with skin and muscle, but she'd wait until the gremlins had gone most of the way back to their holes. Otherwise they might see the flash of her microcannons, and she didn't want to provoke them, didn't want them to associate the darts with her.

How smart were they really? Her mikes and subsystems said they did not have language, only the most basic grunts, although their gestures approached a speech equivalent. That made sense. They lived in a world where there wasn't always air to breathe... and maybe there were predators in the dark of the caves, listening, always listening.

Clara stared at a freeze-frame of the leader's face. For an instant her mind felt as still as the calm around the ship. Then all of the ideas lurking around her crashed together and she initiated her fusion engines.

Get out of here, she thought.

The gremlins' hair distorted but did not exaggerate the size of their braincases, and radar confirmed that their body fur had been trimmed in distinct ways, apparently stylized as well as grown out for warmth and protection. Their eyes were evolved for daylight.

They had opposable thumbs and carried flecks of granite in hand.

They were on the verge of civilization, and Clara understood that this is what scared her most.

Get out.

But the ship countermanded her start-up, no less than four safety features blocking her intent. Clara flinched and went to emergency override. Blocked again.

A new current of air swept across her position, and the gremlins jumped into it, rushing the ship. Clara fired her nano tags in a single burst, wanting only to scare them. More than thirty percent missed or reported suboptimal placement. The rest squawked with data but barely slowed the pack. Then they were on her.

Clara screamed. "Aaaaaa—"

Her voice was such a lonely thing. Somehow that caught and centered her. She had no one else to rely on. She twitched within her box of gel and wire, lighting up all systems. There were no anti-personnel defenses, but if she could outfox the ship she could lift off and that would kill the little monsters, suffocate or bake or pop them. And she had the nanoforge. She could build a cat's claw if she just had the time.

But the gremlins found a seam where her cannons had opened and then another on her belly. They abandoned the first and threw themselves against the new crack in a kicking, hanging mass. They bent back the low-weight alumalloy.

Too late the ship realized the danger. Too late it dumped its protocols and gave her control. The gremlins were already inside, squeezing and twisting through any available space, repair panels, ductwork, delivery shunts. They ruptured the ship's innards like a climbing shouting cancer.

They were human.

"Can you understand me?" Clara put her words through the ship with docking radios and sonar, hysterical now. She needed to convey her fear if nothing else.

They were human. The data was clear. Clara didn't want to

believe it, but the burst from the nano tags was unmistakable. Despite every adaptation these monsters were human beings — and that would make it easier to hunt them.

She tried again. "Stop! Stop! We can talk!" But at the same time she was designing a nerve gas in her forge.

They tore through the ship without purpose, bypassing the diagnostic web that let her track them, ripping into the circuitry of a macroscope instead. It was pointless. It was ... No. Their goal here was the same as it had been out among the weeds. They were not attacking an enemy. They were plundering an unexpected resource.

"Stop!" Clara yelled.

They were savages. Even if they escaped with as much gear as they could carry, even if they ruined the ship and then slowly pulled its guts out piece by piece, the metals and wiring and everything else would only be sharper knives, better ropes, whatever stupid things they could fashion.

"This is your last chance," she said. "Please! Please."

She charged the lines of the macroscope and electrocuted three of them. She also sealed her box an instant before she dispersed her toxin, shutting off her own air, flooding the ship. It was a miniature storm within the night outside.

Thrashing, the gremlins did more damage.

Then it was still.

Clara felt too wild to mourn, but she closed her eyes briefly. Eighteen of them dead... an entire hunting party... Had she just doomed however many others were still in the caves by killing their strongest and smartest out here?

The ship urgently needed repair bots, yet Clara had no trouble convincing it to build a cat's claw first, a whip-fast centipede with articulate saws, both to remove the little bodies and to defend themselves until they were spaceworthy again.

She made sure she had command. Then she sent it to drill out the ship's computer core.

CLARA STAYED ANOTHER year, in orbit, following the gremlins with probes and nano tags. She invaded every tribe and secret, and quickly confirmed her initial reports.

They were as human as any gene-craft like herself. Even with their drastic changes they carried enough baseline DNA to vote and hold an inheritance if those privileges had meant anything in this place.

There was no telling how many generations it had been since their forefathers changed them. The seed ship must have been so badly damaged that even a partially hospitable world seemed like a godsend. This biosphere contained a few odd sugars, but there was nothing poisonous here, and a colonist could probably step right outside and subsist for a lifetime. The problem was how many lives — how few people could subsist. The scarcity of air, water, and food was an impassable limit.

One ancestor had had the vision to see what was impossible and what was not, the long eyes to look past how much would be sacrificed and push for what was best. Before they depleted whatever resources they had left, before their only chance was gone, they'd created a new breed of sons and daughters.

Clara had more in common with these survivors than anyone would think at a glance. Imagination. Grit. The solitude of being different. Yes, the gremlins had lost some of their intelligence with their size. Clara supposed that was a mistake or an unexpected side effect... but they were gaining it back.

They were packrats. They still had most of their ravaged ship down inside the caves, guarding its steel and plastics, thieving from each other, trading with each other, no longer aware of what use these substances might be except as money or superior tools. But on some level they remembered what they had been.

They were people in every way that counted. They cultivated mold as crops. They stacked walls of rock to make reservoirs where steam or runoff was available. The gremlins lived and bred and died, exploring, growing, failing, and succeeding, and ultimately Clara could not bring herself to betray them. This world was worth far more than she could ever spend, but she needed so little and the ship was completely hers now.

She could not rescue them. She could only ruin them. The arrival of normal men might be inevitable, but she could buy them time. Centuries. Would that be long enough for them to regain their intelligence and meet normal men as equals, no matter how small?

Maybe not.

Maybe they were too little to ever be very bright, but the chance was there, so for twelve months Clara forged medicine and tools and books and dropped these supplies to the crater floor. Meanwhile she broadcast her carefully drawn lies back toward known space:

Biohazard. This is an unstable, low-atmosphere world seething with acid bacteria.

Clara put a beacon in orbit to repeat the warning forever. Then she left the pocket planet and followed after her own vision again.

END

Afterword

A lot of the stories I write are present-day tech thrillers — situations that could happen tomorrow — but I've always been a fan of big, sprawling science fiction with interstellar wars, vast gulfs of time, and mind-croggling ideas.

The inspiration for "Long Eyes" was a Golden Age story by James Blish, one of the grand masters. He wrote a novelette called "Surface Tension." Now this was the kind of sci fi written back in the day when the men had steely jaws and the women tended to be wasp-waisted, helpless bimbos except for the hot, feisty redheads who could handle a knife as well as any adventurer. I like to think "Long Eyes" isn't so corny, but it shares some of the major themes of Blish's "Surface Tension," which are loneliness, despair, adaptability, and determination.

Human beings have the ability to overcome nearly any obstacle using their intelligence and their grit. If you've read my *Plague Year* novels, you know these are qualities that interest me.

Crashing a ship on an alien planet is a good way to put people in a fix. Unless you're on TV or in the movies, which present an incredibly simplified view of the galaxy, our species is unlikely to find anywhere that's as hospitable as Earth. We're well-suited to our planet. Even our bitterest landscapes like Antarctica or Death Valley are almost certain to prove more pleasant than the softest environments on an alien world.

I'm not talking about giant monsters with teeth. I mean more subtle problems.

An alien meadow may have Bambi and lush flowers, but there will be nasty parasites and toxins hidden in the grass.

That lovely alien beach? Scalding levels of sodium chloride. Or worms or bacteria.

Safe in my office, these are fun scenarios to play with. For me, writing is a lot like a good game of chess, except I'm not only playing both sides, I'm also the board. When it works well, it's gratifying. So I try to back my characters into corners just to figure out how they're going to escape.

The heroes of "Surface Tension" found themselves in a place so bad, their only way out was to stop being themselves. That's not just a good game of chess, it also speaks to everything which makes us human. I admire that level of storytelling. It's what I strive for in my own work.

PRESSURE

THEY SAID I wouldn't feel a thing, but my dreams were awful — pain and tightness, smothering weight, none of which overcame my excitement. I also dreamed of flying, dreamed that I dove right through the ground and smashed into a spectacular new universe, yet I caught only glimpses of brightness before my eyes ruptured and abrasive rock crammed through my mouth and sinus cavities.

The mind persists in making sense of things, even when drugged and unconscious. It remembers.

Waking was the real nightmare. I had no face, I weighed too little, and raw swelling in my throat choked my voice.

The bite of a needle on one leg helped center me even before the tranquilizer took hold. I stopped thrashing and understood that I was submerged in a tank not much larger than myself. I knew it was a horizontal rectangle, knew I was in its middle — yet I had no eyes. Could my hearing be acute enough to measure distance? There wasn't time to sort through my senses. The ponderous blood-weight of the tranquilizer could not subdue the breathing reflex and I dug at the water with every limb, moving up, *up* —

A hard ceiling punched into the smooth metal protrusions of my face before I reached a surface. There was no air. But I could not drown. I snorted water through the generous filter plate where my nose had been, then expelled a shocking pocket of liquid through the gills beneath my armpits.

For a moment I did nothing more than breathe, feeling each exhalation against my elbows. I almost touched my face, hesitated, then grew interested in my hands and brought them together. The index fingers and thumbs felt no different but my other digits were thicker, longer, webbed.

"Garcia?" Stenstrom's voice was too loud in the VLF transceiver buried high in my cheekbone, distorted by the mumble of other people around him. "How do you feel?"

I thought I heard the vibrations of his enthusiastic tone directly as well, dulled by the water and walls of my tank. They'd told me the recovery tank would be glass and I imagined his entire research team all around my naked body, bristling with recorders and palmtops, every face intent.

Andrea had always giggled when we skinny-dipped together, watchful for neighbors but emboldened by each other's daring, in the early days when we lived at her parents' house in San Diego. Before she got pregnant. "Shark!" she'd whisper, and grab for me. I can be a pensive son of a bitch and her teasing, her smiles, had always been what I needed most.

The thought of her now helped me ignore my embarrassment.

My scrotum had been tucked away, my penis shortened, protective measures that Stenstrom's people swore were reversible, like all of the surgeries and implants. I had that in writing and an eight figure insurance policy to back it, but there's not a man in the world who wants to be cut in that area, no matter the compensation.

"Garcia?" Stenstrom raised his volume painfully.

Answering, I almost swallowed a mouthful of water. Despite all of my training, subvocalizing into a throat mike was very different after the changes reinforcing my mouth and neck. Eating would be a chore.

I croaked, "Drop volume!"

Stenstrom was apologetic. "Is this better?"

"Down, down. Lots."

"You're more sensitive than we expected, apparently. Any other immediate difficulties?"

I kicked through a tight somersault. "Feel great!"

MY PRIDE WAS my savior, my source of endurance.

I spent the longest five weeks of my life in that tank and in a deeper pool, healing, testing, practicing. My feet and toes had been augmented much like my hands, my thighs shortened to maximize the available muscle. I was damned quick. Relearning construction techniques with my new fingers was sometimes frustrating, yet my progress was real and those periods of solitary labor became important to me.

At the surface, in the shallows, doctors poked and prodded and put me through redundant tortures. I had been warned that the study of my new body would be extensive and I did my best not to fear or hate them, but I'd never imagined such intense scrutiny. During my years as a SEAL, I had been like a bug under a microscope, constantly evaluated and scored. Here I *was* the microscope, my body the only lens through which they could measure their work.

Stenstrom tried to be my buddy, as he had always tried, joking and asking what I'd do with the money, yet his possessiveness was obvious. "We'll be famous," he said. "We'll change the world."

I wasn't a slave or a pet, exactly, but I was anxious to get started — to get away from them.

The project had almost selected someone else, a loudmouth much better at politicking than me, but the job would mostly be done alone and they must have thought he'd break without an audience.

I'm sure my Navy files indicated no problems of that nature. I'm the private type, happiest diving or surfing with my laughing Andrea or teaching our boys to swim, feeling my heartbeat, finding the perfect ride, the perfect moment, away from other people and their squabbles and protest marches. I've never understood the urge to merge, never wanted to add my opinions to the bubbling stew of e-media or buy five minutes of fame on iBio. For me, a mob holds no power, no point. Running in circles won't improve the economy, clean the environment, or affect the East Asian guerrilla wars in any way. Hard work is the answer. Honor. Persistence. A willingness to take risks.

The project offered all that and more.

I had to relearn how to chew and swallow, a slow process but strangely more flavorful. Stenstrom said that was only because of the premium foods they'd secured for me, but I had eaten well occasionally in the past and decided my improved palate must be a side effect of the surgeries that had strengthened my jaw and lips. Could taste buds be sensitized?

Learning to see again was also a challenge. From old research with dolphins and orcas, Stenstrom knew better than to surround me with smooth walls. Many of those captives had gone insane over time. That wasn't a concern here, but they didn't want my brain to establish its new neural patterns in wrong or confused ways. Before activating my sonar receptors, which used ultra low frequencies far below my improved range of hearing, they put me in the deeper, irregularly shaped pool.

It was beautiful. I'd lost color but the textures were vivid, stark, each shape imposing. My receptors could also see normally but had no better than 20/600 vision in that mode, which I'd use only for close-up work and to read instrumentation.

I chose complete blindness when calling my family. Rather than face a showphone, I let a computer read and type for me, my throat mike patched into a voder. Site management had encouraged me to limit our exchanges to text only, which was easier to encrypt — and who knew what seven- and four-year-old boys would make of some stiff-mouthed monster claiming to be their father? Brent had only stopped referring to me as "step-dad" a short time ago, and Roberto was still young enough to forget me. The portrait we'd had done before I left was not an image that I wanted to disturb, even though I had been caught in mid-blink and Andrea's smile looked forced, too large.

"I'm doing great, hon, how are the boys?" I asked.

Her response came in stuttering groups of syllables, all emotion masked by the machine: "I used part of the advance money to buy a DFender for our apartment."

It almost seemed like she was having a different conversation.

"Why bother?" I asked. "The house should be ready soon." Smart alarms cost thousands of dollars — just a speck of what I'd earn, but the money was supposed to last the rest of our lives.

"We're still here in the meantime," she said.

The boys gave me no chance to brood over the resentment that seemed so clear in her words. Maybe I only imagined it. "Are you in the ocean yet how far down can you go?" one of them babbled, without first identifying himself, and other said, "Greenpeace rated you a top ten on the widecast yesterday!"

Brent and Roberto both took after their mother. They were rambunctious little monkeys, and gave me the praise and enthusiasm I'd expected. I hadn't realized that Brent could type so fast. The voder spoke his questions much more smoothly than anything Andrea had sent.

Somehow, technical sketches of my surgeries and gear had leaked onto the net. I even had fan clubs with names like Cyborg.org and zMerman. The boys hoped for an exclusive and I decided it was better to play along and celebrate my alienness. I promised to bring them both mementos when I returned. By then, security should have loosened enough for me to take home a few small bits of hardware, something for them to put on a shelf or carry in their pockets.

When Andrea came back on, she was encouraging but brief. "Six hundred four to go," the voder said for her, but I didn't know how to answer. I had lost track of the days left until my contract was up, knowing how long it would be.

"Love you," I rasped, and the computer carried my inadequate words away.

MAPPING THE OCEAN floor was the greatest thrill of my life. Most people probably would have considered it tedious, gliding through a quiet, monochromatic world, but then the only way to get a rise out of most people is to batter them with kaleidoscopes of music, breasts, and talking heads — or to turn off the net and TV. The worst riots always occurred during the rotating brownouts.

Oil and coal were fast becoming memories, and incredible advances in solar power had come to nothing, due to greenhouse clouds and the megatonnage of dirt thrown into the atmosphere by the Nine Days War. With tens of thousands of people still sick from radiation poisoning, no politician would even mention new nuclear plants, and hydroelectric, biomass, and wind generators weren't enough to keep civilization chugging along without interruption.

Aro Corp. had the answer. For months now, crews had been scouting various locales with buoys and remote operated vehicles. The tiny Japanese island of Miyake-jima, dead south of Tokyo Bay, was deemed perfect for political as well as economic reasons. Miyake-jima belonged to an underwater ridge that extended from the Japanese mainland directly into the Pacific current, and its steep southern slope offered powerful updrafts in addition to the normal ocean tides. Aro Corp. planned to build a field of turbines as deep as five hundred feet, using cutting edge technologies like me.

Normal divers max out at three hundred feet and can't remain there long in any case. My surgeries eliminated the need for air tanks. More importantly, a gel solution had been suffused through my bloodstream and organs to protect me from compression.

In addition to performing final, hands-on site inspections, I was also conducting field tests of myself. Before creating other "mods," Aro Corp. wanted to see if unforeseen problems would arise, physical, mental, or emotional.

I was glad for the test period. In three months I would become a teacher and a foreman, caged by responsibility. Meanwhile I explored natural altars of rock and coral, spread my arms to ride rip-currents, and chased quick clouds of fish. One morning I caught a yellowtail. Its buttery flavor was complemented well by sour kelp, and I began to forage instead of eating only from the tubes on my food belt — secretly, truly making myself a part of this environment. The work itself was more fun than difficult, placing beacons and running spot checks on our communications net. The attenuation of radio waves is very high in salt water, even for the military band VLF signals that Aro Corp. had leased from the U.S. Navy. They wanted to be sure they could always reach me, but there were dead areas within the construction zone. During the first twenty days, we added five more relays than they'd originally allowed for in the budget, three on the sea floor, plus two additional surface buoys whose anchoring tethers also functioned as antennae.

The grid was set. The smaller boats that had helped me through this initial stage were replaced by a barge, capable of lowering heavier and larger gear. The first steel cradles for the turbine mounts were coming down.

For a country that had been almost entirely nuclear-powered for decades, Japan had a wretched safety record, averaging two and a half accidents per year. Worse, loss of containment at eleven reactors during the war had done more damage than North Korean missiles. They were desperate for a solution.

Aro Corp. hoped to rev up a quad of turbines as soon as possible, not so much to offset costs but to prove to critics and nervous investors that the idea was fundamentally sound. The complete project, involving hundreds of turbines, channelers, and land-based transformers, wouldn't be finished for four years — and of course Aro Corp. hoped construction would continue for most of the century as they developed other locations around the globe.

I worked nine- and ten-hour shifts, sometimes arguing with Stenstrom when he wanted me to come in. I'm no hero. I was angling for a bonus.

My gung-ho attitude was also based on the fact that my camp on the lee side of Miyake held little appeal. Sleep was always welcome, but any messages the boys had sent tended to make me feel lonely, and then there was nothing to do but wait and brood, composing inarticulate letters to Andrea that I usually deleted.

I was tired when my robot tug brought me to deeper water east of the island. We'd completed inspection of the last sites a week early and the engineers wanted back-up options.

As I kicked away from the tug, a familiar thrill shot through my exhaustion. Beyond this shelf, the sea floor plunged away for *miles*. This place was like another planet, strange and new, and I was the very first.

The squid didn't hesitate. Its only predators were much larger and shaped differently than me. As I drifted into range, holding a small mapping computer to my face, the giant latched onto my left elbow and biceps with its two longer, grasping tentacles. Just weeks before, I might have yelled. But in this world there was nobody who could come to help.

I tried to kick away. No good.

Its eight regular arms spread in a horrible, ash-yellow blossom. When I switched to sonar the squid seemed even larger, backed by a spotty, rising cloud of silt.

I dropped my computer, bumping one of the squid's closing arms. It hesitated, grabbing the small device, but at the same time the pair of stronger tentacles around my left arm reflexively increased their grip. My armor tore open. So did the softer muscle beneath. Blood squirted out in diffuse threads and I was lucky not to suffer a stroke, but too frantic to realize it at the time.

My fletchette gun was holstered on my left forearm, beneath the tentacles. I groped for the knife strapped to my leg, but another of the squid's arms brushed my foot, then seized hold, and I yanked my free hand away before it was also trapped.

"Garcia! Garcia!" Stenstrom's voice felt like part of the adrenaline-pulse throbbing through my head.

I kicked not away from the squid but into it, winning slack from its tentacles, using this moment of freedom to twist sideways. Its arms closed in. My face and left arm led toward the monster's hard, gaping beak. Then my free hand found the gun and squeezed off three-quarters of a magazine, tearing open the back of my left ring finger.

The squid nearly exploded. Its shattered beak seemed to keep opening, spilling flecks of torn innards. The convulsing tentacles yanked my shoulder from its socket and peeled away more armor and skin, but another burst of fletchettes freed me and I swam away.

The current made restless ghosts of its gore and mine.

Consciousness faded to a glimmer, but the thought of sharks kept me swimming—

I DON'T REMEMBER the ride or the hammerheads that came after me. The shouting in my cheekbone, that much I recall. Stenstrom's panic was too intimate to forget. Trying to reload the fletchette gun with one functional arm while clinging to the tug was a monumental task. They say I did it twice, which must be why it seemed like I never finished.

The sea is no place for the weak or wounded.

ANDREA NEVER WANTED me to volunteer, not because of any danger or even because of what they'd do to me, but because it would take so long. We'd argued before, like all couples, silly stuff like who was supposed to take out the garbage, and we'd had bitter discussions after she got pregnant.

At the time I was just twenty-seven, after ten years in the strict, almost exclusively male world of Special Forces, and I had not proved myself excellent family material by butting heads with her son Brent. But until I told her that I needed to leave, we had always found a compromise. She let me name our baby after the father I'd never known — and I agreed to be more lenient with Brent, let him choose his own friends and music and clothes.

We'd never shouted before. She'd never cried before.

"We don't need this," she said, but we did. If we wanted to give Roberto and Brent the education they'd need, if we ever expected to live someplace where sirens and knifings weren't regular affairs, a chance like this was too fat to pass up.

The politicians said the recession had ended in '17, but that was news to us. The SCUBA guide business I'd started after I got out of the Navy failed almost immediately. I should have known better. The tourist trade had been flat for years and my competition, already well-established, gobbled up what little income there was to be had.

We weren't destitute. Andrea subbed as a math teacher wherever she could, we both did spot work for the Park Service, and I made wages on the docks as a mechanic and welder. But I missed the simple vacations we'd taken in the early days, surfing, kayaking. To be reduced to a life of debt, coupons, and freebies was hardly a life at all.

The real horror had been the resentment with which I'd begun to view my family, for needing so much I couldn't give.

On the day before I left, Andrea argued that I'd undervalued my soul. "Two years," she kept saying. "Don't leave us alone for two years."

"We'll talk every week," I promised.

"Two years, Carlos. The boys won't even recognize you."

STENSTROM OPTED FOR a swimsuit when he visited, which was all that I was wearing. To perform their repairs and to let me heal, the doctors had turned me into something of a surface creature again, enclosing my head in a large plastic sphere that piped in salt water, placing me on a table lined with gutters to collect my liquid exhalations. Keeping my skin damp was more complicated. The mist ducts tended to fog the room, so the doctors wore aprons and goggles and long yellow gloves.

Stenstrom had a better grasp of psychology than that.

"What can I do for you?" he asked, not bothering with *how are you* or *hello.*

"Sorry, chief."

"My fault. We should have ordered you to quit for the day. It's not like we were running late." His laugh was a goofy bird squawk that sounded fake the first time you heard it, but he was just a geek — desk belly, pale, with his fingers constantly in his hair or at his nose. "Seriously," he said. "Anything at all."

"Someone to read to me. Someone pretty."

"She can be friendly, too, if you like."

I would have thought he'd be too embarrassed. I was surprised to find that I was myself. Maybe I'd spent too much time alone out there.

My next thought was of my marriage vows, and guilt arrived late. But my first reaction was the honest one. I was basically a cripple here, and the idea of being manipulated did not excite me at all. I'd much rather masturbate, caressed and tumbled by the sea, alone with favorite memories of my wife.

"Someone to read," I repeated.

Stenstrom nodded. "What do you like, oceanography and biology, right?" Standing up, he patted the table rather than jarring me. "I'll have someone come in."

It was awfully cynical, but I couldn't help but think that he was improving at trying to make himself my friend.

I CONTACTED ANDREA days ahead of the schedule we'd set, despite an earlier decision not to worry her. Stenstrom was right. I needed friendly, female attention, and I didn't have to tell her that I'd been hurt.

She wasn't home, even though it was dinnertime. Brent answered and said she was substituting at the community college. That made me angry. I didn't understand why she'd bother with such a low-paying job, especially since she must be incredibly busy, settling into the new house, helping the boys adjust to new schools — but of course Andrea enjoyed teaching, and maybe the fact that we were rich didn't seem real to her yet.

Maybe it was good I'd missed her. Our exchanges had not been going well and I might have said something stupid. Maybe communicating over such a distance, through typed words alone, was impossible.

The boys didn't think so. During my recuperation, they peppered me with messages full of abbreviations and icons that my computer and I puzzled over. They were obviously spending more time online than they had with me around, learning new languages and modes of thought. I was pleased that they remained excited about my accomplishments, but Roberto seemed overly attached to a new interactive he'd discovered, and Brent confessed — maybe bragged? — that he had been caught in two stim sites. I admonished them both to finish their schoolwork as soon as possible each day, put the keyboard away and get outside. Go play in the mud, I said.

Returning to the ocean was unspeakably good, but my days grew more complicated as I coordinated with surface traffic, massive barges that probed the quiet dark with fat, long, phallic drills, blundering through ancient beds of sediment, polluting vast stretches of water with their shrieking as they powered down into the detritus and carbonate. New voices sprang out of my cheekbone, crowding my skull – and four new mods had come through surgery and would join me soon.

This was ultimately what I'd signed on for, and I took close note of each shift's accomplishments, but the joy that it gave me was purely intellectual and I clocked out with the surface crews rather than working overtime.

The best part of each day was making my way to and from my shelter, by myself, letting the currents and whim dictate my course, always discovering new beauty, new peace.

I think I knew what was happening back home.

MOST OF BRENT'S chatter washed over me like a familiar, soothing tide: "Club VR opened a new place downtown and I got to virt Gladiator and I could have done it twice except Uncle Mark is a bracket colon equal sign."

The computer had grown better at recognizing icons, but Brent used so many. This one meant *flathead*, I guessed, or *chicken neck* or whatever. What concerned me was his tone. Brent had once directed this same mean jealousy at me.

"Who is Uncle Mark?" I croaked, the elongated fingers of my

hand tightening into a ball.

I hit the *send* button with a fist.

"WHAT THE HELL'S going on!" I shouted, six hours later when I finally got Andrea online. "After all I'm doing for you ..."

Her response was immediate: "You did it for yourself."

I stared at the shape of the computer as if it were another squid, my thoughts layered and conflicting.

"For the fame," she continued. "The adventure."

"For the money, Andrea! I'm doing it for the money!"

"Would you have let them cut you up if they were going to turn you into a desk, Carlos? You did it for the chance to finally be a fish."

ITS PROW INTO the wind and waves, the barge lowered two turbines on cables, one off of each side. Just hoisting the house-sized cylinders from the deck and hitting the water had taken two slow, exacting hours. The descent itself required five more. During snags and rest breaks, I inspected the squat towers that would cradle the turbines, darting under and around their angled beams, even though we'd already completed our structural tests.

But there was no escaping my thoughts.

Leaving now — quitting now — would be crazy. Reverse surgery and rehab would take almost a quarter of the time left in my contract, and I'd forfeit everything but the signing bonus. We'd lose the home, our future, and find ourselves back in the city scrambling for wages.... And I would never work for Aro Corp. again in any capacity. Even their competitors would have no reason to rely on me, a hard truth that always led me back to the same worry:

Can I ever trust her again?

The weather had been cooperating, but even nineteen-ton hunks of metal will act like sails in deep currents, and close to sundown we realized there had been a miscalculation. Some pendulum swinging had been accounted for — it was a drop of four hundred feet — but instead of a near-simultaneous mounting, we had a double miss.

Each elevator platform had jets which I could use for final adjustments, but they weren't powerful enough to muscle the turbines twenty meters against the current.

"We're twenty east," I said. "Let's elevate forty. Bring 'em back up."

The nearest turbine was a smooth sculpture caught in a web of cables that led upward as far as my sonar reached. ROVs, remote operated vehicles, scooted about or hovered patiently nearby. And when I switched briefly to my fuzzy, nearsighted normal vision, the busy sea became busier, shot through with the ROVs' beams of light. All of this generated surprisingly little noise: the whirring of ROV props, the harp vibrations of the current against the cables.

The first explosion sounded like God had slapped the surface, a bass thunder that reached me an instant after the VLF net surged with voices.

"Was that the engine?"

"Fire! Fire!"

"Number two crane's lost all exterior cables—"

The last bit of information I personally witnessed as the turbine sagged in its web. If it fell, it would roll into the cradle tower and ruin weeks of hard labor.

I swam closer, thinking I might use the platform jets to keep it afloat or ease it to the bottom, but two ROVs tumbled into my path as their operators lost contact. I kicked left. One struck my scarred shoulder and numbed my arm.

I had been assigned an emergency frequency to connect me directly to Stenstrom. Would he be there? The way the ROVs had shut down, the comm room might have been destroyed. I said, "This is Garcia—"

He was near panic. "Can you stabilize number two?"

"I'm on it. What's happening?"

"We're under attack, speedboats, they're widecasting some Animal Earth crap!"

Three small cylinders lanced into the far range of my sonar, moving fast. Smart torps. They were beautiful in the way that sharks can be, sleek and purposeful, a hard swarm of warheads chased by their own turbulence.

I probably wouldn't attract their attention, not being a power source or made of metal — not much metal — but the concussive force of a detonation anywhere nearby would kill me.

I dug and kicked down, *down*—

Tightness in my bad arm made my effort lopsided, slowing me. The buzzing torpedoes grew very loud.

The rift was not deep compared to the plunging valley where I'd encountered the squid, but at its edge was a thick bulge of carbonate. I ducked past, scraping my hip.

That rock saved me by taking the brunt of the explosions, then nearly killed me as parts of it broke away. I was stunned and slow to move.

Animal Earth. The rant-and-slants they'd posted during our efforts here had been based on a refusal to accept our stated purpose. They were *Greens*. They should have supported us, but frothed instead about the blatant destruction of ocean habitats...

I stayed in the rift for two hours, watching, listening, afraid to broadcast on any channel in case there were more hunter-killers waiting to acquire targets. The attack had stopped after five minutes, but our radio communications remained incoherent. Stenstrom tried miserably to raise me on the emergency link again and again.

He tried the general frequencies, too, even sharecasting his public response to the attack. One of the speedboats had been apprehended by Japanese military aircraft, and suspects were in custody. Given the armament involved and the coordination of the assault, Stenstrom suggested that the whole thing was a cover for our competitors in the nuclear or oil industries, and already there were conflicting denials and claims of solidarity from Animal Earth spokespeople.

Finally I began my ascent, goaded by the constant dig of the voices in my cheekbone. At one hundred feet I saw a man, a body, deformed by violence and twisting loosely in the current. We hesitated together in the dim, penetrating glow of the sun.

Then I turned my back on him.

Andrea and the boys were well provided for, and she obviously didn't need me. Brent had never needed me, and Roberto... Roberto was young enough to forget and move on. Let them think I was dead, lost to the tide. The insurance payouts alone would be a fortune.

Four miles proved to be the radio's range.

I kept going into the beautiful dark and never let anyone intrude on my world again.

END

Afterword

"Pressure" is one instance where the afterword might be as much fun to write as the story itself. That's because the basic concept for this story came from a nightmare. I remember opening my eyes, scribbling happily on my notepad and thinking, *Holy cow, I am a sick puppy.*

First of all, I'm a light sleeper and sometime insomniac. Maybe worse, in the middle of the night I often think I'm awake when I'm really asleep. Then I wake up. There's a weird transition from worrying about things that only make sense in the dream state to realizing I wasn't consciously brooding about my projects, chores, and bills, I was analyzing problems and situations that aren't mine and don't actually exist.

What I brought out of this nightmare was the impression of being lost and horribly disfigured. I remembered fighting through my confusion, but I couldn't quite recall the reason for the machines that had been inserted into my face.

At the time, I had a minor head cold, so my sinuses felt raw and weird. Because I'm a light sleeper, I wear ear plugs. Because I was working a clerical job while writing my first novel in my spare hours, my wrists were shot, so I wore braces, too. Because I grind my teeth, I also pop a night guard between my teeth.

My subconscious is a war zone, man!

The head cold combined with various levels of body armor tricked my brain into imagining I was an altered man in a dark place. Changed how? Why? That sense of fear and chaos became the opening paragraphs of the story, and over the next few days I developed it more.

Here's a final secret. You probably noticed some similarity in the climatic decisions of the heroes of "Long Eyes" and "Pressure." They both choose to seek out their individual destinies instead of helping or rejoining their own kind. Partly that's because I'm not much of a joiner myself. All writers are loners to one degree or another. That's a necessary part of sitting with your thoughts hour after hour, day after day.

But in the original version of "Pressure," Carlos Garcia opted out to the Aro Corp. program long before his contract was up, forfeiting all payment in exchange for the necessary surgeries to restore him. The big reveal at the end was Andrea opening the door of their home to find him pledging to dedicate himself to their marriage and their family even if they were poor, in debt, out of work, and unfulfilled.

The story wouldn't sell. I felt like this was the only commercial ending, but editors kept rejecting it.

One of my pre-readers finally convinced me that the problem was the sheer falsehood of forcing the plot in the direction he called the "Disneyland ending." It wasn't true to the character. So I tried rewriting the story the way my friend suggested, and Jed Hartman at *Strange Horizons* bought the piece. Since then, it's been translated into four languages and has played twice on the popular podcasts *Escape Pod* and *Starshipsofa*, so that was a lesson learned.

Let the characters be themselves.

PLANET OF THE SEALIES

PROFESSOR MICHAUD HAD set up camp on the northern slope, which was typically upwind of the site. They wore respirators down inside the excavation — sometimes armor, too — and it was a relief not to wear any gear in their off hours. There was some risk of contaminants if the wind shifted or if an eruption surprised their ferrets, but everyone on the team had been given Level IV gene-mods. They could handle small doses of the gases, dusts, and bacteria that regularly belched up from the pits.

Today the sea wind was thick with the hot, chalk smell of the shore. A woman in orange strode away from the brown prefab camp structures. The land was also brown and the sky, too, was a muddy haze.

Her name was Joanna Mary Löw. She stretched out both arms as she walked, orange sleeves ruffling, as if to snare or fight the hard gusts. The blasting wind felt similar to the conflict alive inside her.

This was a short trail but it was one Joanna took often because there wasn't anywhere else to go. The eroding shore cliffs were strictly forbidden, the excavation site dangerous for its own reasons, and Joanna was young enough to need to stretch her legs even after a day's work. Since earning her job, she'd taken to spending much of her free time among the field of non-hazardous artifacts Professor Michaud allowed them to remove as the search continued for the real treasure. They knew the purpose of only a few of these items and made a game of guessing the names of the rest — the 10,000

Pound Paperweight, the Hyperdrive, and, among Joanna's favorites, the Make-Me-Blind.

The Make-Me-Blind was probably just a kitchen utensil or mechanic's device, a saw-edged set of tongs that opened to the exact spacing of a person's eyes, but the civilization that had made these tools and trinkets was both alien and unmistakably aggressive. Joanna and her line-mates tried to keep things fun during the meticulous, often tedious dig by inventing ghost stories full of conquest, torture, and weird sex.

She liked the Make-Me-Blind because she could chase her sisters around with it. Most of the other artifacts collected here were impressive hulks they'd lifted in via robot, a Stonehenge of metals and plastics.

Joanna preferred small and intimate things, not unusual for a créche-raised clone.

The wind sang queerly through the crushed alloy pipework of the Hyperdrive, which they assumed had been an industrial pumping mechanism although it did, with some imagination, resemble an old-fashioned reaction engine.

Joanna rested her fingertips against its bulk, frowning. Then she hurried across the field to a trio of orange bins where the smallest artifacts were kept. From there she continued on to the 10,000 Pound Paperweight. Within a crevice of this deteriorating stonework, Joanna had hidden a tiny, shiny object she called the Diamond.

Why feel guilty? None of these artifacts were coming back with them. None would be studied or even catalogued. Of the twenty-six members on the team, just four had training in archeology, which they used only as another method of predictive analysis. Their sole interest here, the real prize, was any trace of biological material.

Joanna didn't question their mission, but she worried at herself. She was committing deceit and true selfishness, and for what? For nothing. Her so-called Diamond was only a rust-eaten band of iron crushed around a translucent plastic nub. It was garbage — ultimately useless.

Could the deepening change in her be what the matriarch wanted? Her line-mother must have anticipated the influences of this environment, the effects of separation and competition. Why else the system of individual bonuses for each find?

"I wonder," she whispered, holding the Diamond up to catch the murky evening light.

Joanna felt stronger for her new independence. The senior members of the team were an example of what she might become — accomplished, opinionated, self-reliant.

But she wanted to be allowed home again.

"Löw, Löw." Her implant spoke while she held the Diamond at arm's length and she brought it in close to her chest, reacting with shame. Then she understood she was still alone and felt a sharper fear at the emergency call. "Full crew to the pits. Löw, Löw. Full crew to the pits."

Joanna stepped toward the 10,000 Pound Paperweight and tucked her Diamond away again before running back to camp.

THE FERRETS WERE in defensive mode and altered their hunt pattern as she approached. Worming over the ground, the lithe, furry cyborgs were briefly attracted to the tremors of her footfalls. One lifted its concave face to her as if doubtful.

Joanna's own uncertainty rose into a blood scream before her implant spoke again. The hardware they'd threaded through her cerebrum before she left the creche was a communications device on many levels, helping line-mates maintain emotional balance, but this subtle, mostly subconscious process could also be a handicap. Powerful feelings like fear and pain tended to echo between them. Joanna knew there were many wounded, and she imagined the worst before her line-senior explained: "Quake, there was a minor quake, Michaud's reporting casualties inside the dig—"

Joanna hadn't noticed a tremor, but this coast was riddled with faults. It was constantly settling.

Eight figures emerged as she reached camp, tall giants in

mechanized armor. Katarine raised one steel glove to Joanna as the knot of them pounded by.

Inside the barracks she found Hel in her underwear, prepping one suit, a second outfit hot with the feeds laid down in order.

"Jump," Hel said. "I'll finish this one."

"No." Joanna shoved her toward the ready armor. If a stronger quake hit, if there were dust or gas eruptions, the suits would be their best protection. Joanna couldn't bear to see Hel at risk. The two of them were laterals, closer than most, and Hel had already delayed too long because of her.

Joanna rushed into her armor as their implants spoke again: "We've got five hurt on top and two buried. It looks tight. Let's put our triage by the shed."

"I'm up," Joanna said the instant she was dressed, adding a signature pulse. She moved toward the door. But she'd done a bad job of placing the feed for her left quadriceps. The leg of her suit dragged, and she strained to compensate.

"Joanna, Hel." That was Louise, their line-senior. "Work your way around on the west rim, there's a chance it might be easier to dig through from that side."

They bounded away from camp. Joanna stumbled once and Hel came back to help her stand, patting at Joanna's arm in her fussy way as if it mattered that Joanna's armor was dirty.

"What's wrong?" Hel asked.

"My left quad's only eighty percent. I'm okay."

They cleared a ravine and two sink holes, but Hel grabbed Joanna before a larger jump. "Wait. Can you hop that far?"

"I'm okay."

Neither of them had approached from the west before. In many places, this rim fell away into the brutal surf. The new perspective heightened Joanna's mute, urgent dread.

It was such a strange land, packed into flat steppes, an artificial mountain that had mostly kept its shape even after centuries of quakes and storms. Only brown weeds grew from the brown dirt

— a sterile contrast to the greenery and lush flowers of home. This shore had its own allure but it was a terrible beauty, so much like her Diamond, a dead surface concealing wealth beneath.

Quickly, wordlessly, Joanna and Hel coordinated with the others by grid position and their extensive database of radar scans. The two girls buried in the cave-in had been working Trench Fifteen, which was among the deepest. Recovery efforts would be difficult no matter what angle they tried.

"There's an open rift twenty meters down on my side," Joanna said. "We might save time going through there."

"Let's anchor and get a probe in." Hel knelt in a wide, three-point stance, locking her armor as Joanna crouched beside her, aware of an ache in the ligaments of her hip socket. She grabbed Hel's free arm to better stabilize herself before pushing a wire drill through the surface.

Even away from the cliffs, this place could be treacherous. Professor Michaud often compared the site to an insect mound, a methodical if crude structure, each layer carefully separated from the next but, inexplicably, containing the same hodgepodge of materials. Some had decayed, leaving hollows. Gas vents and fires further disrupted the sediment.

The site was a massive garbage dump, vast enough to swallow Joanna's home colony and six others like it, and her people had discovered ten thousand of these landfills all across Europe, Asia, and North America when they emerged from the ice and tundra above the Arctic Circle six hundred years ago. Expeditions further south revealed more of the same, a world-wide scarring.

This dump, like so many along the fallen edge of California, leached poisons into the ocean. Other landfills had been found near freshwater drainages, which was idiotic yet appeared typical of the breeder civilization.

No one wondered why they were extinct.

Louise made contact again in a quiet, calming voice. "How's that rift look?" she asked.

"Not good, it's top heavy," Joanna said, concentrating on guiding the drill. She uplinked her radar to Louise. "Do you want us to come over?"

"Stay there. Keep searching. I've already got twelve people standing back until there's more room to work."

Joanna frowned at the number. Twelve? A quick grid check showed that her line-mates had been joined by the remainder of the site crew, the third shift, who'd been asleep.

There were three lines cooperating at this dig in what had been equal numbers of ten before a chemical burn killed three Löw and then a viral infection decimated the Suhoza. Replacements, including Hel and Joanna, had brought the total crew back to twenty-six. The line culture could be superstitious about odd numbers, but the Suhoza were still under-strength and it was the Löw and the Michaud who alternated the main work details, so it had been a good bet that one of them would be the next to suffer.

"If I send over two robots," Louise said, "do you think you can dig into that rift?"

"Yes," Joanna said. She felt Hel tense. Her own reaction, excitement, made her strong with adrenaline even though it was followed by guilt. Saving the Michaud girls was no contest. Whoever got to them first wasn't better than anyone else.

"Be careful, cubs," Louise said. "Understood? I just want a second option available if this side doesn't pan out."

THE EXCAVATION ROBOTS were towering, ten-legged spiders, capable of squeezing through narrow holes or extending several legs over a thirty-meter circumference in order to hoist ton-loads of debris. Unlike the ferrets, the spiders weren't cyborgs. They contained no living flesh whatsoever and rarely earned nicknames or affection.

Joanna worked her machine relentlessly, blunting its claws, losing four eyes when she pulled upward too fast and a load disintegrated into shrapnel. Hel was more studious, fishing after the smaller junk that Joanna ignored.

Louise continued to deny them an open link to anyone except herself, shielding them from the Michaud's grief, but Louise could not completely prevent this misery from ebbing through to Joanna and Hel each time she checked in with either or both of them to monitor their progress.

The two girls trapped below hadn't transmitted since the cave-in. Possibly this silence was due to the interference of metals. More likely they were dead.

At first Joanna paid little attention to the garbage as she angled toward the rift. The loose debris was only a frustration. But as ten minutes became fifteen, then twenty-five, her emotions found new focus. Anger.

Her home colony wasted nothing, recycling even their urine to maintain the nitrogen levels in their box farms. The line culture was not only genetically poor. For generations they had overcome energy shortages and cold and isolation. The wealth discarded here was staggering. This same crew of twenty-six could have extracted a city's worth of iron each work week if transportation costs weren't so great. They had too few spiders, too little fuel, and there were a thousand kilometers between here and home, which meant the colonies struggled while this wealth decayed.

It was wrong. It was hateful.

Their line-mother had taught them to view this immense, upside down grave as a powerful lesson, but over time Joanna had felt that wisdom slowly die in her. To confront such waste day after day was irreconcilable with proper thinking. It was as though an entirely new interior landscape had opened inside her.

They had all changed. But Joanna was afraid for herself and so much of what she was experiencing.

She envied the makers of this dump.

"Careful!" Hel swatted Joanna's shoulder, overreacting to a slide. They both drew their spiders out. Hel's machine was pinned for an instant, three legs grinding.

Joanna shook her head. "Okay, we need to start setting the larger pieces as containment walls."

"We need to move further back!" Hel's anxiety cut deeper than her voice, a cold contrast to Joanna's determination.

Joanna resisted when Hel nudged at her again. "No," she said. "This spot is as solid as we've got." She almost didn't ask... "Are you okay?"

Louise interrupted on their implants before Hel could answer. "I'm sending over help," Louise said.

We're doing fine, Joanna thought, but she kept silent, trying to hide her possessiveness.

"This dig is no good," Hel said. "The upper sediment is manufactured items and the next layer down must have been mostly biodegradable. It's sinking."

"It's our best bet right now," Louise said. "We ran into a corrosive spill over here and getting around it will cost us too much time. We'll start digging from the south, too, but right now you're the farthest ones in."

JOANNA AND HEL were alone for another six minutes. Their work grew inefficient, uncoordinated, a truth as unsettling to Joanna as the question still turning like a knife in her heart.

Are you okay?

Hel's loss of composure was a weakness and a danger, but eight crew members approached before Joanna found the courage to speak, because this was not a physical hurt — because she was afraid Hel might ask her the same.

It was normal to feel shock, fear, impatience. Joanna was experiencing worse. She felt resentment and mistrust.

Night came almost in a blink, so unlike the long dusks at the pole. Floodlights preceded the mix of human and spider figures who joined them. The Professor herself led the two groups of Michaud and Suhoza. She had been among those injured in the cave-in, suffering chest bruises and a fractured cheekbone, yet she'd foregone medical attention to join the rescue effort.

Watching her, the pride Joanna felt was soothing. The Michaud were well-made and worthy partners.

"Your entry reinforcements are uneven," the Professor said, rebuking her, and Joanna only nodded when she might have looked at Hel as if to pass the blame. The Professor said, "Why don't you two rest for—"

"No."

"What? Rest for a minute."

"Uh, no, we know this substrata best."

"We have your scans." Professor Michaud walked her machine toward the dig, shrugging four of its legs as well as her own hands in a gesture of dismissal. "Rest."

Joanna turned away, glancing up for the stars but finding only cloud cover. What was happening to her? She'd been right to be concerned. These emotions went against the teachings of the line. To be selfish, to be disobedient, were the hallmarks of breeder thinking, especially in the face of trauma, when a line was meant to close into a circle.

Louise would know what she was feeling through her implant. At the moment, Joanna's turmoil might be mistaken as stress. But Louise would know.

Joanna limped away from the Michaud and was pleased when Hel hurried after her, no matter how she'd been feeling toward her sister. Joanna put one hand on Hel's arm and was rewarded with a small, brittle smile.

"I'm not tired, are you?" Joanna asked.

Hel shook her head.

Joanna smiled back at her. "Let's run a wider sweep in case they need more options," Joanna said.

"Stay with me," Hel pleaded.

"Yes."

They leaned close for comfort as they marched their spiders outward in a semi-autonomous stop-and-scan, their visors flickering with radar and thermal displays. Twice Joanna leaned past Hel to watch the Michaud complete the dig, then drop four spiders into the rift.

"Oh!" Hel flinched and said, "Line-senior?" Her tone was almost embarrassed. "Look at my radar! I've located a huge vein of organics."

Jealousy pushed through Joanna's already crowded head, and she hesitated before joining the link to Hel's spider.

"Excellent work," Louise said. "That's industrial."

"It's, um, I'm estimating two thousand plus," Hel said, which Joanna thought was conservative. Based on the size of the twisting cubic area highlighted in the scan, Joanna's own guess exceeded four thousand. Even if the smaller number was accurate, this find would be among their best.

"What are you doing so far from your dig?" Louise asked, both stern and pleased.

My idea, Joanna thought. *This sweep was my idea.*

"Joanna wanted to make sure we weren't missing a better recovery route," Hel said. She was eager to share the bonus, and Joanna clenched her teeth in self-reproach.

EVERYONE GATHERED ABOVE the rift as the Professor's team unearthed their missing girls, but in the night, in the rarely moving cross of floodlights, it was easy to find a shadow. Joanna stood in semi-darkness.

The casualties wore only respirators and shoulder mecha, which hadn't been enough to protect them. Joanna's emotions were too deep to catalogue when the Michaud brought up two torn, bloody corpses, even though these women were lighter in coloring and slimmer than the black-haired Löw. Death had become uncommon in the line culture as they mastered their genetic codes, and violence was unknown, and Joanna could not have been less prepared for gore and bone.

In some odd way she felt honored, even calm.

Hel trembled beside her. Hel was gripped by a more primal reaction, and yet the Michaud and the Suhoza seemed to share Joanna's mood, carrying the bodies with slow grace.

Standing in the shadows was no protection, of course. Louise and Katarine found Joanna by homing on the signal generated by her implant.

As the two seniors approached, Hel left Joanna's side before anyone spoke, desperate for whatever physical contact could be had despite their armor. "Line," Hel murmured. Louise and Katarine both repeated the greeting, embracing her.

Joanna joined them a moment too late and worried again at this visible mistake.

"Walk with us to your find," Louise said.

"I—" Hel was still shaking. When she moved her head from side to side, *no*, it looked like a larger spasm.

The slightest of glances passed between Louise and Katarine. Then Katarine brought Hel closer to herself, both calming her and turning her away from Joanna.

"I'll show you," Joanna said quietly. She didn't want to leave the group, but judgment was inevitable.

Their foursome split. Hel and Katarine stayed near the Michaud as Louise and Joanna walked away. Underbellies split open with lights, two spiders paced ahead of them, slaved to their movements. One dazzling array of floodlights loped forward smoothly but the other jerked and then swayed as Joanna looked back at the group of human silhouettes gathered in bent, heavy postures of mourning.

MORE SPIDERS HUNCHED above Hel's find, mapping the chaotic sediment layers but not digging. The lines did not, could not, trust machines so completely.

A culture that had survived only by tinkering with its very biology was also one intensely sensitive to change. They could be as hostile towards it as their own hyper-immune systems were towards infection. With a total population of six thousand, her line allowed no room for difference — or freedom.

Joanna walked after Louise cautiously, not trying to protect her strained hip but so steeped in thought that each step was a great process. She recounted each of her failings today, her head swarming with memory and regret.

Their line-mother had celebrated Joanna's childhood skills as a gardener, encouraging her to experiment with otherwise useless blossoms because doing so increased her knowledge of selection and breeding. That had been the start of Joanna's ambition, but always the lesson was one of care and control.

Always the line sought to preempt risk to itself.

Joanna's reverie broke as Louise led her into the midst of the spiders. The robots' long, multi-jointed shapes had never seemed menacing before. Joanna shivered and glanced away but still there were no stars, only the cloud cover. Her apprehension quieted again into something more rueful.

Violence was unknown to the line, yet nonviable members were recycled, whether in fetal screenings or much later, because breeder-like traits persisted among them and must be pruned away.

If earning this job had also been a winnowing of those with anti-social tendencies — if leaving the creche was a test that Joanna had failed by succeeding — she didn't want anything other than her fate. Yes, it would be cruel to kill her now. It was also right. And yet she'd cost the line so much training! Couldn't she still be useful somehow?

Louise stopped beside the nexus spider and said, "I'm going to allocate your find to the Michaud."

Joanna hesitated, caught between hope and terror.

"It's the proper action," Louise said. "It's because of them that we found this batch." Louise watched her closely, aware of her tension. "You haven't patched in."

The deeper link would be her truth. Joanna took the hand that Louise extended, a symbolic joining only, metal glove in glove. Then she tapped her implant—

The nexus spider collated information from all the others much like a line-senior directing her mates. Compilation imaging showed three thousand, three hundred and eighteen Sealies in the main body of this vein, balled up and bagged together by the dozens. Another ninety-one had been scattered as far as ten meters by the tidal grinding of the earth.

It was a superior find, no doubt from a hospital or nursery, and easily worth Joanna's life. On an average day they were glad to recover just five or six diapers from household garbage, most of which were badly degraded and worthless.

Fortunately, Sealies had been a dominant brand throughout the twenty-first century. The synthetics used were almost ideal. Old media advertised Sealies as ultra leak-proof, fluid and odor absorbent, each one stamped with the distinctive logo of a blue, grinning seal.

The breeder civilization had discarded the feces and urine of their infants in such packets by the trillions. The population had been impossibly bloated until the pandemics — and here was their pre-contagion genetic treasure, sheathed in white plastic and poly-cotton filaments grayed with age and mold. Only one in thousands had been mummified by the heat of the rotting landfill, fused with the plastic or otherwise preserved in ways that the line could extract viable DNA, but the poor yield had never deterred them from their hunt. Pre-plague samples were necessary both to reestablish diversity and to further develop superior immunities, intelligence, and life spans.

There were safer places to dig than alongside the California sea, but before the pandemics, this region had been host to an unusual blend of ethnic groups from across the globe. The landfills here were richer because of it.

Joanna's pride was what Louise singled out among her tangle of emotions. "You were excellent today," Louise said, continuing to hold her hand.

Surprised, Joanna flexed, muscle memory betraying the secret of her Diamond. "But the things I've felt..."

"You were better than Hel, tougher and more alert."

"Those are the hallmarks of breeder thinking," Joanna insisted, giddy with relief and love and, still, a razor of guilt.

Louise smiled. "You've been telling yourself too many ghost stories," she said. "It's okay. You're okay. It happens to all of us here, especially because of the implants. Most of what you were feeling was *ours*."

"Line-senior, no. This wasn't conveyance. I know when I'm—"

"You don't. When were you ever in a situation like this? The biggest crisis you've dealt with before today was leaving home. Believe me. The feedback can become its own problem."

Joanna nodded slowly. *Why am I arguing?*

It was Louise who answered the thought. "Your actions prove your heart, cub. Above all you're loyal. And you endured as well as any of us."

"I was selfish."

"Good," Louise said, and when Joanna's gaze lifted suddenly Louise had a new, fierce grin for her. "Yes. Good. We're not just out here to dig up Sealies."

Joanna began to smile back. "I, sometimes I thought..."

"You're quicker than most, cub."

"Sometimes I thought the matriarch must have planned for the ways I'd feel, even *wanted* it."

"Our line-mother was one of us, a digger, before you and I were born. It's been that way now for three of the past four generations."

Joanna stared. Then she laughed at the idea of herself ever becoming eligible for a senior position. "But they teach us that leadership is internal," she said.

"In the creche, they have to. Ninety-five percent of the line never leaves home, cub." Louise grew quiet again. "We're weaker because of it."

This notion seemed even stranger, and yet Joanna understood. In the colony, life had been well-ordered and predictable. The line itself was equally tame, at least in comparison to the veterans of this site crew.

"We're starting to change," Louise said. Her voice was more forceful now, like a promise, and Joanna felt a bright, rising fire of self-worth.

The hostile lands stretching endlessly from the pole held too many resources to be ignored, too much sheer *room*, but to recolonize Earth would also demand new skills and capacities, new strength, new destinies.

"Thank you," Joanna said.

END

Afterword

Like a lot of my stories, "Planet of the Sealies" began with the setting. First I had a place. Then I added people and problems.

This bleak future was the offspring of a very simple chore combined with yardwork. We live on a good-sized lot with mature mulberry trees, which I trim myself, partly to save the money, partly because I enjoy the exercise and working with my hands, and mostly because — at least in California — the most prevalent philosophy toward mulberry care is to cut them back every fall. I mean all the way back.

Personally I think this is a scam invented by pruners in order to generate more work for themselves. Yes, mulberries are fast-growing trees, but I see mulberries that have never been trimmed, and they look like trees. That's nice. Alas, the original owners of our home bought into this scam. For decades, they had their trees shaved year after year. By the time we moved in, the mulberries were barely more than thick, six-foot stumps. Of course they grew in a bushy mess! No one ever allowed them to shape into trees, and there was nothing left on top but scar tissue.

Over ten years, I've encouraged the trees to become trees again and reach for the sky, but it's involved some careful work, sort of like *bonsai* training, except with the judicious application of a chainsaw. Occasionally I've had to clear out large parts of their branches in order to make room for the larger upward growths.

Then I hauled truckloads of biomass to the dump.

The dump was a fascinating place. It was *miles* wide, like a strange, endless prairie where the bulldozers roam and seldom was heard a living sound except the scavenger birds. Maybe more interesting, there are no prairies on the California coastline. We live near the eastern, inland shores of the San Francisco Bay Area, where the waterline is surrounded by dry, rolling hills, gullies, and watersheds.

So where did this prairie come from? I started to do some research. Back in the 1950s, when the region really began to boom after World War II, guess where the city and state governments realized would be the easiest, cheapest places to use as landfills?

The low spots.

See, what you do is find a good hill where you can bring trucks and throw the garbage down the hill. Keep doing this until the low spot fills in. Bulldoze it to pack it down. Keep filling. Then move on to the next low spot.

And those watersheds that happen to be downstream of the gullies you've just filled? Heck, those birds, fish, frogs, raccoons, and squirrels won't care! Oh, wait, the watersheds flow into the ocean next. And the toxins that leak into the Bay will swirl around and end up on the beach where the people go with their children...

The blind stupidity of the situation bothered me. Yes, a technological civilization will generate refuse. Understood. You can't recycle or burn it all. But you don't shit where you eat, especially not when that old saying can be meant literally.

The dumps aren't only full of inert junk like plastic. They also become the home of everything we throw into our household garbage — cadmium, copper, nano silver, mercury — and the feces of our babies and our elderly. Yes, there's a small, growing movement toward cloth diapers, which have their own problems with increased electrical and water use, not to mention adding to water treatment demands, but do you realize how many disposable diapers a child goes through from birth to two- or three-years-old? Have one. You'll find yourself up to your elbows in poo on an hourly basis, my friend.

All those diapers, thousands of them each year, combined with millions of batteries and old appliances and light bulbs... that kind of mess wasn't something I could leave alone. So I sent Joanna Löw and her clone sisters underground to investigate.

PATTERN MASTERS

SAUBER WASN'T CRAZY. He'd planned on never hitting the same place twice. He even kept a check-list — near the toilet, in case it needed to be destroyed in a hurry. But two hundred and nine days crawled past before he'd bagged every store in Berkeley and Oakland, so it seemed impossible that anyone would remember him at Greenwald's, his favorite. His first.

Sauber was at the register before the girl stopped him. "Those are mine," she said, reaching out.

He held the packet against his chest. "What?"

"Look at the label."

Of course he'd already studied it carefully. Thirty-six exposures, regular 35mm film. Jennifer Crisp. The address, written in delicate cursive, was just two blocks from here.

Adrenaline spilled from his veins into his gut.

The girl was half his age, peasant-faced, her nose like a ski jump — yet her breasts were perfect, small and neat, her white bra outlined against her thin white blouse. At five-nine or ten, she had at least an inch on him and maybe ten pounds.

Sauber made a show of examining the packet with a smile. Then he said, "Right, geez, these all look the same."

He'd practiced the words so many times that he managed to sound bored. It still wasn't convincing. The green envelopes were *exactly* the same except for the personal information each customer jotted down.

The girl's fingers closed on the packet. Sauber knew he should let go — let go and stop grinning like a chimpanzee. But her skin was smooth, wonderful. She wore more rings than he could count in a glance.

She smiled back at him and said, "You sure would've been surprised when you got home."

Sauber's eyes lifted toward the security cameras. What were the odds that he'd pull this packet from the wide drawers just as its owner arrived? One in a thousand? Higher, given the vagaries of timing. Much higher.

He wasn't crazy. He'd been set up.

The photo department at Greenwald's was tiny, crushed in back between two rows of over-priced groceries and the bright, gigantic counters of the pharmacy. He'd shopped here before, scouting the place, and knew that his quickest exit was through the rear. But were the stock room doors unlocked?

"Don't worry about it," the girl said, as the heavy-set photo clerk stepped out from behind the register. The man's eyes were lost under wiry dark brows.

Sauber turned to run.

Her grip was unbelievably strong.

The two of them fumbled the packet and it careened off the back of Sauber's calf as he spun away. The sharp-cornered impact felt like a knife.

He hit a rack of disposable cameras with his shoulder, kicked through the avalanche of small yellow boxes, fell, got up, slammed into a swinging door. In the dim, confusing maze of the stock room, two men shouted at him. He reached daylight sooner than he'd hoped, scrambling under a giant truck and around a corner before he stopped to look and listen.

FOUR BLOCKS OVER, he thought he saw the girl again behind the wheel of a dented VW Bug.

THE SPRAWLING CAL Berkeley campus was Sauber's second favorite place in the world, a sea of loud young voices, firm bodies. Their hairstyles and ridiculous piercings — lips, noses, once he'd seen a *forehead* ring — always made him smile. It was a safe, colorful environment where anonymity was the rule.

Today it seemed like the kids weren't ignoring him.

Black grease from beneath the truck coated his butt and both knees, and his thoughts felt very loud. He kept his head down and his feet moving but avoided the shortcut behind the clock tower. The thought of that narrow alley made him edgy.

Sauber had always planned on bluffing his way out of a confrontation. Causing a scene would only make him more memorable. All he had to do was apologize and then "realize" that he'd tried the new digital service, the one that Greenwald's sent out for an extra day, and presto-kazam he was just another moron you might joke about with your husband over dinner.

He'd panicked. His streak of bad luck wasn't letting up and he'd gone stupid over a simple coincidence.

If the police did know about him, they wouldn't bother with an elaborate sting operation and sexy decoys — they'd come to his apartment. Now they had his fingerprints. A description.

Outside the science building, three girls and a hairy boy stood in a ring playing hackeysack while another girl circled them, crouching here and there with a pocket camera. "Kick it up, kick it up," she said. Her jeans were very tight.

Sauber felt his anxiety lift for a moment, wishing he was that boy, imagining he had such friends.

He couldn't stop now.

A NEWSPAPER STOOD precisely on end against the door of his split-level. Sauber stared. *The Montclarion* was a free publication that he'd given up on trying to have stopped — yet it had never been left anywhere except in his spotty, muddy strip of grass. He hurried forward and opened all four locks.

The small apartment wasn't anything great — its only real window faced right onto the street — but the entrance was fairly private and he didn't have to share and it had only taken two heavy tarps and a little soundproofing to transform the bedroom into a decent workshop.

Sauber threw the newspaper into the trash and went to the fridge. A blink of red caught his eye. The answering machine. Two blinks. Sauber hesitated, then walked to the counter.

He tried to remember the last time someone had called. A salesman. His ex didn't even have this number.

Then the phone rang and Sauber yanked his hand back.

He took a step toward the front door but turned and strode to the bedroom, propelled entirely by instinct. Guarding that doorway, he stared back at the phone. His heart beat so hard it seemed to squeeze his lungs down against his stomach.

The machine still had Deb's tired voice: "Hi, nobody's here. You know what to do."

Silence poured out of the speaker into his home. He heard a faint scuffing like someone shifting from one foot to another. He didn't move. The caller hung up.

When he ventured forward to hit the 'Play' button, the first two messages were the same expectant quiet — someone listening.

THE WORKSHOP WAS an awful mess that he'd planned on cleaning this afternoon, but he was restless, nervy. He still needed at least one more score.

He grabbed a different jacket and a Niners cap, tucking his hair up to further change his appearance, remembering clean pants at the last minute.

He had that bad sensation of suffocating again as he stood outside his front door, triple-checking the locks. But nothing happened. No one approached. *Nobody is watching you*, he thought.

The congestion downtown was comforting: beggars, skate punks, businessmen. He became invisible.

He caught glimpses of different lives through the windows and sliding glass doors of the university dorms — a hideous red leather couch, the smell of grilled cheese. A bare-shouldered woman singing under the turbine roar of a blow drier was his favorite. At the sorority house, zero progress had been made on the steel patio fence that they'd been building since July.

Long's Drugs seemed deserted and his feet clicked loudly against the gleaming tile floor. He fingered through the Ds and Es until a row of flower-heads drawn across the top of a packet caught his eye. Amy Ellison. She had an off-campus address. Roughly one in thirty people got impatient with alphabetical groupings and marked their packets outside the space provided, to make theirs more noticeable. Stars, looping circles, jagged black scribbles. Sauber found these choices very revealing.

He splurged on some candy bars and paid cash. If he got lucky, this one might be the end of it.

In the parking lot, the girl from Greenwald's stood waiting against her dented VW, arms folded, a smile tucked into the corner of her mouth. Sauber was so surprised that he walked straight over, awash in a perverse sense of relief.

Someone has *been watching me*! he thought.

The only question that occurred to him was so intriguing he almost shouted: "What are you doing?"

"What are you," she countered. "All these pictures."

Her eyes were blue-green, very sharp, and her eyebrows had that same razor quality, thin and perfect. One of her incisors was half-gone, chipped off. A tomboy. How much did she know?

"I'm Nina," the girl said.

"The name on that packet was Jennifer."

"It wasn't mine. I was just trying to start a conversation."

Sauber hoped his smile looked right.

"So what's the secret?" she asked. She had a habit of shaking her head to one side when she finished speaking that he liked. She was rude, confident, crazy.

"I'll show you," he said.

HE GOT HER inside because she moved the same way that she talked, without hesitation — not getting into her tiny car with him, not parking on the dark street, not at his front door.

She finally wavered in the doorway to his bedroom, the toes of one shoe crackling on the heavy tarp laid over the carpet. Sauber worried that it smelled funny. He worried that he couldn't see her face. He should have cleaned.

"Jesus," she said.

He came up behind her. "Who else knows about me?"

"This is amazing—"

In most ways the sculpture was a departure for him. Deb probably wouldn't have recognized it as his. The work was too busy, too bright, too anthropocentric.

The base structure conformed to a human shape — his own, he imagined telling interviewers — because he hadn't wanted the piece to overwhelm with sheer bulk. It also had to fit through the door. Yet its every surface was flat, aside from a concave dish where the face should be. An oversize dish. None of the proportions were correct, the left biceps squashed into a pyramid, one hip no more than a dangling cube, the fingers of the right hand represented by flat, ten-inch strips.

The man-shape appeared to run or jump or perhaps just swoon, perhaps all three, it depended on where you stood and what was visible of its skin.

The skin, of course, was a mosaic of pictures.

Nina stepped forward in a rush and paced through snippings, cans, power tools. The man-shape danced with her. She said, "This is absolutely amazing! You'll be famous."

Deb had always promised the same. Poor Deb.

Small and large, cropped or whole, color, black-and-white, at first the hundreds of images shotgunned the mind. Then the eye found a place to rest. And then patterns emerged.

Nina paused as a particular grouping caught her. The right

shoulder. Sauber nodded to himself. The skin there consisted of healthy young men, some shirtless, one nude, many playing to the camera. Along the arm were tuxedos and brides, homes, children. Further down the ribcage the young men merged abruptly with a series of infirm seniors, bald, baggy — and still monkeying for the camera, gumming pizza, fencing with canes.

The skin was full of such contrasts, ghettos and pristine deserts, parties and intensive care units. It was illuminating and magical and at the same time utterly horrific.

It drew Sauber's eyes away from her.

He'd lived with this tapestry of stolen lives for eight months now, longer than any other work, and still it had the ability to make him forget himself.

He moved closer just as Nina brushed one fingertip over the mosaic. She pulled back, eyes wide. "Sorry."

He slapped its jaw. "Indestructible."

The base structure was concrete mixed with epoxy, the sort of thing to use as a shield against a nuclear blast, and he'd triple-laminated the skin and planned to hit it twice more when he finished. Sauber had yet to skin the right calf or the great empty dish of a face — although he'd contemplated leaving that concave blank, hungry, groping. Or maybe that was too obvious.

He'd already thrown in several conspicuous jokes: a life-sized ear precisely where it should be, drunkards mooning the camera on the rump. Such literalism gave idiots something to understand, and in Sauber's experience it was crucial to market to numb-ass television zombies who wouldn't recognize their own existence without having their hands held. There were more of them than anyone else, after all. Therefore they had most of the money, and their choices skewed everything.

He wouldn't be using his own bedroom as a studio and surviving on credit cards if he'd done a better job of commercializing himself when he still had grants and a wife and free warehouse space provided by the university.

"It's almost filled in," Nina said, caressing the back of the right calf. "Will you use a picture of me?"

Someone would surely object to his placing a group of young women way down on the leg when the young men graced the shoulder, no matter that the space in between was filled perfectly with themes of age, professions, shots of guys shopping and girls watching sports.

This was Bezerkley after all, so packed with liberal freaks that during the Vietnam War, their city leaders had actually proposed seceding from the United States of America.

Someone would cry *sexism* and Sauber dreamed of protests and media frenzies. He wasn't stupid. He had learned that talent wasn't enough to sell — and controversy was publicity. He might even get national coverage after people started recognizing themselves inside the skin and filing lawsuits.

"Please," Nina said. "I'm better than anything in here."

She lifted a Greenwald's photo packet from her purse. Thirty-six exposures, regular 35mm film. Jennifer Crisp. She'd stolen it herself!

Sauber reached for the packet and Nina flashed her chipped tooth at him and laughed.

Moments later, they began to spread other lives across his kitchen counter, their fingers bumping together again and again, warm, eager.

"That one's ridiculous," she said. "Throw it out."

"You won't find a camera owner in the world who doesn't line up their friends and tell them to smile."

"In a parking lot. Jesus."

"But don't you see what's happening, the blonde's always in the middle and the fat one's on the end again. There's a whole series here. The dynamic—"

"Boring! Throw it out."

"OOH, LOOK AT all that sushi, the colors are—"

"Come on, these Barbies don't have any imagination, they're just posing again. We got a bad batch."

"JESUS. NOW THIS lady needs help."

"Are you kidding? I love this shot."

"It's of a *wall*, Sauber. The camera must've gone off by accident."

"...there isn't space for it anyway."

SAUBER DIDN'T OBJECT when Nina swept both sets of pictures into the garbage in great, messy handfuls. He liked the way that she pinballed through her decisions. Typically he'd brood over shots for days, even those he knew he wouldn't use, gleaning clues and patterns, groping his way into different realities.

She clapped her hands together. "It must have taken forever to get all the pictures you needed."

He shrugged and nodded.

"I can show you whole libraries of stuff. Edgy. Weird. We'll download whatever you want."

"Download."

She flashed that tooth again.

PARKING IN HER neighborhood was impossible. Nina beat her hand on the steering wheel impatiently and Sauber hid a smile as they glided up the street and down again.

Even in low gear, they moved faster than he could walk, allowing only time for fleeting impressions. It made him drunk. The Berkeley hills were thickly populated and the steep lots demanded unusual architecture — houses with rooms lined up like train cars, tiny yards on top of jutting roofs.

Her place reeked of candle wax and incense, a tiny attic studio at the same level as the uphill street. Her kitchenette looked directly out on the tires of parked cars. Sauber loved it. He imagined eating breakfast at the window, watching shoes match up with vehicles as each morning commute began.

City maps covered the short walls — the same map, Berkeley. He stepped around her rumpled bed for a closer look as she booted up a shiny new tangerine iMac in the corner.

Tangled, angled lines had been sketched in a rainbow of colors across the black and white grids.

"What's all this?" Sauber asked.

She said, "The big one by the window is you."

NINA CHAVEZ HAD worked in credit fraud protection for less than a week before she grew obsessed.

"Look," she said, pogo-sticking an index finger across the city, "this guy's so anal he'll skip the gas station right next to his house and drive all over town looking for a deal even though he must spend twice what he saves just cruising around. Same with his groceries. Same with his dry-cleaning. Almost never the same place twice."

"Wow, neat, okay."

They stared at the hectic patterns and finally Sauber had to touch the map so he could feel the man's days.

Nina made a low sound in her throat, cat-like, pleased. He turned and saw that her lower lip hung open one slight, inviting fraction. Her eyes shifted toward his. Sauber looked away, but he thought maybe her gaze had flickered down to his mouth too.

He said, "What about this guy? He's just two big blots."

"Electronics freak." Her tone was boasting. "He's always in the same couple shops. Probably he uses cash for everyday stuff. I'm sure he doesn't have any other cards, we barely approved him and he's already at the edge. Minimum payments, always late."

"And me?"

She held his eyes, not smiling. She smelled terrific, like mango, he guessed.

"You're in a world of hurt," she said. "I've written off almost three grand for you as merchant error or duplication in the last two months, otherwise you'd be maxed."

Sauber had to sit down.

There were a few big purchases he'd kept waiting to pay for, but he'd thought... He didn't know what he'd thought. Deb was the math wizard.

The idea of losing the very last of his possessions, his tools, the sculpture — no. He would become a thief before selling off what remained of his soul. The realization made him glad and sick. Two or three robberies a month might be enough and he knew dozens of stores intimately now.

Nina perched on the end of the bed beside him, intent on his face, but he was afraid to let her see his eyes. He was afraid of what her reaction might show.

The bundled sheets were ripe with her scent, worn soft. He snuck his fingers deep into their folds.

"It's okay," she said. "I can buy you more time."

THEY STOOD SHOULDER to shoulder by the filthy window, examining his map. The trails he'd established weren't as curiously random as the penny-pincher's or as compulsive as those left by the electronics freak or those of a woman Nina called the Porn Queen — but nevertheless his pattern had intrigued her. It shrieked of desperation. Most people didn't use credit cards for eleven dollars at the grocery store every other day, much less for a buck seventy-five at Peet's Coffee.

Sauber had also drawn big cash advances at the end of the past two months, she assumed for rent, and he was constantly visiting hardware stores and craft shops.

"I had to know what you were doing," she said.

Like the others, his map bore a tiny label at the bottom. Nina's handwriting was all sweeping jags and flares: Timothy J. Sauber, thirty-eight, 1113-C Bishop Dr., teacher, salary range $19,750 - $23,000.

Resentment crept through him as he understood that ten thousand computers and clerks had him pigeon-holed. He'd never thought of himself as an instructor; it was just a job, a trade-off for studio space and a paycheck; and yet unseen armies considered this a vital definition of his being.

Nina bumped his hip with her own. "You think I'm nuts?"

"I think your maps are great." Her maps were alien. "I think we see things most people don't."

She made that low sound again, *Mmm.*

THAT NIGHT AND the next were ideal. Sauber wished someone could take a picture. Nina sat cross-legged or happily lay belly down on the floor, shuffling her maps and colored pens and the print-outs she'd stolen from work. He typed carefully at her computer. Sometimes she got up and stood behind him, sharing. Sometimes she laid a hand on his shoulder.

The first sites and galleries she'd suggested seemed to lack authen-ticity. The scenes were too spectacular: sleek girls painted by dance lights, a skier cutting through sprays of powder. But he was capti-vated by the promise of wealth.

They chuckled together over morons posing with their pets, even fish tanks, and took turns reading aloud from personal web pages and Facebook. Entire families were on display, labeled, often with short bios and home addresses.

"That's crazy," Sauber said.

He got excited over a poorly lit shot of an all-girl garage band fronted by a heavy teen in a wheelchair. Nina showed him how to download files and to use her printer.

"How much does this special paper cost?" he asked, but she just shook her head.

He caught her smiling at him six times.

When she was in the bathroom, he smelled her bed again and felt the inside of her jacket. He never wanted to leave this quiet, oddly shaped apartment. But he was gentlemanly. Before ten o'clock, he excused himself.

Nina held out a key. "I love watching you work," she said, "but I'm at my job all day. You shouldn't have to wait."

The damp fog and cold did nothing to quell his exploding mind. He would've said *I love you too* but it was too soon.

STRIDING DOWN THE hill seemed effortless. Inspiration struck as he passed a jam-packed mailbox. Sauber stuffed his pockets with everything that wasn't obviously a bill or advertising, then hurried on.

The night was full of lighted windows like big TV screens, all tuned to family dramas.

When he got home, his answering machine had two messages, only silence again. He smiled to think that she didn't know what to say, either. He would have called back, but he wanted to keep the stolen mail a surprise until he could see her face.

NINA SEEMED TO purr, humming, growling, as she marked one of her maps to show the five addresses where he'd taken mail. She could not sit still, bumping his side, throwing herself on her stomach, climbing back onto her knees. Sauber's eyes rarely left the hem of her skirt.

"Listen!" she kept saying, "listen to this," smoothing out personal letters and waving a postcard from Washington, D.C. Every phrase was wonderfully mundane.

Finally her energy carried her to the door.

"How about some take-out Chinese," she said. "I'm buying."

As they exited her building, she took his hand like a little girl, smiling, tugging him up the hill to her car.

SHE SPED BY an open space right across from the restaurant and pulled into a dark lot. She turned off the engine. Sauber took off his seatbelt but paused with his fingers on the door when Nina touched his other hand.

"Wait." She gazed at the busy street — random pedestrians, a pack of thirteen-year-olds smoking cigarettes under the brilliant lights of a corner store.

She brought his hand to her sculpted leg.

Together they pushed her skirt up to mid-thigh. Then she parted her knees.

Nina was loud, maybe deliberately. Twice people on the sidewalk looked around as she ground down on him, her face turned to the window. Beneath her skirt their skin overheated like putty, but his scalp felt chilled — his feet, his gut.

He was so distracted he didn't finish until she'd exhausted herself and slumped against him. His release was abrupt, an afterthought.

She laughed against his neck and buried him in her hair.

WHEN SHE CAME home on the fifth night, he had a pot of canned ravioli waiting but Nina ignored it, pawing through the stacks of paper by her printer.

"What the hell is this?" she said.

"Read the parts I marked, it's really incredible."

"You spent all day in a chat room?"

"Yeah! It's almost like watching people think."

"Boring. All they do is complain."

"It gave me an idea for a new piece!" He dripped sauce on the stove-top, gesturing, and she started to say something but he couldn't stop. "Imagine an American flag constructed out of special computer monitors, ticker-tapes maybe, one stripe would be these anti-government loons, the next would—"

"I can't cover for you forever. What happens when you're out of money? You'll be on the street."

"I'm almost done, I have enough pictures now."

"Give me your key. Get out of here. Go finish it so you have something to sell. Otherwise you're dead meat."

BUT HE COULDN'T stay away. Not because of the sex or her wicked smile, because of her computer or — as Deb would insist — because he was subconsciously delaying the bleak, tiresome process of marketing himself to yups and straights. No artist enjoys explaining why beauty is beautiful, pimping for $12,000 civic improvement awards, wasting days hoping to impress gallery managers with over-crowded schedules.

He couldn't stay away because of all these things.

He got spooked about the mailboxes he'd ransacked and hiked around the long way, approaching her house from up the hill. He wondered how many passersby were tempted to crouch down and peer through her kitchen window.

He wondered how long Nina had been two-timing him with the chubby guy assembling radio equipment on her desk.

It was the electronics freak from Map #6.

JUST A WEEK before, Sauber probably would have left, let it end, and turtle deep into his work. But Nina had made him bold. He eased up the narrow, creaking stairs to her attic, taking the steps in random batches of three and two, waiting for noise from other apartments, the rattle of plumbing, television laughter.

Initially he thought Nina had several men in her place. He thought disgusting things. Then a shriek of static made him realize that, of course, the voices were radio broadcasts.

Nina was loud: "Try that one! No, no, go back."

She was like a kid with a new toy.

Sauber considered ways to win her again.

Then she said, "How about some take-out for dinner? I know the perfect place."

HE MUST HAVE slept some that night because he dreamed he was back in her cramped stairwell. With the logic of nightmares, he pushed her after he had already fallen and they lay together in a shattered heap, the chubby guy reassembling them incorrectly—

SAUBER MADE THE call the next evening. Waiting for Nina to pick up, he finally realized it wasn't her who'd left those silent, searching messages.

The chubby guy knew where he lived.

He was sick with jelly-hard blood when she answered. Sauber wanted no part of a grudge war. He wanted out.

"It's done," he said. "I thought you should see it first."

THE UPSTAIRS NEIGHBOR always banged when Sauber used his

power tools, and sometimes the people next door beat on the wall so hard that he imagined they'd break through.

He was pretty sure everyone was home from work when Nina arrived — it was after seven — so he began shouting as soon as he'd locked the door behind her: "You whore, you little whore, who else is part of your harem?!?"

Nina had walked directly to his sculpture, which stood now in the middle of the living room. She turned and stared, but someone next door was quick to thump on the wall and suddenly she was yelling too, her small hands shrunk into smaller fists. "I saved you!" she said. "You don't—"

"Who else knows about—"

"You don't have a chance without me!"

She advanced on him, aggressive as always, chin up, legs scissoring beneath her skirt. She probably figured that if she twitched her hips for another ten seconds, he'd mount her right there against the kitchen counter while the neighbors listened.

But Sauber had carefully placed his electric saw on the shelving alongside the door.

Nina froze when he grabbed it. Then her arms lifted out from her sides like a woman on a tightrope. She made a noise like a word, "Nuh."

She screamed over the high whine of the saw, lurching back as he jumped after her with the churning blade held up between them. Just to destroy her composure was intensely gratifying. He laughed and she screamed again and he thought he heard his neighbors panicking somewhere beyond Nina's voice and the snarl of the saw as he pressed it down through the upholstery and the wood frame of his couch.

It couldn't last, of course, this chance to master her.

He hurried when he wanted to dally, beyond excitement, near hysteria, adding his shrieks to hers.

Too soon there were sirens outside and the first shout at his door was a woman's: "Police, open up!"

He held them off until the media arrived, sixteen more minutes, cramming his hand over his gasping laughter now. The cops couldn't seem to negotiate without hollering since there was a door between them and a terrific circus outside as residents evacuated and news vans jammed the street.

Sauber was too familiar with confusion and fear to have difficulty pretending. "What are you doing!" he yelled back. "What are you doing!"

"Sir! Sir, just open up!"

He had allowed Nina to circle around him as the sirens approached, and she'd clawed at the door hard enough to leave one fingernail on the carpet before escaping. If he was lucky, that would be the last he ever saw of her.

His landlord would be furious, yet Sauber had been careful to damage only his own furniture, and eviction proceedings in renter-friendly Berkeley moved with all the speed of a drowned worm. A charge of disturbing the peace was probably the worst he'd face. Nina wouldn't press charges — assault with a deadly weapon, whatever — because she had too much to hide. Even if they stood him in front of a judge for obstructing a peace officer or resisting arrest, Sauber had no record. They couldn't jail him.

He only hoped Nina never understood his true intent, because he didn't think he could outsmart her twice.

Soon enough she might suspect, unfortunately, if everything worked out right. If it was a slow night, local news footage of his sculpture might get thirty seconds or more in a million homes across the Bay Area, and that was exactly the kind of notoriety that started bidding wars.

Sauber wasn't crazy.

END

Afterword

The technology is dated now, but people still use cameras with film, and I continue to see photo processing departments in drug stores.

"Pattern Masters" is one of two stories I wrote before my wife Diana and I went digital. Because I'm a disturbed monkey, I constantly wondered what would prevent me from taking an envelope full of pictures that weren't mine. The drawers where the photo department keeps the finished envelopes are self-serve. They alphabetize them. You're supposed to find your own, then bring it to the register with the rest of your shopping.

The cashier never bothers to check whose name is on the envelope. He just rings it up.

So... Would other people's photos be more interesting than mine? Were they having better vacations, bigger homes, crazy sex on camera, or training ninja dogs able to walk a high wire above gasoline-soaked flaming metal spikes?

All writers are voyeurs. We like to get into other lives and times, or we wouldn't be writing, and most artists I know are the same. Whether they paint, sculpt, act, or sing, we share that urge to capture some aspect of the human experience.

Eventually I got to know the girl in the photo department enough to ask what she saw. "This must be an interesting job," I said.

"Sometimes," she said. But mostly she just sat by the same machine, wearing the same white gloves, looking at almost-the-same groups of people standing in almost-the-same groups and smiling.

I thought that was interesting, too. There were patterns in our lives that most of us didn't see — only the girl at the photo counter. Mundane or not, the pattern was there.

One of my childhood friends is a sculptor. He's gone on to design artwork, statues, and other structures in city parks, inside libraries, in front of Target stores, and at the tram station outside the Denver Broncos' stadium, but first he suffered through a long stretch of poverty as he developed his portfolio and his reputation.

As a wedding present to Diana and I, he presented us with a four foot salmon left over from a fountain he developed for a sidewalk near California's state capital buildings.

"This is cool," I said. "Can we put it in our yard? I mean, is it weather-proof?"

"It's cement mixed with epoxy," he explained. "If it was bigger, you could use it for a shield against a nuclear blast."

So that's how Sauber's statue was born.

CANINUS

THERE WAS DEFINITELY something wrong with the dog. Cancer, maybe. An eleven-month-old shepherd should be its own riot of energy and noise. This poor girl sprawled on the examining table like a pile of yarn, utterly lethargic, offering no resistance to Diana's manipulations, wincing at the light and breathing shallowly. Her mild fever couldn't account for this stupor. Diana would test for parasites, but office files showed that the shepherd had been wormed on schedule.

Cancer at this age would be unusual, like leukemia or cystic fibrosis in a child. The world was a cesspool. Diana knew anger wouldn't help, yet she felt a familiar dull heat surge through her chest. Sickness was such an insult.

"You say she's better at night?" she asked.

A pit bull of a man, short and pudge-faced, the owner spoke in a grunt. "Not much," he said.

Diana glanced at the window, where late afternoon sunlight lanced through the drawn mini-blinds. If the summer heat was adding to the shepherd's problems, the briskness of the air conditioned office should have perked her up. As Diana's last walk-in of the day, the shepherd had been kept waiting most of an hour. Plenty of time to cool down. Diana guessed there were other periods of improvement during the day while the owner was at work, and that he must be imagining a pattern where there wasn't one.

"And she's not eating," Diana prompted him.

He shook his head.

"Are you sure she hasn't been fighting?"

"What?" He shook his head again.

"This isn't a self-inflicted wound."

He blinked, then stepped forward with a frown. Diana gently sifted her fingers through the shepherd's neck ruff to expose the newly-healed bite marks that she'd discovered. Some dogs were limber enough to gnaw open the base of their own necks in a vain attempt to destroy fleas or mange, but the angle of these punctures was all wrong. The attacker had come from behind and above. Strangely, it was a tightly localized pattern rather than the body-wide bruises and cuts typical of a fight. Diana might have thought that a rutting male had latched onto the shepherd, but the poor girl wasn't in heat.

Even more bizarre, it almost looked like the scars were layered, as if the bites had been inflicted over a period of time.

Diana was surprised that the owner hadn't noticed the wounds when they were fresh. The shepherd's jugular vein had nearly been opened. There must have been plenty of blood.

"My fence," the owner said. "She can't get out."

Diana didn't argue. He could believe what he wanted.

As a vet, Diana preferred dealing with chatty folks because they were easier to judge as care-givers, but off duty she favored the company of more quiet types. She enjoyed making her own sense of things, rather than being battered with the obvious. This made her something of a stranger in Gen M culture, but her pet huskies, Sam and Sandy, were enough for her. The three of them led a small, satisfying life together.

Diana had recently spent her thirtieth birthday alone in a hot bath with a book and some wine, and didn't regret it a bit. Invisible beneath the layer of bubbles, her slim hands had recreated the perfect lazy urgency that her ex's fingers had once built inside her — without his roughness or his greedy kiss.

Pretending, alone, was new for Diana. But she knew what was good for herself. She hadn't moved from the suburbs to the San Francisco peninsula to find new friends but to escape her old ones, who'd ridiculed her for becoming such a solitary cliché after the divorce. *Spinsters aren't supposed to be veterinarians, they're librarians*, Beth had said, laughing.

People could be such shitty idiots.

DIANA WAS GLAD to lock the front door behind the owner. She had more than an hour's work ahead of her, yet there was a slim chance that she could get in a quick walk afterward. The days were still getting longer.

As she glanced through the window over the empty parking lot, calculating the sun's fall toward the blocky horizon of highrises, Diana felt a strange sense of foreboding. She had always admired animals for their heightened instincts, which seemed quicker and more honest than complicated human emotion. She'd tried to adopt that centeredness herself and to act on hunches as if they were fact. Leaving her ex had been a test of intuition, and a successful one.

Diana wasn't sure yet whether she trusted the owner. He seemed to love his shepherd. He obviously combed the poor girl regularly, and he'd protested about being separated for the night... but Diana had never seen an animal so close to catatonia except when abused.

Back in the examining room, Diana noted that the shepherd's listless demeanor did not change now that they were alone. The poor girl's glazed stare made her feel guilty for being so concerned about getting out in time to get some exercise.

Finding a vein was surprisingly hard — and when Diana succeeded in drawing blood, its pale color made her frown. She was also glad she was wearing latex gloves. Human beings were not susceptible to most canine diseases, or visa-versa, but she always had to be extra careful to avoid carrying something home to Sam and Sandy.

In her closet-sized lab, Diana pulled an old microscope from the shelf and squeezed a tiny drop of a sample between two slide plates.

It proved to be mostly plasma, the red cell count too low, the white corpuscles swarming furiously.

The shepherd was dying of what appeared to be a viral infection, which made it all the stranger that the bite wounds had healed so cleanly. Diana had never seen anything like this.

She gave the poor girl a dose of Claivax, a wide spectrum antiviral, then two shots of vitamins. Unfortunately it would be at least seventy-two hours before the samples she'd mail to BioDyne were processed, animals being a last priority, but if—

The shepherd spasmed upward from the table like a gout of fire. The dog was fluid muscle and gnashing teeth.

Diana fell away, cracking the base of her spine against the counter. She instinctively raised both arms to protect herself as the shepherd coughed and spat.

Training made Diana move forward to help, her hands reaching out now, but fear caught her in mid-stride. She stared.

The shepherd convulsed, paws and muzzle drumming on the table, and then the poor creature also froze. Just as quickly, the shepherd relaxed, her head and legs dropping to the table with gentle thumps. It was over.

Diana stepped forward, then hesitated again. She saw blood mixed with the shepherd's spittle.

The poor creature was dead.

THE RECORDING ON the owner's answering machine seemed uncharacteristically jolly. "No one's home right now, so leave us a message," the man said.

She didn't. The last time a patient died in the office had been right after New Year's, and the family was right there to take the Siamese home.

Diana knew there were heavy plastic body-bags somewhere, but she was too upset to remember whether they'd been put in storage or were in one of the examining room's half-dozen cabinets.

She focused on the shepherd. Internal bleeding, heart failure, possible stroke... Such a powerful allergic reaction to Claivax was unheard of, and Diana tentatively decided that the shepherd's death could not be related to the injection.

She cleaned the floor and table slowly. Tending to the corpse became a meticulous ritual, a kind of penance. Then she called the owner again. Still no one home.

IT WAS TWILIGHT before Diana walked out to her car, still shaken and thinking queerly. She glanced over her shoulder twice, provoked by an unidentified feeling. It felt like fear. She told herself that guilt was only natural.

Bad things happened to good people. That was the stumbling, random way of the world. Her mother liked to say the important thing was how each person dealt with their burdens.

The city looked different, hard, sterile, even threatening. The surreal pinkish hue cast by the streetlamps only heightened her strange mood. Waiting at a stoplight beside a hulking bus, fenced off from the dark sky by power and phone lines, Diana realized she'd passed through three entire blocks without seeing a single tree or any vegetation whatsoever except a few weeds struggling up from the sidewalk.

This was no place for animals, or for humans, really, living in boxes stacked ten high and in the straight narrow canyons between, reabsorbing their own filth and pollution through lungs, stomach, and skin.

She'd wanted to be anonymous outside of work and to be her own boss in a private clinic — but she spent her days treating claws fractured on concrete, irritated eyes, asthma, digestive disorders, and bones and bodies smashed by cars.

It was a losing battle. The sheer density of the population was the very reason that the city was so inhospitable... And yet she was content here, both at home in her own little space with Sandy and Sam, and at the office where she met so many other animal lovers and their companions.

Pets softened people, awakened compassion and a sense of

responsibility in them, traits that all too often otherwise seemed nonexistent.

Lost in her musings, Diana drove right past a parking space just half a block from her building. By the time she realized her luck, another car had pulled into it.

She found another space down by the corner.

That spider-light feeling whispered up the back of her neck again as she stepped out of her car. She glanced around. Full darkness had come. Illuminated windows cast a hazy gleam upon the rows of parked cars. She saw nothing.

Then a low, sneaking shadow detached itself from the blackness beneath a station wagon. Inhuman eyes gleamed back at her. Diana's heart jumped and she took a step back. Then she grew angry with herself.

Men were something to be scared of — muggers, rapists — not a neighbor's dog or some stray. Yet she was very aware of the distance to her front door.

The compact shape paced closer, strong, deliberate, its glinting eyes never wavering from her.

Diana spun and ran.

SHE FELT STRANGELY sad to see Sandy and Sam, who trampled each other — and her — in their eagerness for contact. Thoughts of the dead shepherd were like a tapeworm in her mind.

Sam and Sandy sensed her anxiety, the way they understood all her moods. They calmed quickly and she knelt to meet them, and all three became a roving pack hug of fur and comfortingly familiar smells. Sam and Sandy were husky-lab mixes, smart, loyal — and stinky. Diana could never bring herself to rob them of their identities by washing them, because scent was a canine's most crucial sense.

Visitors might have considered her ground-floor apartment somewhat ripe, but she didn't have visitors.

After giving both huskies an individual scratching and nonsense murmurs of praise, Diana led them to the side door. The so-called yard was only four feet wide but it ran the length of the entire building. It was just enough room to toss a ball. The landlord refused to let her install a pet-door, but, like most dogs, Sandy and Sam had an amazing capacity to hold their bladders all day.

Back inside, both huskies got a chew treat for being so wonderful and Diana allowed herself a glass of wine.

She put a pot of spaghetti sauce on the stove, diced some garlic and green onions, then went to her room with a second glass. She distracted herself from memories of the ugly day with glances at the mirror, smoothing her nylons from her calves, opening her blouse from her small, perfect chest, knowing that true escape would come later in a hot soak, knowing—

Sam and Sandy howled, not their usual throaty bark but a panicked yelping.

It felt as if the doses of adrenaline from earlier in the day were still in Diana's bloodstream. Her limbs surged with fear and clumsy strength. She threw down her blouse and rummaged through her nightstand, then ran.

Sam fell silent before Diana reached the end of the hall, as Sandy's baying took on an even higher pitch.

There was another dog in the living room.

Sam pressed against the intruder, his nose ducked submissively low but his tail at stiff attention, his hips cocked and hind-legs quivering, enthralled. Diana glimpsed his red penis as it grew erect. Sandy, still baying, fell quiet and also ducked her head as the intruder turned on her, as if its sparking eyes were some sort of weapon.

The utter *wrongness* of the huskies' reactions sent a heavy pain tumbling through Diana's entire body.

"Sam!" The word came out as a howl.

Empty of thought, only instinct, Diana thrust her .32 forward and fired twice. Directly behind the intruder, small blossoms of splinters burst from the side door.

Less than ten feet separated them. Diana sighted carefully and fired again. And a third crater appeared in the door.

The locked door.

Sandy squeezed under the loveseat, moaning, but Sam seemed oblivious to the gunshots and began to awkwardly hump the air. The intruder was also unaffected.

Conscious thought returned to Diana in a cold shocking swarm as the intruder faced her, its lips drawn back from a mouthful of unnaturally large fangs. Part of Diana noted clinically that its nose was dry and scaling, its paws misshapen.

It was the shepherd, the dead shepherd, whom Diana had left zipped in a heavy bag inside an industrial refrigerator.

Would silver bullets work? No, that was for werewolves and this was no oversized hulk of muscle — it was a shadow, a mesmerizer.

Vampire.

The clues had been there all along: the multiple bites where another *caninus* had fed repeatedly on its seduced victim. Diana had also noted the shepherd's weakness, lack of appetite, and bad reaction to daylight. Had an infected human somehow managed to pass the curse to a favorite pet, immortalizing it, or had the werewolf and vampire legends always been confused?

Diana thought of the Claivax. The drug had caused a violent reaction from whatever had been incubating in the shepherd before it had died, but vampirism was clearly more than a viral disease — more powerful and more evil.

The shepherd had died.

She was certain of that.

It had died, and then it had resurrected. Perhaps the Claivax had even forced the transformation as the paranormal disease grew beyond some critical level in response to the drug's attack. These creatures must be extremely rare or even the conveniently dense feeding ground of the city would have long since been overwhelmed.

Wood and garlic were supposed to be weapons—

Even as Diana began to turn toward the kitchen, the shepherd pounced. The logic blasting through her head vanished. She fired once more, point-blank. The shepherd didn't notice. It slashed at her forearm and unprotected chest as they fell together. Diana felt blinded more by horror and the suddenness of motion than by pain.

The floor slammed awareness back into her, an awareness shot through with agony. The shepherd dug through her soft belly and scraped its fangs against her flexing spine as she thrashed, her scream reduced to a wet sigh.

But the shepherd wasn't interested in her. It did not feed. It turned and left her as everything went black.

Diana dreamed that Sandy was burning. The high note of Sandy's yowling bespoke complete helplessness... and silence fell again as Diana woke, dull and hazy.

She saw Sandy creep out from under the loveseat stiffly, compelled, as the shepherd stood waiting. Satisfied by this total obedience, the shepherd moved past Sandy to Sam, sniffing briefly at his maleness before latching onto his neck. He collapsed with a loving groan.

Diana wept, clawing weakly at the carpet, only vaguely aware of the sticky red bog spreading through the soft fibers beneath her or the flecks of meat that her hands encountered.

Why had the shepherd come here? Because she was its last memory? For revenge or sheer evil? How intelligent could it be?

Then she remembered how it had simply walked away after neutralizing her as any sort of threat. Vampires thirsted for their own. Perhaps it had scented Sam and Sandy among her things and fixated on them as its first meal. *Why* no longer mattered.

Steadying her arm demanded more physical strength than her body seemed to contain, but Diana's mind had shrunk to one rigid point and there was energy in desperation.

Her first shot was bad. It took Sandy in the flank as Sandy stood watching the shepherd bleed Sam. Sandy yelped, waking from her trance, and Diana shot her in the face. Sandy crumpled.

The feasting shepherd didn't lift its sopping muzzle from Sam's neck until Diana put a bullet through Sam's chest — not until the blood flow stopped as Sam died.

It was the best that Diana could do. The cleanest.

The shepherd rushed toward her again, slavering, and she fired the last bullet up through her own mouth.

END

Afterword

No, the heroine isn't actually my wife. Yes, the real Diana has a self-possessed beauty and intellect, but we've never had dogs, nor marital trouble, and the real Diana is a marketing analyst, not a vet-turned-detective. We've never lived in a major urban environment, either, which is why the character Diana seems both intrigued and repelled by the endless concrete of her unnamed city. To me, cities feel like a bizarre torture to inflict on yourself. I don't care if it's easier to find a good Thai restaurant. I get claustrophobic.

Like "Pattern Masters," "Caninus" was written during my horror phase. This was a few years before "Twilight," but vampires have always been popular, and I thought a vampire dog was a nice twist — not a werewolf, but vampirism in animals.

Animals wouldn't develop an elaborate, immortal society, developing their secret clans and secret rules. They'd operate on instinct. That struck me as cleaner than the sometimes indulgent, long-winded books about human vampires and their lovers, slaves, wannabes, hunters, and rivals. This story was meant to be a short, sharp shock.

It also came from my fascination with the human-pet relationship. As a boy, I grew up with dogs and cats, but now as a husband and a father myself, we're too busy earning a living, raising our family, and maintaining our home to give enough attention to a pet.

My impression is most of my neighbors are too busy, too. Energy costs more than in my parents' time, which means everything else costs more, too — food, clothes, utilities, everything. People work harder now than ever, and yet we're the only household on our street that doesn't have a dog. Because I work at home, I often listen to those dogs barking in lonely, neglected misery for hours on end. The fact is dogs are pack animals. It's wrong to leave your friend alone in a fenced yard or a garage or your house while you're at work all day. They need stimulation, and they will create it themselves if necessary. Hence the noise. The dog is staving off madness.

I'm sure I'll get in trouble for saying so, but here it is:
Too many people talk a good game about how they love their pets like members of the family, but dogs should be treated like children. They need constant attention. If you can't provide it, don't own a dog. Of course they're cute and fun, but it's absolutely not cool to treat an animal like a toy you can take out when you want, then ignore when you're busy. That's selfish, even cruel, and the cranky writer next door doesn't appreciate the barking, either.

"Caninus" emerged from a long love of monster movies mixed with curiosity and frustration. Why bother to have a dog you won't care for? They cost money. They fill your yard with crap... or the street, if you're inconsiderate enough to let your dogs run loose because you don't want to clean up after them... and the trail-heads near the open space where we live are encrusted with the mummified poop of ten thousand dogs excited to be free at last. They've become an incredibly artificial niche species. I don't get it. So just for fun, while we're on the subject, I've included a bit of free-verse called "Eighth-Acre Blues" that appeared in a college publication called *Kokopelli's Seed*.

EIGHTH-ACRE BLUES

I am
held here
and these wood walls
this patch of green
and single tree
is all
I've ever known
save for faded
memories of
sisters and brothers
who shared
a mother's warmth

Here
I am well-fed
but
each meal
is the same
as the last

When they let me
out
on my chain
it is I who leads
the guards

They yank us
back
by the chokers
we wear
when another captive
and I try to
exchange greetings
of silent scent

I like it outside
but
beyond my confines
I often hear
the false cry
of an Evil

It masquerades
as one of us

Its mechanical howl
controls me

Frenzied
I bark back
but always
the horror fades
and leaves us
prisoners in peace

Sometimes
at night
we howl
too

Afterword

I hope it's obvious that the idea here is of a small, captive, almost-sentient race scattered across an environment they barely understand. Sometimes I wonder what pets think of suburbia. Sometimes I wonder how they'd react if they gained more intelligence as in "Planet of the Apes" or the clunky, ancient thriller "Day of the Animals."

A lot of pets are well-loved and have every basic need provided for them. It's a life of luxury. And I'm very, very glad I'm not one of them.

EXIT

THERE WERE RATS in the soufflé again — whole ones, this time. Stevens wasn't being subtle anymore. Fine. These babies were impossible to miss, unlike the little clawed feet sprinkled into last night's dinner.

Last night I'd told Dr. Hallwag that he had twenty-four hours. NORAD refused to give us any more time.

We were down to roughly one hundred and eighty minutes now, with nothing to do but fill our neglected bellies. My squad and I had been gofers, muscle and security for the scientific staff of this subterranean compound; my duties were through; what remained of the equipment had been gone for and muscled into place, and security was only a rude joke.

I poked at a leathery tail jutting up from the middle of my plate (Stevens wasn't being subtle; he was *sculpting*) and stifled an exhausted giggle. It was a bad idea to get started. I might not stop.

Beside me at the cafeteria table, Corporal Watters set her fork down with a sudden, precise movement.

Good, I thought, *she sees them, too.*

"Lieutenant," she said, "Stevens obviously has it or he would have quit this crap. I hoped he was... just making some kind of statement."

"It's your turn."

Watters shook her head. "I took care of Riggs."

"But I did Carrington and Rudowski. I'm one ahead."

She frowned at me, surveyed her plate, then rose and strode toward the kitchen.

"Get me a sandwich while you're in there," I said.

Watters must have been wound tighter than I thought. Her first shot was bad. I heard Stevens scream before she shot him again.

THE VIRUS — when perfected — had been intended to be a merciful means of conducting war, like spraying enemy lands with an incapacitating form of LSD and then simply walking in. When the fevers and hallucinations wore off, their troops and leaders would find themselves defeated unconditionally. Bloodlessly.

We would never know which scientist released the proto-forms of the virus, or even for sure if it had been an accident. Did it matter? I had watched the security camera back-tapes as I transmitted them to NORAD, but saw nothing definite. C Block was closed off now, sealed the instant that the sniffers belatedly detected the leak, and I had been too short-handed to send a detail in there merely to search for clues that might not exist.

The situation had been lousy from the start. Most of the people capable of solving the problem, and most of our supplies, had been lost in the chaos that ensued before C Block fell forever silent. The staff trapped behind the automatic gates all went violently insane as the proto-viruses made their subconscious fears as real to them as their skin.

Over the past two days, most of my small command had also succumbed. Hazmat suits were no protection. One proto-virus had spread much faster than anyone could have guessed and was now incubating within us all.

There was no exit, no salvation, unless Dr. Hallwag pulled off a miracle. Even then NORAD might incinerate us with a baby nuke just the same. How could they be certain we weren't pretending to have conquered the virus out of desperation?

Three lives meant little weighed against the possibility of loosing the virus upon the American populace — and the world.

HALLWAG DIDN'T LOOK up from his microscope when I stepped into his makeshift laboratory, eating a turkey on white. It wasn't much of a last meal, but it didn't have any mice in it. I'd checked four times.

He appeared as neat as ever, even wore a red tie under his lab coat like a flower at the base of his neck.

"Doc, you hungry? Take five. Maybe a short rest'll help."

He didn't respond. A centrifuge spun on the counter beside a rack of tissue samples. Some of that flesh was mine. I rubbed at the gauze wrapped around my forearm.

"Doc!" I sprayed crumbs.

He leaned back from the microscope and I saw that his face was a pale mask. The neatness of his clothing was inadvertent.

"Dinner?" I said, but he shook his head and returned to the microscope.

LESS THAN AN hour left, the alarms I'd set at the exit went off. Watters and I drew our sidearms and ran.

Hallwag screamed as we stalked toward him. Who knows what he saw — who or what we were in his eyes. "No chance!" he shrieked. "No chance!"

Watters shot him cold.

Hallwag had managed to open three of the locks. One more correct code-keying and the elevator would have powered up, the gates opened. How he'd deciphered my codes I couldn't guess. Maybe he was just that much smarter than me.

Watters and I studied the closed gate for a long time. I almost reached out to the keypad. But the virus would leave with us.

She said, "How about dessert, lieutenant? My treat."

We walked back into the compound.

END

Afterword

This "short short" is the first piece of writing for which I was ever paid. The second was a spaceships-and-dopplegängers story called "Fellow Travelers" that I didn't include in this collection because, reading it now, it makes me wince.

"Travelers" had a good, spooky idea, but at the time I hadn't learned enough craft to execute a larger story. "Exit" avoids that pitfall by holding itself to three characters, three scenes, and one simple if frightening concept.

"Exit" was also among the last entries in a tradition perpetrated by the Moscow Moffia, a writers' group centered around Moscow, Idaho, where I lived for a year and a half after leaving college. They ran writing challenges and published anthologies of "Rat Tales" — short stories whose conceit was that each story must start with the same sly, opening line, "There were rats in the soufflé again." After that, you were on your own.

In its heyday, the Moffia and other writers included in the "Rat Tales" anthologies included such giants as Dean Wesley Smith, Kristine Katheryn Rusch, Kevin J. Anderson, and John Brunner. Most of them had moved to higher circles by the time I arrived on-scene, but one of the prime movers behind the group was writer, editor, and superfan Jon Gustafson.

Jon died several years ago, but he was among my first friends in sci fi. I'd never heard of science fiction conventions. Jon worked as one of the prime movers behind MosCon, which drew people from all over the Northwest for twenty-two years in a row.

I fell in with Jon and his crazy friends not long after settling in town, entered that year's writing challenge, won first place, and was paid $5 to have "Exit" included in the MosCon XVI program guide book. I was also awarded a free membership to the con.

Next year, he paid me $60 for "Fellow Travelers" and ran it in the guide book, too.

Maybe that doesn't sound like much to call home about, but MosCon's guests of honor that year and the next included legends like Roger Zelazny, Gregory Benford, and Phil Folgio. Even better, in a small twist of fate, "Exit" ran alongside a reprint of a story by Doc E.E. Smith, and "Fellow Travelers" appeared with an exclusive, advance excerpt of a novel called *The Tides of Tiber* written by Buzz Aldrin and John Barnes. The publisher, Tor, granted Jon the right to run this excerpt purely based on his reputation in the field. I was included in the same pages. That was heady stuff for a young, would-be writer, and I've always been grateful to Jon for his encouragement.

Since then, "Exit" has been translated into five languages worldwide, reprinted twice in English (not including this collection), and appeared twice as podcasts.

Not bad for five hundred words and a tasty breakfast.

MONSTERS

HIS NAME DOESN'T matter. He had a job in which he invested forty-odd hours of his life each week, a car that was only two years old, and a small apartment with a view from the kitchen window of an undeveloped hillside where the sun came up. Because of this, he usually breakfasted standing at the kitchen sink whereas he ate most of his dinners in front of his girlfriend's TV. His days passed with little adventure or romance — a speeding ticket here, oral sex on the hall carpet there; hardly the stuff of legends — and he was content.

As he pushed through the theater's heavy door with his shoulder, protecting an armload of popcorn and soda, some kid in the front rows yelped like a puppy. He barely noticed. His girlfriend jammed a finger into his ribs as she brushed past, even though it was her snacks that he'd drop, and he said, "This whole place is designed for us to sit dead-center. The picture, the sound system..."

She flashed her smile and shook her head. "Some tall dork always plunks down in front of me."

"No one's even here." He didn't much care what his vantage point would be for this "sweeping Victorian epic," yet by appearing to give in now he was more likely to win a later dispute. He'd already racked up big points just by agreeing to see a movie completely lacking gunfire or killer asteroids.

In front, the kid who'd yelped was on her feet, rubbing her butt and talking in a squeal. The woman beside her said two short syllables in an embarrassed tone. The kid shook her head. The woman growled something that sounded like *okay fine* and they moved over a couple seats. That was all.

On the far left side of the theater, he sat down next to his girl-friend. Something hard and very thin lanced into his thigh and he stumbled up, careful not to spill his Coke. "Ow. Man!"

"What?"

He thought she'd jabbed him — payback for his earlier sermon on the top ten most boring aspects of chick flicks, but his wound really hurt. Her idea of fun was to pinch his nostrils shut when he over-slept or to deflate his bowling scores. And her puzzled grin became a frown when she saw his expression.

"Look," he said.

The tiny steel shaft was almost the same color as the maroon upholstery, but specks of bright metal showed through a dry sticky coating of red-black.

His stomach lurched as he realized the crust was blood, some instinctual need to purge himself. He would remember that feeling later on restless nights, in muted hospital rooms, during slow dead hopeless hours.

There were other moments that he could resurrect in his mind, heartbeats in which his body reacted before he could think. Most came playing roller hockey — saves, scores, falls that should have resulted in broken bones but because of a last second lunge or judo-like roll had cost him only bruises. Others were more alien and random — a sense of knowing a strange woman that went beyond physical attraction — shadows of fear — an aggressive predatory urge when bumped on a crowded sidewalk.

Instinct, primal emotion, seemed in many ways quicker and more powerful than the intellect.

"Man. Oh, man." He rubbed at his flank exactly as the kid in the front row had done. The dim lights went out. Previews started as he investigated his seat.

In the dark blue flickering glow of an ocean storm, he found a note taped to the underside. It was only three letters long.

HIV.

In the brown gloom of a courtroom scene, he shouted at the audience. Three people hollered back at him to shut up. He tried again, panicking, but his girlfriend tugged on his sleeve. She didn't care about them.

HE WENT STRAIGHT to the emergency room. Two hours passed before the insurance papers were complete and a doctor was available. The desk nurse suggested that he leave and visit his primary care physician the next day.

Sweating, certain that he could feel the disease scratching in his veins, he pleaded that money didn't matter, he wanted to see someone now, right now, please.

His girlfriend sat as close as the hard plastic chairs would allow, holding his hand, while a parade of strangers kept them waiting — a guy his own age whose shattered forearm seemed to have an extra wrist, two children with dog bites — none of whom honestly seemed in more danger than himself.

"It was a prank," his girlfriend said.

They stared at the tile floor.

Later, she whispered, "Doctors can kill it with drugs on the first day, I think."

He lifted his head to kiss her in a sudden delirium of fear and need. She leaned back, avoiding him. In the day to come, he would understand her reaction as an important lesson — that he was ultimately alone in this no matter how many times his parents and friends promised to be there for him.

The thick dirty flood of hate passed quickly, but for a moment he trembled with energy. He almost stood up and shouted. He almost hit her. Then he slumped back in his seat, already defeated, already dead, pushing her hand away and crossing both arms across his chest.

Her eyes were horrified. "I'm sorry," she said.

"You can't get it kissing somebody," he said.

"I'm sorry."

WHEN THE ER doctor told him HIV infections cannot be detected for six months, disbelief clogged his head. For most of a week he managed to hope, numbly, that nothing had happened. Then police technicians announced that the needles did indeed carry a virulent strain. Every professional he visited put the odds at ninety-plus percent that he was blood positive because his puncture wound was rough and deep.

He'd become a different man with what felt like someone else's future. It lay in wait for him ghoulishly.

Great strides had been made in minimizing and controlling the effects of the disease, but there was no cure and might never be. In fact, most researchers had given up on overcoming the virus. The current focus was on creating a vaccine to prevent infection in the first place. Protease inhibitors could drop HIV to below detectable levels, and with care and some luck he might live most of his normal life-span — yet how normal would it be?

Each day he lived out sixty years in his mind, breathing in claustrophobic phantom mobs of might-have-beens and cruel visions of himself as a bed-ridden husk. The effort was exhausting, lethal, and he tried to shut down his mind. There were more danger zones than safe areas now. He needed to be smaller.

He kept busy. Another new lesson was that action of any sort was better than waiting, worrying.

"Stay positive," a therapist told him, not understanding the irony of her word choice.

"You've got a long time ahead of you, son," a specialist promised.

THERE WERE NO fingerprints on the needles or the notes. Interviews with theater employees and the small number of moviegoers who'd come forward generated not one lead.

If there had been any point, any profit, it could have been the perfect crime, but it was only perfect madness.

A ninth victim discovered more needles in the coin return slots of three payphones down the block, but again there were no clues or witnesses. Short of receiving a confession, the police might never be able to explain who had done it or why.

He'd become a statistic. For what? He dwelled on lunacy, though greater minds than his had offered only more questions or cures that helped few at best. Monsters in all their many forms were a perverse cancer that would have been abolished by now if evil was not inherently part of the human being. Shooting sprees, arson, child molestation — the insanity had become so constant, most people tried to ignore it.

Others sought out chaos and pain, some to feast, some to heal. In the days after the theater incident, he was harassed by both types. And half a year later, when tests proved that eight of the victims were blood positive, the circus started again.

He was a minor celebrity in the media, especially the tabloids. There were plenty of other crazies and their deeds to celebrate (*Golf Club Killer Bludgeons Neighbors*; *Sabotage Kills 4 In Subway*), but he and the other infected victims were walking dead and this insidious aspect played well — as did the fact that their only mistake had been to sit down. Everyone sits down. On buses, in restaurants, at ball games. Everyone.

His notoriety wasn't anything that a man could properly capitalize on, of course. Women would never clamor for space in his bed. Employers wouldn't compete for him. His buddies started picking up the tabs for beer and food, but very soon he was seeing less and less of them.

Some of this distancing was his own fault, partly because he ran to see every specialist his insurance would cover, mostly because he couldn't stand rehashing what had happened or getting maudlin about the good ol' days.

Much of the gradual separation was their doing, however, and he quickly learned who was a friend and who had been a mere acquaintance.

Losing his girlfriend was the hardest.

Her pity hurt. Her revulsion hurt. Memories hurt. Hope and regret and wishes hurt. She was experiencing her own myriad of anguishes, but he didn't care. He couldn't afford to.

He'd stopped answering his phone during the blitz of calls from media, friends and family — and from oblivious telemarketers who made him smile bitterly. The plaintive voice on the machine no longer sounded familiar. He erased all her messages.

A LAWYER APPROACHED him with the news that six of the other victims were filing a liability suit against the theater, a national chain which was at least sure to settle out of court.

"I'm in," he said.

What had happened could hardly be considered the theater's fault, but protracted phone calls and paperwork and meetings with representatives of his insurance company had him frightened. Money meant more doctors, more treatments.

He visited the lawyer's office twice but continued to avoid the other victims despite his therapist's suggestions to join group sessions. He didn't want to know those people. In a sense, he wished he no longer knew himself.

HE HOPED WORK would be an escape. All he wanted was to be ignored. Instead, he was avoided, a different thing altogether, which he deeply resented. His first life had been full of casual contact — handshakes, the brush of fingers when exchanging files — but now he walked in a ghost world, isolated and damned, unclean. Once he caught a woman emptying out the coffee pot in the break room after he'd poured himself a cup.

"You need an outlet for your anger," the therapist told him. "Paint. Play music. Let it out."

He blasted ten thousand spaceships on his PlayStation and smashed baseballs at the batting cages until his hands and wrists throbbed. He went skating but ached deep in his soul when confronted with rollergirls whose firm-bodied health had always been the stuff of fantasy.

There were dating services that linked HIV-positive singles, even heterosexual drug-free singles. He'd never have oral sex again or experience intercourse without the sensation-killing barrier of prophylactics — mixing viral strains at random would only hasten his decay — but the possibility of intimacy did exist, no matter how sad and unappealing. Nonsmoker, professional, likes movies...

The note left in his cubicle read: *Faggots rot in hell*!

He should have laughed at this ignorant cowering bluster. His therapist would have been proud. Yet it was a full minute before he stopped shaking and unballed his fist from around the crumpled paper. He showed it to his boss, establishing a record, then did his best to provoke his suspects, visiting their cubicles often, volunteering exaggerated reports of his treatments and future symptoms.

With luck, they'd strike again. Another lawsuit meant more money. And he enjoyed his plotting with fierce joy. It was wonderful to be the aggressor again.

THE SKINNY OLD woman in the free clinic that only charged fifty bucks had trouble finding his antecubital vein. The inside of his elbow might as well have been a dartboard.

"Here," he said, with all the patience he could muster.

Flying out to California had not been a great idea — his mom made him chicken soup thirteen times in two and half weeks, and his dad no longer seemed capable of looking him in the eye — but he couldn't afford a real vacation. The liability suit had yet to be resolved, and he'd missed too much work during the past year.

There was solace in resignation. Even a bad game of golf with his dad was better than rotting alone. Iced tea tasted as good as ever. Fresh-cut grass still smelled amazing. But the yuppie foursome that played ahead of them ripped his heart. The breeze had been full of the men's advice and cheerfully crude propositions, the women's laughter.

He should have been one of them.

Let go, let God, was his mother's mantra, and he tried to believe it. He practiced meditation now, energy-channeling, color therapy. Unfortunately, these were acts of desperation instead of than real faith.

Anger flared in him like a migraine when the old bitch missed his vein for the third time. Familiar, powerful anger.

He'd hoped to get through the summer without subjecting himself to more blood work, but his doctor wanted to try a new anti-viral and needed a fresh count. His insurance, which had begun clamping down, declared this an elective process, so instead of visiting real professionals he'd come here, exposing himself to a lobby full of sicknesses borne by other people who couldn't afford better care.

Even worse was the humiliation of revealing his secret to new people. The dark-eyed receptionist had been polite but he knew what she was thinking. He wished she wasn't so pretty. He wished no one was that pretty.

The skinny old bitch forgot to apply pressure after she withdrew the hypo. He grabbed a cotton ball from her supplies and jammed it down on the puncture himself so that he wouldn't bruise. He almost said something caustic, but in his new life he'd encountered plenty of workers who were ill-trained, indifferent, condescending, too busy.

It did not surprise him that trust was a mistake.

"THERE'S NO NEED for alarm," said the man on the phone. "We just want you to come down for retesting just to be safe."

Rather than disposing of disposable needles, the silly bitch had washed them with hot water and soap, thinking she was doing good, being thrifty. Her training had consisted of two four-hour classes and she would have continued to mix and match blood-borne diseases in unsuspecting people except that a more experienced co-worker happened to observe her at the sink.

Of the more than five hundred people this woman treated, only eleven proved to be infected. Various officials declared victory.

Six of those eleven had passed through the clinic immediately after him. Ironically, all were healthy twenty- or thirty-somethings, for the most part sexually active, in their prime, exactly like he had been not so long ago. All six had chosen to be tested for HIV merely for their own peace of mind after seeing too many community service commercials.

Now they had his strain of the virus as well as the Hepatitis B he'd picked up from a man before him.

He remembered a few faces and articles of clothing from the waiting room, a strident voice, nothing more. What had happened wasn't his fault — it had never been his fault — but he felt a connection that had never existed between himself and the other victims of the movie theater incident. Perhaps he was weaker now, after months of constant isolation and loss.

He tried to seek them out, but confidentiality rules made this difficult, as did a circle-the-wagons mentality on the part of the clinic, which was already under threat of several lawsuits. Neither of the two women he managed to track down wanted anything to do with him. One was hysterical. Both seethed with blame. He understood, yet it might have helped to create a special tribe. People to die with.

Hepatitis would ravage his compromised immune system.

WHEN HE WOKE the next morning, the sun was strong and promising and two fat scrub jays screeched energetically in the flowering shrubs. He watched them without expression.

He'd finally achieved the narrow thoughtlessness that had eluded him for so long. He understood *why* now — knew what dark instinct had driven the nameless monster who'd killed him, no matter how random and insane as it must seem to the healthy, the secure, the happy.

He had been infected in that theater in more than one sense.

After breakfast, he stabbed himself with a dozen needles and went out to boobytrap some park benches.

END

Afterword

"Monsters" must be the most disturbing piece of fiction I've ever written, and I say that as someone whose first novel opens with five billion people dead.

The heroes of *Plague Year* are murdering cannibals — the heroes! — but this story bothers people more. I think that's because the protagonist of "Monsters" deliberately turns to evil. In the end, he chooses to walk into the darkness, whereas Cam and Sawyer and the other survivors of *Plague Year* have no other option.

I got this idea from a newspaper article, and, later in the story, the nameless hero reads about other mindless attacks both large and small. A lot of people are unhappy. Some of them try to make everyone else unhappy, too.

Why? What drives them to spread the misery instead of working to reduce it?

Sometimes I think it's a failure of imagination. Many of us are short-sighted. We can't see beyond our own immediate needs, and I think that's incredibly sad. It's also scary as hell. "Monsters" is upsetting, but it's probably also the best story to emerge from my horror phase. Too often, life is horrific, and it's hard to argue that "Monsters" doesn't capture that feeling.

ROMANCE

THAT THE ODDS were always against them must have been part of the appeal.

He was a dark stranger with a Glock 9mm that never left his reach and suitcases full of cash belonging to another man. She was book-smart, lonely, restless, the only daughter of that other man — a greedy and fear-plagued mob boss who treated her like a treasure, like something to be counted and displayed.

He had wasted his life earning percentages. She'd lost hers dreaming of freedom.

He spoke to her gently when they met in her father's house and she murmured a polite response, and their watchful eyes conveyed a promise meant for no others.

They escaped that bleak world together.

Her skin was hot silk, his kiss devouring, her murmurs an invitation as well as a demand for more.

He found work hammering nails while she took tickets at the zoo — mundane jobs that delighted her with their ordinariness. Their apartment was tiny and had only one window. It was a perfect nest.

She taught him laughter and intimacy with notes and whispers; by loading his dinner with jalapenos; by sharing her education. He taught her less meaningful things such as how to count cards, stack beer cans, clean handguns. They were content.

The men who tracked them down brought a terse message: *Come back. Now.* She surprised everyone by pulling a pistol.

They escaped again, this time deep into Mexico. She read him poetry while he massaged her neck. They slept late and basked in each other's heat.

One day her father himself appeared, backed by twenty men.

The siege lasted two hours. They killed six. Their wounds were horrible, their spirits undaunted, their final shared smile a loving, bloody grimace of fierce beauty.

Last chance, her father called through a bullhorn from the smoky yard, and she killed the bastard who'd stolen their dreams with a lucky shot snapped off from the hip.

They died in a firestorm, triumphant like all doomed lovers, together forever.

END

Afterword

Like "Exit," this short short was conceived for an annual fiction contest, this one held by SLO Nightwriters, a writing group of which I was a member for two years while living on California's central coast. "Romance" didn't do as well as "Exit." As I recall, it placed fifth or sixth, but I've always liked it for its compact elegance.

Yes, it's cliché. But it's elegant. You won't be surprised to hear that I was watching a lot of Quentin Tarantino movies at the time.

NURTURE

SHAWNA PLACED THE jane doe's age at mid- to late-twenties. Her age. She'd never cut someone who could have been her friend before, and she hesitated twice before pressing down on the scalpel.

Like Shawna, the jane doe had been taking care of herself, exercising, eating enough greens, trimming her nails and bikini line, unlike the sloppy bastards who came in full of taco grease and wearing the same boxers that they'd had on for a week. You could read people's lives by how they'd treated themselves. The jane doe had expected to kick ass for another seventy years.

It was sort of like seeing herself on the table, and Shawna got spooked, which made her mad. Here in the city, people weren't bothered by anything — screaming on the next block over, naked homeless people — unless you slipped into a parking space they'd been waiting for or held up the line at the ATM. Shawna punished herself by proceeding slowly with extra attention. Otherwise she might not have catalogued the subtle deformations in the woman's temporal lobes.

At first the withered specks, just slightly whiter than the pale yellow sponge of so-called "gray matter," were something that Shawna assumed to be part of the head trauma.

Probably the victim of a hit-and-run accident but considered a possible murder, the jane doe had been smashed by a vehicle going in excess of forty miles per hour. Her blue shorts and the fluorescent green impact gel on the soles of her running shoes had been alien swatches of brightness in the quiet, tiled lab until Shawna removed and bagged them.

This was Shawna's first solo autopsy, which she'd been permitted only because Oakland PD had already taken samples of the orange-colored paint imbedded in the jane doe's skin — and because the cause of death was so obvious: fractured neck, impacted cranium. Shawna's boss expected her to finish the paperwork and return to other tasks, but she had always been meticulous.

Close examination revealed that the withered pinpoints were a preexisting condition, which didn't make sense, given the jane doe's youth and obvious health.

Shawna had seen plenty of weird stuff, of course, even though she'd only been an assistant M.E. for three weeks. In med school, it had seemed like every other case study dealt with some abnormality or affliction — and after she washed out, her new instructors had nothing but horror stories. Few people grew up wanting to inspect corpses as a career, although it paid well, and many medical examiners took a perverse pride in cataloging "unique freaks." Nature was wild. Second stomachs, missing genitals, hair growing inside the skin rather than out from it — living structures were too complicated to be cookie cutter perfect. In fact, perfection did not exist. The immaculate businesswomen who made Shawna feel so much like an imposter, like a hick, were in reality all mascara, padded bras, and hair gel, doomed like everyone else to allergies, shag carpet eyebrows, toe fungus, or irritable bowel syndrome.

The jane doe must have had some difficulty processing her senses. It wouldn't have been anything as dramatic as autism, but Shawna knew enough neurology to suspect that sound and smell especially had been dim for the dead woman. A specialist would be able to tell more.

Could the jane doe's inattention have contributed to the accident that killed her?

WHEN SHAWNA EMERGED from the basement lab, there was still some sunlight left, but she didn't stop to enjoy it yet. She double-checked the side door to make sure it was locked, then hurried up out of the box-like well of concrete that housed the stairs, which reeked of urine and was littered with cigarette butts again. Homeless people often camped there... but why did they pee and leave garbage in the same place where they slept?

Once out of the stairwell and near her car, Shawna paused to examine the bruised sky. She'd never seen sunsets like this back in Ford County. There wasn't enough pollution back home.

"Rush hour" had ended ninety minutes ago, but in Shawna's experience the maddening congestion of cars was permanent. Errands that had taken her thirty minutes back home — dry cleaning, groceries, gas — now required most of two hours and her whole day had to be planned accordingly.

Every sixty seconds or less she found herself backed up at a stoplight with dozens of other vehicles, most of them containing only a solitary driver like herself. It was horrendously wasteful and stupid, but nobody was going to the same places on the same schedule. Someday someone would invent a better system. Meanwhile they all hated each other for being in the way.

Shawna hated feeling so self-conscious, too. Singing along with the radio helped pass the time, but whenever they came to a halt she shut up, looking neither right nor left, keeping her expression neutral, like a mannequin. The natives simply ignored the world outside their shells of steel and glass, chatting on cell phones or picking their noses.

At home, her neighbors were at it again, their TV cranked up so loud that each voice made the wall buzz. Shawna had taken down her family photos almost as soon as she'd hung them because the rattling of the frames only increased her irritation. She had gotten better at ignoring the noise, but she still wasn't sleeping well. Months ago she'd started off nice, apologizing for being bothered, but lately she'd taken to banging on the wall and harassing the landlord's answering machine. No one cared.

MR. MORROW, AS Shawna's boss insisted on being called, showed little interest in the brain deformities of the jane doe, who wasn't a jane doe anymore but Joan Kristyn Tarwater. Mr. Morrow was right that they were behind on their case load, yet Shawna didn't think that excused doing less than a thorough job.

The updates to Tarwater's file offered little personal history and no record of health problems, not even something as subtle as dizziness or fatigue, but Shawna was transfixed. Twenty-nine, single, an admin assistant for a fax and copier sales company, Joan Tarwater really could have been the friend Shawna had been looking for since moving to California.

"Joan's condition may have contributed to her death," Shawna said.

"The client," Mr. Morrow answered carefully, "was killed by severe head trauma. That's all we need to know."

The bloated old coot had obviously been down in Autopsy for ten years too long. His office was above ground, but he kept the blinds three-quarters shut, allowing no more than a dim shine. Shawna didn't like the way the place smelled, either. Even the meat-and-disinfectant stink downstairs was better than Mr. Morrow's gastronomic endeavors.

"I'd like to get a specialist's opinion," Shawna said. "Joan's family has a right to know..."

Mr. Morrow shook his pumpkin head. "There's no room in the budget for that. It's just not necessary." He waved her back to work. "Get used to not always having all the answers."

SHAWNA MIGHT HAVE forgotten about Joan. She worked ten hour days while Oakland experienced one of those bizarre cycles where the elderly gave up, the sick wore out, and coronaries and accidents struck down the out-of-shape and the unwary. But that four days later, she found almost exactly the same abnormalities in the frontal lobes of a seventeen-year-old boy. His name was Steven Huff. The police report said he'd fallen off the roof of his three-story home while goofing around with a friend. Maybe they'd fought. Steven might have escaped with nothing worse than a broken leg except he'd failed to clear an awning, spun around, and landed head first.

Shawna decided not to bother Mr. Morrow. The lazy coot was obviously mostly concerned with keeping their 'files closed' rate above par. But she had to wonder if the bizarre cerebral deformations would have been found in any of the six skulls that she hadn't opened during the past four days, or in any of the eleven that Mr. Morrow had handled himself.

In 1977, a stunning incidence of childhood arthritis had led a group of Yale physicians to identify a new bacterial disease transmitted by ticks in a small Connecticut city called Lyme. About the same time, a wasting sickness predominant among homosexual males in San Francisco had caused scientists to discover HIV. There were more examples like this than Shawna had fingers and toes. Nature was not all postcard beaches, fuzzy animal babies, and flowers. Parasites and viruses were a normal part of life — and it was only the energy of trained professionals that initiated the battles against such killers.

Shawna saw both an opportunity to help and, maybe, a second chance at medical school.

She scanned MedNet during breaks and lunches, entombing herself in the windowless file room, the door shut to avoid questions, knocking back cold coffee as if it were shots of tequila. She tried a variety of key words, uncertain at first if she was wasting her time. Many private offices and even some major hospitals had yet to upload their files — and yet if anything there was too much information, too many undiagnosed curiosities of the cerebrum. Nature was a tricky bitch, complex, sometimes cruel. The human race still knew very little about their own bodies.

Shawna ruled out major afflictions like retardation and other obvious handicaps. Joan Tarwater and Steven Huff had both been healthy, functioning individuals, at least on the surface.

That was the interesting part.

SHAWNA HAD NO authority to begin an investigation or any experience conducting one, but she was painfully unsatisfied with the police department's verdict. They just said it was open case, which meant they would ignore the file unless some new information hopped up and bit them on the butt.

It was tough to blame the police for this, given how badly outnumbered and overworked they were, but a human life should never be shelved so perfunctorily. Joan was more than a computer file to Shawna. Worse, if she had discovered a new brain disease, it was crucial to learn what caused it and how it could be stopped.

Shawna sent blandly worded e-mails to Steven and Joan's physicians, Joan's gynecologist, Steven's teacher, even their dentists, stressing the need for discretion, not sure what she was looking for yet hopeful that a clue would arise. She planned to visit their families before the end of the week, but her regular work could not be put on hold, especially now that Mr. Morrow was allowing her some real responsibility.

Joan Tarwater had lived in a duplex set practically under the freeway. Idling in the middle of the street, Shawna gawked at the building until a delivery truck honked behind her. She'd thought her place was awful. The view here was of massive concrete pillars and perpetual shadow, while the windows of what must be converted attics peeked out on four lanes of hurtling traffic.

Shawna had driven here on her own time, and at six-thirty in the evening, the wide mud lots under the freeway were packed with residents' cars, an impromptu parking lot. There wasn't room anywhere else for all those vehicles now that everyone was home. Shawna finally squeezed into a bit of red curb nearly three blocks away, obstructing a fire hydrant but hoping that the city ID she put on the dash would save her from a ticket, although it seemed unlikely that anyone was enforcing petty laws in the area.

She kept one hand in her purse as she walked like she'd seen other solitary women do. The theory was to scare off muggers with sheer potential. *What caliber are you packing?* The small plastic rod of her pepper spray wasn't especially reassuring.

The front steps and handrails of Joan's building were coated in grime. So were the windows that Shawna had thought were tinted. Exhaust, dirt. Maybe those were her first clues.

If there had been a police seal on Joan's place, it was gone now. A neatly scissored section of brown grocery bag tacked to the door gave upcoming dates that the apartment would be shown as well as the landlord's phone number. Shawna wondered what had happened to Joan's belongings while she dug into her purse for a notepad. She wondered who would attend the funeral.

She knocked on the door opposite Joan's, not feeling nervous until footsteps creaked toward her. She managed a smile when it struck her that she was being examined through the peephole.

Whoever spoke could have been male or female: "What?"

Shawna held up her little wallet, folded open to display her city employee's health benefits card, which had her photo, and a generic business card used by everyone in the office. "I'm Shawna King, Oakland M.E. I wanted to talk to you about your neighbor for a minute."

Three locks snapped open and the door yanked inward. Black, very tall, the man was bald except for a salt-and-pepper mustache and gray eyebrows. Shawna wouldn't have matched his reedy voice with his body. He had seven inches and at least sixty pounds on her, which would have made her wonder about his caution not so long ago — but paranoia was very natural here.

"Which neighbor?" he asked.

"Joan Tarwater, right across from you."

"The police came by already."

A lie came surprisingly easily, as did a bored tone of disgust. "They managed to lose their transcripts," Shawna said.

"Typical." He seemed to take satisfaction at the thought of incompetence, and actually smiled as he gestured past Shawna's shoulder. "Well, she was a real bitch, I can tell you that much, always telling everyone where to park, how loud to play our music. It wouldn't surprise me if she got bumped on purpose."

For some reason, Shawna felt mad at him. *Well*, she thought, *who gets along with their neighbors in this city?*

BUT JOAN'S CO-WORKERS at CNG Copiers thought she was a bitch, too, and weren't hesitant to say so.

Two days had passed since Shawna began her slapdash investigation. She'd had no luck with her e-mails or with the phone calls she made to press the issue, not even after arguing with a file clerk or threatening a receptionist who wouldn't put her through. None of the professionals in Joan and Steven's lives had anything definitive to offer. Steven had been a minor disciplinary problem at school, and had teased some of the pets in his neighborhood so badly that the cops had been called, twice, yet that was all very normal stuff for a teenager.

Shawna was swinging in the dark at this point, hoping to nail down some preliminary characteristics or symptoms before she submitted her report. After that, her discovery would be open game for better trained and more prominent people. Shawna hoped to luck into attaching her name to it first.

She'd found excuses to open up the skulls of an elder stroke victim and a drunk who'd smothered in bed, yet neither of them had showed abnormalities. That was good news, really. Shawna felt disappointed.

Getting through security at the CNG building was much easier than convincing Mr. Morrow to allow her a long lunch "to take care of errands." He never spoke to her anymore without mentioning their workload, and she never laid eyes on him now without wishing that she could tell him off. Fortunately, there was room for them to avoid each other most of the day.

The ladies who'd shared a small glassed-in office with Joan Tarwater were a modern Tweedledee and Tweedledum — tight StairMaster bodies, short, simple hair, and an abundance of attitude. "Joan's job wasn't exactly what you call demanding," the first lady said, and the second didn't even try to hide her catty smirk. "Talk to Prince," she muttered. "Joan used to date the hairball."

Shawna spent fifteen minutes looking for Jim Prince in a maze of gray cubicles before she was told she was on the wrong floor. In the elevator, she wished bitterly that she'd gone back to Dee and Dum and shaken some politeness into them.

Jim Prince was a pale young man with rumpled clothes, rumpled hair, and dark puffy patches under his eyes. He hunched over his desk, practically hugging it, but let go to grab at Shawna's ID. "Let me see that," he said

"I just have some very simple questions."

"I'll try to give you some simple answers." His laugh was a quick bark. He dropped her wallet onto the desk, perhaps an inch closer to her than himself.

Shawna tried to keep her voice cool. "Joan may have had a disease. Were the two of you intimate?"

He didn't react the way she'd hoped. If anything, his belligerence increased. "Sure. But we were safe, you know? What kind of disease?"

"Did she ever complain about feeling nauseous or dizzy? Or have any problems with her hearing?"

"She complained all the time." Prince barked again. "She was a queen bitch, you know, her way or the highway. So I told her to get cranked."

If Shawna hadn't learned that assholes were as common as cracks in the sidewalk, and if she hadn't been stepping so far outside the bounds of her job, she might have checked with the police to see if Prince was on their suspects list. His intensity seemed out of place, even for an ex-boyfriend.

But no murderer would act so obvious.

NO ONE CAME to the door at Steven Huff's residence, although Shawna was certain she glimpsed somebody through the drapes in the front window. She knocked twice, then pounded until she scraped her knuckles. She was tired and hungry and knew she'd be late back to work, and she didn't look forward to keeping her mouth shut as

Mr. Morrow lectured her about responsibility.

Walking back to her car, Shawna stumbled in the tiny scrap of yard because she wasn't looking where she was going. Just a few blocks away, the I-80/580 interchange dominated the hills, a tangle of no less than six overpasses sweeping through and alongside one another. The roaring traffic sounded like a storm tide, violent and unstoppable.

Could pollution be the common denominator between Joan and Steven? Nature was clever, karmic. It always gave back what had been given to it. Lately the papers had been full of the state's efforts to remove a fuel additive from gas supplies and production after traces of this chemical had been found in their drinking water.

Driving away, Shawna slowed at a corner and shook her busy thoughts from her head, studying the street signs. Somehow she wanted to bypass southbound 80 and get to 580.

Checking her mirrors for police before making an illegal left, she noticed a yellow car in her rearview. A moment later, she noticed it again. It had made the same awkward turn after her. The car was an older four-door.

Shawna groped in her purse for her pepper spray as she made another sudden left at random. Bad decision. The street narrowed to one lane as she passed a dumpster and then loose piles of flattened cardboard — and then there was nowhere else to go. The walls were broken only by a few barred windows and occasional side-alleys that would have been too narrow to turn into even if they weren't full of pallets loaded with boxes and green produce.

The yellow car did not follow.

Shawna took three measured breaths, but she didn't let go of the pepper spray, ticking her thumbnail over its textured grip again and again. *Paranoid*, she thought. *I've gotten just as paranoid as every-one, impatient, irritable, and stupid...*

She didn't like the way she was changing.

She considered going home, not her cramped, noisy condo, but *home*. She had friends there and two guys she'd known well, a third she'd been interested in. Odds were that at least one of them wouldn't have hooked up with anyone else yet. Things moved slower in Ford County. In fact, life there was too slow, but there was a lot to be said for peace. She could find work, wait for a veterinarian's assistant job to open up... But failing med school had hurt her badly, and Shawna wasn't sure she could ever settle for a regular job like waitressing or running a register. For one thing, she still had school loans to pay off. More importantly, being a professional had become a treasured part of herself. It was too late to ever go back.

The street ended in a T, but a parked truck blocked the left branch. Idling in the right branch was the yellow four-door.

Shawna stared, frozen, with her foot on the brake. Her car was at an angle halfway through the tight turn.

In this light, the other car was the same shade as the paint that had been dug out of Joan Tarwater's flesh. It was also much heavier than her late-model Honda, and when it lurched forward it shoved her car back a full yard, shattering her plastic fender.

Shawna's seatbelt tightened across her sternum like a broad fist. Her pulse was deafening. Mixed with her heart's thudding were footsteps that rattled over the hood of her car. She tried to shake off her shock.

She didn't recognize the man who threw open her driver door. He slapped aside the pepper spray as she thrust it forward, his palm blocking the brief squirt of fluid — and when he slapped the same hand back across her face, her right eye exploded with more than pain. It burned with pepper spray.

He dragged her out, smashing the air from her as his blunt fingers punched her breast. The panting against her cheek smelled like cinnamon. For an instant, they stood motionless between her open driver door and her car, the man embracing her tightly from behind. Shawna's mind churned, but at the same time she felt as thoughtless as a rabbit.

"Shit, dude, gimme room—"

There was a second man. A baritone. Shawna glanced around, sucking air to shout for help.

Jim Prince stood directly behind the first man, near Shawna's car, leveling a small automatic pistol. "Gimme roo—"

Then she was moving again. The first man pushed her away like a dance partner, his hands controlling her hips. In her peripheral vision, Shawna sensed motion as Prince took aim.

She went limp, dropping straight down, putting as much of her weight as she could into her right foot as she kicked at the first man's ankle. Her heel ground across the bridge of his foot and slammed into his shin. He toppled toward her.

Prince's wild shot blew the back of the man's head off.

Seconds later, Prince stepped forward, almost standing over her, as Shawna wasted time dragging her arm across her eyes to clear the sticky red spatter of blood. His scream felt like her own. She tried to roll away, but the first man's twitching body blocked her.

Prince fired. The bullet struck the asphalt beside her, then bounced up through the skin of her thigh into the open car door. Plastic specks burst from the stereo speaker under the armrest.

An idea knifed through her, and Shawna swung her left hand up against the outside of the door, fracturing both bones in her wrist, feeling nothing. The door swung over her and slammed the pistol from Prince's hand, twisting him around, bringing him to his knees. His weight trapped one of Shawna's legs, but she rose into a sitting position and bashed him with the door again.

And again. And again, yanking her twisted, sprained leg free of his half-conscious body, putting every muscle into the swing of the door. Again and again and again.

OF COURSE SHE had to explain everything, first while she lay in a hospital bed, then later in more detail. Eventually she gave well-rehearsed speeches, although it was seven months before public announcements were made — twenty-eight weeks in which Shawna was allowed to play at least a supporting role in the autopsies of Jim Prince and his accomplice, in subsequent tests and experiments, and in the new investigation of Prince's murder of Joan Tarwater.

Shawna was hardly a star among the many neurologists, pathologists, and assorted Ph.Ds, but she worked long hours and made a name for herself, a place for herself.

It was the beginnings of a real career. In retrospect, that made the entire ordeal worthwhile. She'd become a success.

Ironically, the police reached nearly the same verdict as they had before. They attributed Joan's murder to Prince and closed the case, but there just wasn't enough information to discern what argument or simple evil had made him do it.

Prince and his buddy must have come after Shawna out of fear of being caught, but it had been an incredibly reckless thing to do, given the number of witnesses who'd seen her at CNG Copiers. They might have hoped to pass it off as a mugging or rape gone bad. Or maybe they hadn't worried much about the consequences.

Shawna had nightmares that their motivation had been something deeper — the fear of being *discovered.*

Could Prince have known he was different?

Was it possible that he and Joan had shared some instinct that was the basis of their attraction? If so, that would be more irony. The same reduced sensitivities that made them different had no doubt led to friction, then hatred...

Parts of Prince's frontal lobes were literally shrunken.

More disturbing in some ways, however, was that Prince's accomplice had proved normal in every way. One hundred percent normal. Aggression and stupidity would not be erased from the human race simply by curing this cerebral disorder.

Medical examiners across the nation were quietly told to gather more information. They began to open all of the skulls in their morgues. But the initial report, after seven months, offered more questions than answers. The disorder was widespread, affecting maybe one person in fifteen, almost entirely in urban areas — but it did not seem to be caused by anything so obvious as pollution, advanced bacteria, or a virus. None of those things had been ruled out as contributing factors, and wouldn't be for years to come, yet they were extremely reluctant to label it *learned behavior* as Shawna had suggested.

Shawna was certain. That it was affecting kids like Steven Huff seemed proof enough.

They were doing it to themselves.

Nurture could be just as strong as nature. Every day people deliberately shut down parts of their minds to escape the noise and congestion and sheer emotional impact of their lives. Ignoring so much so often became more than habit. It caused atrophying, a defense mechanism that did more harm than good, because people with limited empathy, patience, and self-control would have a greater tendency toward confrontation and risk.

The papers and TV had a spectacular time with the news. Conspiracy theories flooded the Internet. Politicians and religious leaders bemoaned economic woes or liberal social programs. Hotlines were established, studies funded.

But nothing changed, of course. There really wasn't anything to be done.

SHAWNA QUIT HER job and went home.

END

Afterword

I wrote "Nurture" when I moved back to the urban sprawl of the Bay Area after living for several years in small towns in Arizona, Colorado, Idaho, and on California's central coast. There was an amount of culture shock. I especially hated how much time it suddenly took to run simple errands.

On the coast, I used to rollerblade to the grocery store with a backpack. In the Bay Area, it became a 15 minute drive in each direction, plus several minutes to hunt around for a spot in the store's overloading parking lot. Yuck.

"Nurture" is the only "trunk story" in this collection — the only story that never sold anywhere — and I can tell you why.

Editors didn't like this piece because it doesn't have a neat, perfect ending in which our brave young heroine identifies the cause of the epidemic, confronts it, and defeats it. One of the fallacies in storytelling is that every story needs a tidy wrap-up. We're trained to expect it: three acts and a climax. Sometimes I get complaints about *Plague Year* and *The Frozen Sky* for the same reason, but, like "Nurture," those stories deal with planet-wide disasters.

Planet-wide disasters aren't something you tidily wrap-up. The best you can hope for is an uneasy peace and hope for the future. The world is just like that. Civilization is too large and too complex to pack into an hour-long TV episode.

I felt it would unrealistic, even false, to put Shawna in a prominent role in an internationally-coordinated crash program to develop some kind of super-vaccine. She's a rookie assistant medical examiner. And introducing a new bevy of characters, all of them biologists and toxicologists and secret agents, would step beyond the bounds of this story and begin an entirely new one.

Ultimately, her individual choice to live as well as she can, in the best place she can, needed to serve as the final note in this story. That's the wrap-up. She wants to be happy and safe. We should all be so lucky.

GUNFIGHT AT THE SUGARLOAF PET FOOD & TAXIDERMY

FORTUNATELY THERE WAS always one more moron coming down the road. Otherwise Julie would have had to find a real job, or move again, but she loved it here in Big Sky Country as they bragged on their license plates — the high rolling plains, the slow winters and sweet, pungent summers. There was room to think.

Trolling for hot-heads, drunks and fools wasn't exactly big money, yet Julie enjoyed every minute of it. First there was the waiting, tucked away in the brush with her remote controls and a thermos of tea, letting her mind roam or whispering on the radio until some joker passed by in his gun-racked truck. Always a *him*. Usually tossing out Coors cans and cigarette butts. Cigarettes! In many ways the people here were a century behind the rest of the nation, and proud of it.

The little man in the sports car was a surprise.

As he sped around the turn, his headlights flashed over the silhouettes of Julie's deer standing in a meadow. Of course her beautiful beasties didn't run. Then his brake lights flared and he stepped out wearing a nice jacket, no hat. No lonesome country band thumping on an old cassette deck.

Julie had come north to escape labels and stereotypes, and

recognized the irony of her thoughts. She wanted to be a better person. But the fact of the matter was that her victims tended toward a demographic particularly easy to reduce to cartoons: single syllable name, beer gut, filthy pants.

Shorty here did not fit the bill. Julie didn't think he was even driving an American car, given the low shape of it. Maybe an Audi. He looked like a suave TV villain there at the edge of his headlights, trim and spare — and barely five-foot-five.

When he pulled the compact Uzi submachine gun, Julie's headset distinctly said, "Oh no."

Julie froze, her left thumb jammed down on a button, her right hand still pulling on a joystick. In the meadow, the doe's tail twitched and twitched and twitched while the buck's head reared back so far that its antlers gouged its own spine. Any local would have jumped back in his truck.

Shorty opened fire on full auto. Both deer burst apart into flecks of real hide, white cotton stuffing and metal gears.

"Yeeeeeeehaw!" he screamed.

Already lying prone, Julie squashed her breasts so flat that they migrated into her armpits as the distinct snap of a bullet went overhead. Highsong had let her choose the location and set-up tonight, and her first priority was always to hunker down out of the line of fire. Way out. Some of the drunkards would make superb material for anti-NRA commercials, blasting away like they were General Custer combating the Sioux Nation.

Shorty quit only when the buck's head winged away and its savaged body remained standing. He lowered his Uzi and gawked.

Typically the next stage of the game went smoothly. This wasn't west Miami. The Great White Poacher knew he'd been tricked, and humiliation doused his adrenaline. Highsong would crash out of the woods in a monster SUV, lights flashing, loudspeaker booming. The men about to be ticketed were often indignant, and enough California retirees had invaded the land that now the words *entrapment* and *lawyer* came on a regular basis, yet only twice had Julie seen somebody wave a rifle threateningly. Never had anyone actually taken aim. But they weren't packing machine guns.

"Uh, Highsong?" Julie whispered into the radio. She snuck a hand under her belly to see if she'd peed herself.

His voice was a groan: "What!"

"What're you gonna do?"

"We. What are we going to do. I don't know."

Shorty had finally twigged that a deer, like every other living thing, requires a head to stay on its feet. He cut glances left and right as he scuttled back to his car.

"It's a huge bust, don't just let him go." Now that she knew she was okay, Julie got mad. She didn't think of herself as sentimental, but Bongo the Buck out there had survived almost two dozen arrests and twenty-eight gun wounds, three arrows and one rock. Now there would be no more. Neither poor Bongo nor the doe, still too new to have a name, would ever do a job again.

Julie also felt a leaping tickle of excitement. This was way beyond the usual combination of trespassing and hunting out of season at $238 a pop. This was the big time. She hissed, "You smash out onto the road like always and I'll back you—"

"Shut up and stay down."

"Highsong—"

"If you move I'll shoot you myself."

Julie fumbled for her binoculars and jotted down most of the license plate before the little man roared off.

He was headed straight into Sugarloaf.

BEING THE ONLY black woman around for at least three states, as she liked to say, Julie Beauchain would have been notorious even if she wasn't a mad scientist. That made it easy to get dates, but she still freaked when total strangers addressed her as *Miz Boo-kane* or *Boy-shane*.

Julie did not prefer the hostile anonymity of urban life. It was just that her first thirty-four years of existence hadn't done much to teach her that human beings could be polite and neighborly and honest. Yes, this region was favored by white supremacists and had been the last refuge of the Unabomber, but in a head-to-head collision, Florida's battalions of drugs lords, smugglers, militants, pimps and psychos would barely break a sweat kicking butt on Montana's worst.

She liked the mountains. She still laughed at the way that so-called cities *ended*, fading into open country, unlike the gargantuan concrete sprawl of Miami-Dade. The police here let you out of a speeding ticket with five bucks paid on the spot, even for doing a hundred and ten on the ruler-straight highways — and you could forget to lock your car and still find your stash of five dollar bills behind the sun visor.

Highsong drove back into town sedately, not at all interested in catching up to the man with the machine gun. Julie squirmed on the bench seat of the 4x4 Suburban as the radio bled static. Finally the voice of Sheriff Tom came in answer, mumbling, "Haven't seen him, Bow-shane."

"He was headed right at you."

"Well I'm looking up and down main street right now."

Tom Young had never been enthusiastic about Fish, Wildlife & Parks stationing a new unit locally, viewing them as competition instead of as allies, and a few months ago he'd grown openly difficult. The silly pecker had gotten himself nabbed for hunting out of season, twice on the same day.

Julie felt certain that the sheriff's second shooting had been vindictive. Men would let pride get the best of their intelligence every time, as if deer could somehow mock them. Her small experiment in social conditioning was a total failure in that regard, since her decoys must be bitterly cursed across the state. Everyone knew. And yet each four-hour sting still averaged at least one bust. Some guys were simply too full of testosterone to pass up a target.

She tried to keep her voice calm, glancing at Highsong for approval. "Sheriff, there's only a few side roads between here and town. Why don't we each take a couple?"

As usual, the sheriff didn't answer immediately. Then: "Sounds like a goose chase to me, Bow-shane. There's lots more turn-offs than that. You just don't know the area."

"Neither does this guy, he's not local."

"Well we'll keep an eye out for that license plate."

"Sheriff..."

Highsong patted her knee and Julie let herself be distracted, looking down from the dark road ahead to her leg. Lately her weekday partner had grown chummy — and not in a brotherly way, she hoped. His hands were giant and scarred and always nimble with equipment, colored like cinnamon to her chocolate. Julie had memorized an excessively poetic list of the places and ways she wanted to be touched.

She scooched away from Highsong on the long, bed-sized seat, tucking her own small hands into her lap where they couldn't do anything embarrassing. "Out," the sheriff mumbled against her crotch, and she slammed the square microphone back in its cradle.

Highsong might have smiled. Julie opened her mouth but then shut it, angry with herself for being flustered.

When the two of them were lying out there in the cool empty night, murmuring into each other's ear, she imagined her curves against his angles. She imagined being married twenty years. She and Highsong never babbled, but they shared the obvious passions for wildlife, for hiking, for camping out. He was surprisingly obsessed with global politics and always asked about new developments in her work, and it was only on the drives back or sitting face-to-face over burgers and pie in noisy Mother's Tavern that they couldn't find any words.

Somehow that made her crush all the sweeter, and as irritating as hell.

Even romance was different up here on the plains.

BACK AT HER shop, unloading the remains of her deer in a cloud of cotton fiber, Julie sneezed directly into Highsong's face. "Oh jeez, I'm sorry!"

He mopped at his cheek, unflappable as always. "I needed a shower anyway."

"Sorry! Really. How about some coffee or something, I'll show you my new mini." That was not an innuendo. Over their five months working together, Julie had grown terrified of spooking him, because if Highsong was indeed courting her it was in some infinitely patient Indian way. She tried to be all business. "This is a hundred times better than the decoys, really, I took some of those little lawn gnomes—"

"Julie, it's late," he said. "Next time, okay?"

But he wiped at his face again as he stepped away.

SHE WAS TOO upset to stay home. Still, she knew better than to go hunting an Uzi-toting maniac by herself.

She drove out to Shaug Nurseries as the moon rose.

Their stings were typically set up on private land owned by Drew Shaug, partly because it was a challenge to find more than a foot or two that Shaug didn't own for miles in any direction, mostly because he didn't appreciate trigger-happy cowboys running around the same woods as his grandchildren. Julie couldn't wait to hear his thoughts on assault weaponry. Shaug was employer, landlord or both to most of the local population, and no doubt he'd put a boot in Sheriff Tom's lazy backside.

From the highway, the lights of the nursery resembled a miniature city. She passed four gates before turning in, but Florida millionaires would have laughed at the Shaug residence. It was a plain ranch home within shouting distance of a sprawl of employee cabins, and the land in between was crowded with partially disassembled tractors.

Headlights rolled out to intercept her.

"Hey there, Boy-shane." Bob LaChapelle was Shaug's foreman and quite the charmer. His pickup truck was bigger than her pickup truck. Julie seemed to own the only small size Nissan ever sold in the state of Montana, and LaChapelle smiled down from the window of his giant Dodge Ram as they jawed like two riders out on the range.

"Mr. Shaug's buyin' seedlings in Europe," he said. "Want me to pass on a message?"

"Um, I guess not. Thanks."

She had already swung her truck around when she noticed an odd pattern of reflections in the dark window of Shaug's house. Looking back, she repressed the impulse to hit her brakes and then barely avoided steering into a ditch.

A car was easing down the jeep trail behind the garage with its headlights off — but its waxed hood glinted in the new light of the moon as it rocked back and forth.

Shorty's sports car.

JULIE DROVE MUCH further down the highway than she wanted. The open road felt like a stage and she had to go more than a mile before a rocky knoll concealed her. She made a U-turn, switched off her lights and then cruised back again, wondering how she'd stop without touching her brakes. She supposed she should have bashed out the taillights.

Her truck was personal property rather than an FW&P unit, so no radio. Highsong never answered when he was off-duty anyway. Typically he let his machine get the phone, too. Why? What was so important he couldn't be interrupted? She'd been to his trailer six times and had scrutinized the long living room and the kitchen especially for any sign of a woman's presence, but his home, so much like his face, was just too damn uncomplicated.

Julie let off the gas before she reached the north gate and turned in. Too fast. She yelped as her truck jolted through a pocket of mud, then yanked on the emergency brake. Finally she stopped. Her head thrummed with adrenaline.

She made too much noise rummaging through the mountain of boxes and bags in the truckbed, and stopped getting enough oxygen to think before she found what she wanted. That was okay. It was easier just to be muscle and a pair of eyes.

Most of the employee huts were dark. One seemed packed with people, talking too loud, laughing.

She came across Shorty's car in the shadows behind a row of greenhouses, its hood ticking as it cooled. He'd actually kicked in his taillights, and Julie smiled to think of him cursing his way over the hills and through the woods. Someone who lived here must have shown him that back route. LaChapelle? He might have been standing guard, waiting for Shorty. But why? What were they doing?

Julie blundered around the garage in time to be pinned by a slash of light spilling from the door of a double-wide trailer. *Bond, James Bond*, she thought disgustedly. Two men stepped inside, one small, one regular. Good thing they didn't glance back. She must have been a heck of a sight mincing along on tiptoe with her arms wrapped the decapitated, long-necked heads of a doe and a trumpeter swan.

She wedged herself into the muddy shadows under the trailer, beneath the living room window, and forced herself to work slowly. She was using new gear for the first time and wanted this field test to be a success.

She raised the swan first, bumping the trailer's wall with its beak as she thrust its face up to the glass.

"—king pinhead, you're smoking it yourself!?"

"Man, why don't you just relax."

Julie triple-checked the tape recorder she'd spliced into the wires falling from the swan's neck. Then she grinned. A swan's eyes were too small to be replaced with cameras that she could afford, so she'd plugged in high-gain microphones instead.

"Look at you." That was LaChapelle. "Look at your face all squinty and bloodshot. You know cTHC is *addictive*, right?"

"Just testing the product."

Shorty's voice was slower and deeper than she would've guessed, maybe because smoke had made his throat raw. Marijuana. THC was the drug in marijuana. Her brother had sucked it down the same way mom soaked herself in rum and coke.

Shorty said, "You wanna do business or what, man?"

"Do you? You almost got all of us shafted tonight playing Canuck Cowboy."

This just got better and better. Shorty was Canadian. Were they smuggling across the border? How much pot could you stuff into a sports car? It would make more sense just to grow it here with all these greenhouses and horticulture experts...

Julie performed quick surgery on the doe's wiring while she pinned the base of the swan's neck between the trailer wall and the back of her head. Then every muscle in her neck seized up. She leaned away, clumsily grabbing the swan before it hit the ground. If LaChapelle looked out now he'd think she was putting on a puppet show.

The doe had nightvision camera-eyes, of course, which she'd spliced into a DVD recorder. Staring at the tiny screen in her lap,

Julie lifted both animals again and zeroed in on the faint outlines behind the drapes.

"—even carrying a gun like that?"

"Wanna try it? Let's have a toke and go blow the tits off some stuff, buddy, you should see—"

"We're not buddies," LaChapelle said quietly. "We're business partners. And I think our other partners would be very, very unhappy to hear you're taking chances. And testing the product, you idiot, cTHC is *addictive*."

See THC. Canadian? Camouflaged. Cocaine. Cockamamie. Julie was too revved up to play Wheel of Fortune.

A bad ache knotted her shoulders again and she twisted her butt around in the dirt, trying to find a comfortable pose. It couldn't be done.

Shorty had what must be a briefcase and laid out several small items on the table, the first hot enough to show on infrared. A nifty little incubator. But LaChapelle gave him no money as far as she could tell, only paperwork, and Shorty muttered his way through a few lines: "The select crossbreeding resulting in concentrated THC has proved independent of the plus nitrogen fertilizer." He laughed. "You guys really think you're rocket scientists or something."

"Just bring it back to the lab, all right?"

Concentrated THC. They were retooling the plant to sink its teeth into people like tobacco or heroin.

Could Mr. Shaug know about this? He didn't need more money, that was for sure, and it didn't fit with his protectiveness of his family... LaChapelle and some cronies were probably looking to cash in on the side. Julie wondered why they were using a lab across the border, but it must be tough to find people with the right training, especially out in the middle of nowhere.

Busting an international biotech drug ring! She was going to be absolutely *buried* in venture capital money, and she couldn't wait to see the look on Sheriff Tom's face when the grumpy old boob realized she was his best friend in the world.

She was going to have to let him in on the glory.

DESPITE ITS FABULOUS name, the Sugarloaf Pet Food & Taxidermy was merely a three-room cabin set beside a warehouse in a dirt lot graced with two trees and a sagging fence. By rights the place should have been named something more along the lines of Beauchain Security, but Julie hadn't thought it prudent yet to draw that sort of attention. In any case it was Highsong who'd christened her shop, with mischief in his often unreadable dark eyes, and Julie had blown a hundred and forty bucks getting a sign made in the hope that he might feel a possessive twinge each time he picked her up.

She did not sell pet supplies. Highsong was a tease. He found it amusing that she had six bird feeders and threw snacks to every mutt in town, yet packed her warehouse with armies of dead beasts. Most of it was FW&P work, of course, although she did perform some regular taxidermy since it was decent money and also generated good will among the townies she'd busted.

Tonight her cabin seemed stuffy, too small. It had been one wild ride of a day — a new day now; it was twenty minutes after midnight — but things had ended well. Sheriff Tom had goggled at her recordings and actually stammered *thanks*. He said he'd go straight to the nursery as soon as the state police arrived. He also warned her that she stood some chance of trouble herself, having no authority, no warrant, but Julie pulled her tapes out his hands and told him to say he received an anonymous tip. Big deal. The man really was dense sometimes.

Heading home, she'd considered a drive out to Highsong's place with a sixpack to celebrate. But what if he wasn't alone?

She was putting water on for tea when twin lights flashed across her window, then again. She leaned over the hot stove to peek out. Speeding into her lot was a sports car, *the* sports car, followed by the sheriff's hard-top jeep.

"God no," Julie said.

Too late it all made sense. *Idiot.* How else could LaChapelle have known that Shorty machine-gunned her decoys?

Now she had maybe twelve seconds before they got inside, and used three grabbing her phone and punching 911. Then she wasted two more realizing that calling the cops might not be the best idea. What if all six members of the Sugarloaf sheriff's unit were in on the deal?

The slam of car doors felt like malfunctions in her heart. Julie forgot to think again as gunfire blew through her front door right over her head.

Originally she'd drawn up the killer lawn gnomes as a gag. In Florida, however, people crammed their yards with shiny plastic flamingos and miniature windmills and such. She'd realized there would be a paying market — and a trio of elves had been standing on her coffee table because she thought she might lure Highsong inside for a little show-and-tell.

Julie dove back behind her kitchen counter as Shorty kicked through the door. He goggled down at the weird greeting party he discovered inside, then snorted and started to kick at them.

The first elf misfired, its jaunty green cap rocketing off to the left. The second either aimed or launched poorly. Its taser-leads bit into the sofa with a flash of white electricity, at least twenty inches off-target.

The third elf rammed its juice home directly over Shorty's heart. His chest seemed to explode into ashes.

Julie screamed, expected buckets of blood. An instant later, though, her cabin was saturated in tasty blue smoke. He must have been carrying a personal stash in his pocket.

He toppled like Goliath onto the ceramic elves.

Coughing and wheezing, Julie rose from her hiding place and ran for the back door. Her feet felt huge, weightless, like soft balloons pushing her skyward. She was looking down at them when her face encountered the door and then her butt met the linoleum.

Oh jeez I'm totally schnockered! she realized, and sat there owlishly counting her own thoughts.

The sound of two gunshots slapped her like her mother's palm. She pushed herself upright. But the small, neat holes in the door stopped her again. *Just missed.* When she looked around her vision seemed dim — they were shadows thrashing toward her in great swimming motions and everyone was yelling.

Suddenly she was outside, wrapped in fogbanks of smoke. Then she could see again. The stars glittered and the chill air felt exquisite on her neck. She made sense of the fact that she was wearing only floppy socks and knew she couldn't run all the way back to Florida. She sprinted toward her warehouse instead.

"Goddamn goddamn goddamn!" Sheriff Tom chanted behind her.

She slammed the door on his anger and dropped to her hands and knees, sensing bullets like she had radar. Her consciousness felt huge and sensitive and vulnerable, as if every hair on her head had been squeezed full of brains like toothpaste.

She rolled right, then popped up beside a work table as the door crashed open with a resounding metal gong. The vibration felt so intense that her fingers wouldn't close on the master remote she wanted. Groping for it through the jumble of tools and wiring, she cut herself on a band saw and that raw hurt was the promise of death.

But LaChapelle wasn't handling the smoke well either. He went completely bug-nuts, shooting away from her — shooting her pets.

The black bear's only moving parts were its neck and one foreleg, yet even positioned on all fours it was nearly as tall as a man, a hulk of claws and teeth. Shotgun blasts echoed through the warehouse. Then she activated the rest of her toys and Sheriff Tom also opened fire, shrieking in fear.

Julie had not invented the robo-decoys. That honor went to a Wisconsin taxidermist. She had, however, made improvements as word got round and poachers grew wary.

The migratory elk were capable of walking stiffly and waddled forward in a slow-motion stampede, bumping and bonking each other. Julie realized with surprising passion that she had to take them to Hollywood, here's the pitch, live-action *Bambi* crossed with *Night of the Living Dead*. They formed a shaggy wall of muscle from which Sheriff Tom and LaChapelle could only blast meaningless, fist-sized hunks.

High in the rafters, a mass of shadows flopped and twitched.

She'd run out of working space in autumn, when gun lovers were permitted to kill beautiful fuzzy things and her decoys had to be put away. And in winter, Fish, Wildlife & Parks focused more on maintaining habitats than on trapping the few hunters enthusiastic enough to brave the elements.

Her birds nested on sheets of plywood laid across the open rafters — and her turkeys and sage grouse could all walk. The lone bald eagle and platoon of ring-necked pheasants could all open both wings. They carried the immobile owls, cranes and swans to the edge.

It was Biblical, a rain of fowl.

Most of the palsied horde crashed down upon the elk or her work tables, but enough hit their targets that Sheriff Tom vanished from sight and LaChapelle was driven to his knees, hacking on old dry feathers.

He put one last shot into the ceiling as Julie charged in for the *coup de grace*, high-stepping through the flapping mess. She brained LaChapelle with a duck and kicked him four times for good measure, then drove her bruised knee into Sheriff Tom's belly when she was bumped from behind by an elk still diligently marching its way forward.

THE PARAMEDIC KEPT pressing his thumb down on the skin beneath Julie's eyes, checking her pupil response to see if she was concussed. She had repeatedly lost track of what she was saying, fascinated by the blizzard of red and blue lights. The confusion of emergency vehicles and personnel seemed roughly equal to the congestion inside her stoned brain.

"Look up," the paramedic kept saying. "Can you look up?"

"Let's go over it again," the state trooper said. "They followed you into the warehouse..."

"Right." Julie tried to point and nearly fell over. She'd squeezed three industrial-size tubes of epoxy over the pile of robo-fowl, binding LaChapelle and Sheriff Tom into a surreal cake of beaks and bodies that would have to be taken apart with a power sander, no doubt painfully. As for Shorty, she had simply hit him with the taser again because she was unable to tie him up, having unfortunately glued her right hand to her own hip.

She gestured with her chin instead and saw Highsong among the milling uniforms. His head was also turning, searching, and Julie's first impulse was to hide. She was very aware of her own sour adrenaline breath and lumpy afro — but with the sudden clarity of the smoke, Julie understood that this might be her best and only chance.

He spotted her as soon as she started toward him, shuffling. Then his eyebrows went up. Did she look even worse than she thought?

She was confrontational: "So what was so important you couldn't even come in for a cup of coffee earlier?"

He hesitated, then grinned and shrugged, an expansive motion that was unlike him. "Left-over tacos and a two volume biography of Eisenhower," he said.

"What?"

"I just didn't think we should rush things," he said.

Julie stepped closer and Highsong brought his open arms in, enfolding her.

And when she kissed him, he kissed back.

END

Afterword

"Gunfight" is my *Butch Cassidy & The Sundance Kid.* My parents took my brother and me to see *Butch Cassidy* at a drive-in when we were kids. It made a huge impression, not least because we were each given our own bucket of popcorn.

When I grew older, William Goldman became one of my favorite writers and a man I've studied for his craft. Go read *The Color Of Light* or *The Princess Bride.* (Yeah, yeah, I know you've seen the movie version of *Bride*, which was adequate, but go read the book.) Goldman's technique is deft, spare, and honest. Even better, he always delivers a rollercoaster ride of surprises and reversals.

I didn't process any of this when I was eight. Not consciously. Sitting in our station wagon's front seat beneath a sixty-foot screen, here's what I learned: Guns are TOTALLY AWESOME! And cliff-jumping! Horse chases! Explosions and bank robberies!

It's a mystery why I didn't grow up to be an outlaw.

Julie Beauchain ranks among my favorite characters because she's fun. I'm a fun guy. People who know me — my friends and family — are still trying to figure out why I write dark novels like *Plague Year.* That's because my parents also let me read books like *The Stand* and *On The Beach* before I was twelve. Gritty drama resonates even more deeply than all-for-laughs adventures like *Butch Cassidy.* Like I've said, the things I admire the most about human beings are our strength and intelligence. But I enjoy a good romp.

"Gunfight" was sparked by a *Newsweek* article about a Wisconsin taxidermist who aided local rangers by creating robot deer, which they used to entrap poachers. That was the coolest thing I'd read all year. Instantly I knew I wanted to write my own story, and I have family in Montana, including an uncle who runs one of the largest nurseries in North America.

Sugarloaf is a fictional town, but the landscape is real.

One more thing. Sheila Williams, the editor at *Asimov's*, was brave enough to ask me for a sequel to "Gunfight" after taking a lot of heat from an abusive nut who objected to what he perceived as the subversive pinky-pie liberal agenda embedded in this story. After all, the heroes are a black woman and a Native American, whereas the evil sheriff and his cronies are white guys. Obviously I'm trying to indoctrinate the youth of America. White, bad! Color, good!

Well, no.

For me, Julie's race was nothing more than craftsmanship. I am not a *Manchurian Candidate* brainwashed by the mainstream media who's now regurgitating the same self-hating message of the weak, socialist left. Relax, man! Science fiction is supposed to be a literature of ideas. Its fans don't tend to be people who purposely limit themselves, and yet more than one white supremacist has also taken me to task for the cast of *Plague Year*, which features a Latino and a genius Jew.

I'll talk more about their weird accusations later in this collection in an essay called "Rose-Colored Demons," but, like my protagonist in "Monsters," I think people sometimes can't see past their own problems. In fact, a lot of times, people consciously or unconsciously wrap themselves in their pain, their own failings, and their hate, which distort everything.

Julie being black was a deliberate decision with one goal. Yes, I got a nice bit of poetry comparing her skin color with Highsong's, but the main intent was to introduce an additional layer of tension to the story. For a genre writer, suspense is critical, and it's not difficult to find outsider themes in nearly all of my writing.

Now back to Butch Cassidy... er, I mean back to Julie Beauchain...

A LOVELY LITTLE
CHRISTMAS FIRE

SOMEONE WAS SMART enough to call her. Even with the Army and DHS on scene, the governor had tapped her personally. *Miss Beauchain?* he said on the phone. The job couldn't have been any dirtier, but that kind of compliment was better than cash, neck rubs, or beaches, so Julie grinned as she turned into the moist stink of the bugs.

"Watch the ceiling!" she yelled.

"I'm more worried about the floor," Highsong said.

Julie waved her TI gun as she hit the stairs, glancing back at him through the office space. "The ceiling is hot—"

Highsong wasn't moving. "We're three stories up," he said. "If the floor lets go, you won't be so excited about making our bonus."

He couldn't have stopped her any faster if he'd smacked the wide part of her jeans. Julie froze and then turned on the fourth step, exasperated — in part because he was twenty feet away. A dozen low cubicles separated them. Highsong could be as stubborn as a rock, but the truth was they made a fine pair. Julie was aware that they both looked out of place in this well-organized call center, dragging guns and packs into the maze of desks. He was six and a half feet of Irish/Cheyenne, a mix almost as exotic as her own African/Arabic/French ancestry, and lean and firm in comparison to her curves.

"It's not about the money," she said.

"Isn't it?"

"It's about doing well."

"Then why is your radio off?"

"We don't need help."

"Always the superhero."

Watching him, Julie shifted beneath thirty pounds of sensors and other gear. She never felt the weight when she was running — only when they stopped to rest in the late July heat — and the mischief in her heart grew as she took in Highsong's posture. Spine straight. Arms folded. His protectiveness made her happy, so she flirted with him by stamping her feet up and down two stairs in a spontaneous little salsa dance. Maybe she put more hip into it than necessary. *Ba boom bang bang.* Her thoughts were like a drum. *I love you.*

"Seems safe," she said, lilting the words.

"If you fall through—"

"You wish."

Highsong's mouth twisted as he fought with a smile and won. His scowl deepened. Then he started toward her through the cubicles. "Just be careful," he said.

Julie laughed. "They haven't made a bug yet that's got more brains than— Yaaah!"

The stairwell exploded overhead. Julie fell. In the first seconds, the avalanche was only noise, a stampede of footsteps and crashing boxes, but then she was overwhelmed by hundreds of small, shiny objects and cardboard and a leaping man. He was Caucasian. Brown hair. Brown beard. He wore a backpack even larger than her own.

"Run!" he screamed.

Julie tumbled into an unladylike heap on the floor, her elbows and knees spread to catch herself. Instead, the man squashed her flat when he put his shoe on her pack. Everywhere, the small trinkets clattered down the stairs — silver balls and red balls and gold stars — and Highsong shouted behind her. He might have tried to intercept the man. Julie heard someone bang against a desk, another shout, and a sharper *crash.*

She yelled, "What the—"

Then she got a face full of bugs. The stairwell was buried in winged termites. They were slick, yellow, damp, stinking. Julie shrieked and clawed both hands across her mouth.

"*Yuck!*"

Blinded by the swarm, she tried to get up. Someone grabbed her shoulder. Highsong. No one else would have waded into the bugs for her — but he was still supporting her when he slipped, yanking her sideways. Julie bounced off the wall. Highsong hit the floor. She landed on him.

Fortunately, the termites were dispersing. Julie spit in disgust and looked around, not unhappy with her position on Highsong's chest. There were bugs in his hair and bugs on the floor and Julie giggled to shake off the lasting sensation of creepy little feet against her skin. But it was too hot to stay together. The office building was stifling in the summer sun, so she patted his arm affectionately and began to roll aside.

Highsong grabbed her waist. "Wait. You okay?"

"Hey!" Julie said, not fighting too hard.

His free hand went to the absurd junk on the floor, distracting her as he lifted a clump of trinkets — a glittering blue-and-white ball, a plastic snowman, and a red-nosed toy reindeer. Julie wrinkled her eyebrows in confusion. Highsong smiled. "Merry Christmas," he said. Then he kissed her.

WHAT HAD THE other man been doing in the building? This part of town was supposed to be clear, but some hold-outs had stayed to fight the bugs themselves. There were also looters, thrill-seekers, and other assorted fruitcakes. The man was probably stealing as much as he could carry. He was about the twentieth unauthorized person they'd seen today.

Julie rubbed a bruised elbow as she and Highsong worked to kill the termites. It was messy. The bugs were in the walls and file cabinets and a translucent squirming mass of yellow bodies burst from an easy chair in one office. The air was hazy with winged termites and dust. They had a hard time finding the nest. Julie used her thermal imaging gun to locate the worst pockets in the walls as Highsong created some breathing room with his glue sprayer. They laid down bait and pheromone beacons.

As it turned out, there were already three queen colonies. *Heterotermes aureus machovsky* moved fast — too fast for an eleven syllable name. Julie called 'em *machos* for short, like nachos, even though their creator's surname was pronounced *ma CHOV ski*. Lance Machovsky. His babies were smaller than most termite species but acted like they bled methamphetamine.

The bugs had ravaged most of the building's top floor, which seemed to be dedicated to management offices and storage for discontinued items. In back, endless boxes had slumped to the floor, chewed apart by the machos, leaving flecks of bright wrapping paper and cardboard and what looked like eighty-six billion Christmas ornaments and other holiday goodies like pint-size Marys and Santa Clauses. Julie crunched through the debris with an alarming sense of guilt.

"Is this going to put us on the nice list or naughty?" she called back to Highsong, wincing at each *krnnch* and *pop* of snowflakes, elves, and holly beneath her boots.

"You know which list you're on," he said.

THEY WERE DUMBER than pigs to mix work and romance, of course. Julie's grandpa would have said Never poop where you eat, with stronger language, but Julie Beauchain and William Highsong had been partners in the Department of Fish, Wildlife & Parks before they were lovers. Neither of them wanted to quit the job. Putting in for a transfer would have created another problem, most likely moving one of them too far across Montana to see each other regularly. So they had rules.

Rule Number One: Keep your clothes on during your shift.

"Stop it!" Julie said, laughing as she skipped away from Highsong outside the office building. But he caught her easily. The sidewalk was empty. The road was empty. Julie let Highsong take her pris-oner again and they nuzzled right there beside an abandoned car for anyone to see, no matter how filthy they were with grime and sweat.

"I'm glad you're all right," he said.

"Next building," she said.

"That guy could've broken your neck."

"And you let him go."

"That's right." Highsong touched the sensitive skin behind her ear and Julie shivered.

"This is business, not pleasure," she said, even as she ruined her own attempt at severity with a wink. She loved to encourage his play-ful side — was that the Irish in him or the plains-riding Cheyenne? — and she felt especially glad for it now. The silence was worse than the bugs.

Missoula, Montana was hardly a major metropolis with a popu-lation of 60,000, but it seemed larger in the preternatural quiet. As far as she could see, the downtown blocks were lifeless, resonating only with the sound of distant helicopters. She smelled smoke and gasoline.

"Let's move," she said. "We're behind schedule."

"Yes, sir."

That earned him a whack and another approving kiss. The truth was that Julie wore the pants in their relationship. At least she liked to think so. Highsong was hardly a cliché TV Tonto, yet he seemed content to follow her lead, in part because her head was just louder than his. Most of their gadgets were Julie's inventions. Their noto-riety was also because of her tech skills. Two days ago, every public servant in Montana had been called into duty at all levels — city, state, and federal — but few Fish, Wildlife & Parks rangers like themselves were actually in combat.

Missoula had been under DHS quarantine for thirty-plus hours as the 4th Infantry and units of the National Guard tried to control the infested areas. Martial law was in force across most of Big Sky Country and neighboring Idaho.

"Scanning," Julie said as she tried the glass doors of the next building. The ground floor was retail, a coffee shop and a women's clothing store. Both were locked. Very few people had obeyed the requests by DHS to leave their businesses and homes unsecured. No problem. Highsong took his pry bar to the coffee shop door and they were in.

Julie was already fairly sure the place was clean. Even sitting still, machos ran hotter than normal termites — and these bugs never sat still. Her TI gun had only penetrated through the windows into the front room, but if there were machos anywhere in the coffee shop, she would have picked up movement or trails outside where the bugs were squeezing through the slightest gaps around the windows, doors, or vents. That was how they'd tagged the office building next door. *H. aureus machovsky* was voracious. Even with more than enough dry wood or paper to sustain a colony, the machos always sent scouts to expand their foraging area.

Julie and Highsong swept the back rooms of the coffee shop, then moved to the clothing store. Minutes later, they broke into the first of eight apartments on the floors above. It was hot work. Their grid consisted on two full city blocks, which they were expected to clear before sundown, so the pace was relentless. Sweep each room. Leave bait if suspicious. Chart their maps. Keep moving.

"You can't buy a work-out like this," Julie gasped at the top of three flights of stairs. She hoped Highsong would smile and say *You don't need the exercise, babe.*

The big lunk just nodded and said, "No kidding."

Julie laughed. He gave her quizzical look — yet as much as she liked to argue, there wasn't time. She would bring it up again in the shower, though, he could be sure of that.

"You're some date, Highsong," she said.

"What are you talking about?"

I love you, she thought, but she was careful with those words, hoarding them to herself. It was better to joke. That was how their relationship had begun, light and easy, and for the most part Julie was okay if it stayed that way. Except she was crazy for him. Who was she protecting?

"Scanning," she said as she approached the next building.

Inside, they refilled their canteens in a men's room sink and snacked on the sodium-laced Buffalo Wing chips and bland cheese sticks they found in a break room, scavenging like the machos. Unfortunately, their packs were nearly empty of beacons and bait. Soon they'd be forced to hoof it back to their FW&P jeep, which they'd left down the block.

They emerged into the late afternoon sun with less than two-thirds of their quota done. Julie's disappointment made her mad, which seemed to heighten her senses. She felt on stage in the empty city. Maybe that was why she noticed the change in the air. There were voices around the corner of the nearest intersection.

"You hear that?" she asked. "Either we've got more civvies who should've evacuated or there's another bug team poaching our grid, and I don't want 'em making any kills that are ours. Let's get in their face."

"We could use the help."

"Whose side are you on?"

"Let's just call it in," Highsong said, but Julie marched away from him. They could have driven, but their jeep was in the other direction, and Julie wanted to surprise the other group if possible.

She was still two buildings from the corner when the voices turned to screams. "Look out!" a man yelled as Julie broke into a run, the TI gun swinging in one hand. Her pack jostled against her shoulders. Highsong quickly passed her and she doubled her effort, cursing under her breath. What she wouldn't give for legs that long.

He beat her to the intersection. Then they froze. The five men and women in the street were unauthorized persons, that much was clear. No uniforms. No gear. They'd also dropped a lot of money when they panicked, breaking away from the doors of a check cashing operation. Machos rushed from another entrance to the building as if the two-story structure had opened its mouth and breathed. The fog was an evil yellow. Great tendrils of bugs swept over the paper bills on the street and absorbed the screaming people.

Three of them made it to their pick-up truck, beating madly at their hair and faces. They left a duffel bag and their friends behind in the swarm.

"Jimmy!" a women shrieked from the pick-up.

"Freeze!" Julie yelled. They ignored her. The engine roared and the full-size Dodge Ram lurched toward Julie and Highsong through the bugs, trying to intercept one man. The other guy had charged in the opposite direction.

Neither Julie nor Highsong had any real weapons, so Julie faked it. Her thermal imaging gun looked like a Martian death ray with its stubby barrel and a side-mounted display as round as a dinner plate. Julie pointed it at them, shoving it forward in a classic gunman's stance. Someone inside the pick-up shouted. The vehicle jerked.

Highsong blasted them with his glue sprayer, hosing down the windshield and the open passenger door and the schmoe they were trying to rescue. The schmoe fell down, coated in a sticky gray mess full of hundreds of bugs. At the same time, the pick-up swerved again — its driver blind — then submarined magnificently into the street front of a laundromat, sending glass through the sky. Alarms went off. The neon TOPWASH sign slipped and then detonated against the truckbed.

"Holy crap," Highsong said.

Julie had almost lost track of the fifth bandit, the one on the far side of the bugs, but he flinched and looked back at the noise. She saw his brown hair and beard and recognized the extra large pack.

"That's the same guy from the Christmas place!" Julie yelled, running toward the billowing swarm.

Highsong caught her arm. "Let him go," he said.

"What!?"

"These people are hurt. I need help."

Julie glanced at the moaning schmoe in the street and the dazed bandits inside the truck. None of them had fled in the same direction as the fifth guy. Was he even with them? "Highsong, we can't let him get away! Something's not right about—"

"Get on the radio or I'll glue you myself," he said.

THE STATE POLICE and 4th Infantry platoon who responded came in two patrol cars, two gun-mounted Humvees and a half-ton Army truck. Julie was taken aback. She wouldn't have expected more than the patrol cars even if they'd captured Butch Cassidy and the Hole In The Wall gang.

The arrests derailed them from their bug hunt. Julie hated to give up on her grid, but the police sergeant wanted their statements and the platoon captain dispatched his men into the infested building. "I guess that's enough fun for one day," Julie said to Highsong, leaning close as she watched the cuffed, bruised, and bandaged robbers led into the back of the truck. "Um. Wanna take a bath?"

"Yep."

No nonsense. That was what she liked about him. Lord knew she generated enough malarkey for the two of them. Is that why you haven't asked me to move in with you? she wondered as they got into the sergeant's patrol car. One of his men would drive their FW&P jeep back to HQ.

The outskirts of the business district looked like a war zone. Five huge fires crackled in the Wal-Mart's parking lot, sending smoke over the city like winter clouds. Civilian truck rigs and Army vehicles jammed the streets, suddenly forcing Julie's escorts to stop and start through the traffic — empty trucks leaving, full trucks arriving.

Ash ticked against the windshield as Julie stared out, biting her lip. All of the incoming rigs were swaddled in ungainly fat bulges of plastic. The soldiers unloading the trucks wore respirators, goggles, and jackets despite the summer heat. Others patrolled the lot with glue guns and flamethrowers.

They were burning Christmas trees — hundreds upon hundreds of Christmas trees. The whole scene looked like a demented Satanic fantasy. Say something funny, Julie thought, but her mind had gone blank. She loved Christmas. Growing up, the holidays were the best times in her life, when she and her mother visited her cousins in Tampa and mom put on a convincing veneer of normality, drinking less, hugging her more, even joining in for carols and cooking and corny old movies like It's A Wonderful Life.

Watching the trees ablaze was like incinerating those memories. Worse, Julie knew this was one of the smallest burns in Montana. Rumor was there were uncontrolled fires in wide swaths of forest just east of Missoula on the Continental Divide. This hell consisted of a tiny number of trees. By the last count she'd heard, barely a thousand had been reduced to charred stumps on the Wal-Mart's flat asphalt lot. These trees were being cut from city parks and open spaces — not only to be destroyed but tested for termite samples.

Each pyre had a white tent set beside it. Technicians in yellow protective gear strode back and forth from the incoming trees and their tents with clippers, jars, chem kits, rakes, nets, spectrometers, and laptops.

"It's like Plan 9 from Outer Space," Julie said at last, turning in her seat to keep her eyes on the Wal-Mart as they broke through the heavy traffic.

"You all right?" Highsong asked.

He must have heard the slightest hitch in her voice, which left Julie both unsettled and pleased. "Sure," she said. "I'm great. Hungry. Can't wait to get out of these clothes."

That drew a glance from the cop at the wheel, a white guy with freckles. Julie smiled to herself, feeling better.

The trees aren't my fault, she thought.

Headquarters was in a preschool around the corner, which seemed goofy, but the school offered a neat space with lots of tables for the DHS and military officials who were running the show. They'd also wanted to be close to their field labs.

As soon as the cop parked his car, Julie hopped out and bee-lined inside, looking for Agents Coughlin or Reaves. Once again she felt that jarring sense of the surreal. Hard-voiced men and women sat among laptops and radio gear, surrounded by rainbow-colored charts of the ABCs, the solar system, and smiling cartoon dinosaurs.

She found Reaves first, a tall, thin man with thick wheat hair. He was on the phone but Julie said, "We have a problem."

Reaves recognized her without a second glance. He covered his phone with one hand and nodded. "Hey, sure, we heard about your little gang of banditos. Nice work. Just help the cops and I'll do what I can to keep the paperwork to a minimum. Thanks."

"No. Listen. I need property records and access to your criminal database."

"What?"

"I'm onto something bigger than robbery," she said. "Can you help me with property records?"

It was a place to start. How were the two buildings linked? The saboteur might be attacking rival businesses in order to destroy the competition — or was it personal? Maybe he was nothing more than a disgruntled employee. Julie's instincts said no, but they needed to test that theory, too.

Reaves frowned at her. "What exactly are we talking about here, Miz Bo-Chain?"

"Someone's planting bugs in the city."

"You mean bringing them in?"

"Yes."

Reaves lifted one hand and shouted across the room. "Leber! Hey, Leber!"

The other guy was white, too. They were all white, except for the Hispanics and blacks in the Army and a few Asians and Hispanics among the federal agents. Montana was not a diverse state, certainly not like Florida. Julie was accustomed to being the only black woman for miles around. New acquaintances usually stumbled over her Bayou name, mostly in an effort to get it right but sometimes only to mock her. *Missus Boo-Kayne. Miz Boy-Shane.* That the governor had pronounced it correctly spoke of his willingness to invest in her, but Julie always felt the stigma of being an outsider.

"Leber, this is Bo-Kayne," Reaves said. "She says she saw some-one bringing bugs into the city. I want to know where they hit, how hard, and why. Look at our DTs again. Get me something fast."

"Sure," Leber said. "Come over to my station."

DTs weren't a new thought for Julie, either. The media was rife with speculation that domestic terrorists had released the machos despite announcements to the contrary by government officials. These white boys in their five hundred dollar suits had all the answers — they said they knew who'd created the termites and why — but Julie didn't trust them. Not entirely.

Highsong joined her in the HQ as Leber walked her through the same questions half a dozen times, challenging everything they'd seen. That was his job. He was a federal investigator. Leber wasn't condescending but he didn't take her at her word, either. Too often, he doubted her. Was she imagining it? Yes, she had a problem with authority that could be traced all the way back to her mother, ol' bourbon brains, and her father, who'd skipped when she was five. That wasn't the issue. Julie preferred to think she was simply a per-fect fit for the American West, loaded with independence, spirit, and know-how.

For example, it was deeply quixotic for her to make fun of Dr. Lance Machovsky's name, but Julie had been suspicious of this whole plate of worms since the DHS briefings, which, well, had been too brief.

"You're certain you saw the same man?" Leber said, trying again to deflect her.

"Yes. Look." Julie was losing her temper. "Someone's either try-ing to take out the competition or settling a grudge or both, and they don't care who else gets hurt."

"I understand your concern," Leber said.

She fumed while he tapped blandly at his computer. Was he delaying her? Why? Maybe they just didn't want her causing a fuss. DHS seemed to specialize in turning out these smooth, unflappable men, who, in turn, conveyed only calm and confidence to the public.

DHS said the termites were just one of many gene-splices under development by private and government bio research teams in response to the agriculture industry's issues with blight and pests. Global warming would increase crop threats throughout the twenty-first century. Manmade attacks were also a real possibility, and DHS and the White House officially — quietly — supported efforts to meet such dangers.

Machovsky worked for DawnTech. The field test they'd chosen first was directed against a comparatively humble foe, so-called pine rust, a fungus that had decimated Montana's holiday economy for three years running. It infected blue spruce and every species of fir — in other words, the most popular Christmas trees in the nation. Between the blockades and the lawsuits out of California, Oregon, and Colorado, where the rust had spread with imported trees and seeds, Big Sky Country was taking a huge beating. Nurseries made up fifteen percent of Montana's economy. Not all of them were Christmas tree farms, of course, but the entire industry had suffered.

Heterotermes aureus was a desert termite. It could not survive in the damp, cold north, not for long — not even in the summer. That was its failsafe. Machovsky had crossed his bugs with the black fly and with the rust itself. Fly genes accelerated the machos' metabolism. The rust genes meant they were dependent on the fungus as a nutritional source. *H. aureus machovsky* was intended to pick and choose its way through a diseased farm at a hysterical pace, then weaken and collapse after exhausting the supply of rust-sick wood.

Breed fast, spread fast, die fast. That the machos could survive without the rust was a surprise adaptation. Whoops.

"So what happens next?" Julie asked, gesturing at Highsong and herself. "We want to help — *before* this guy brings more bugs inside the quarantine. We both know the city, and we're good with our hands. Can you put us on the team?"

"I'll be in touch," Leber said.

"When? Today?"

"I'll be in touch," Leber said.

IT WAS A brush-off. Julie and Highsong left headquarters with no answers. She was only generating more questions, such as where did the saboteur get not just one queen colony, but several? How would he gather thousands of bugs in order to pack them into the city? One man alone couldn't collect and preserve a colony.

Julie didn't like the over-reaction to the gang of bandits, either. Yes, an entire Army division was in-state, but there were also 60,000 refugees and the fires and a pandemic on their to-do lists. No one had twenty men to spare unless they were nervous about what she and Highsong might uncover at the site. Who was worried? The feds? Somebody local? Could she trace the orders to send a full platoon back into the tangled chain of command?

As soon as they were outside, Julie pulled her iPhone and tapped in a Los Angeles-area number, gazing up through the ash.

It only rang once.

"Beauchain?" A young man.

"Em, you're going to like this," she said.

His voice rose in pitch. "Am I hallucinating or are you calling me on a cell phone?"

"Listen, I just—"

"Idiot." He hung up.

"Oh boy." Julie turned to Highsong and slung her arm around his waist, feeling tired and lost and glad to have him. "We should just go back to my place," she said.

"Nah." Highsong squeezed her. "Let's get in some trouble first."

HER PLACE WAS a cot in a big tent surrounded by big tents where DHS was housing civilian law enforcement groups on the north side of town. Highsong had been assigned to a men's tent nearby, but they walked to his pick-up truck instead, which hardly offered any more privacy, lost in a sea of vehicles that other cops, rangers, firefighters, and workmen were using as sleeping quarters and offices. People were everywhere in the vast parking lot.

"You pervert," Julie said.

Highsong didn't react, opening the cab and waving her inside. His laptop was squirreled away behind his seat. He gave it to her and scratched her back as she typed at the machine. DHS had wi-fi over most of the camp. It was sluggish with traffic, but that was good. Julie's emails would be like one little mouse in the on-going circus.

It's your favorite idiot, she typed.

Forgiven. I've seen the news. You're stressed. What's up?

I need some background, she typed. *Can you poke around for me?*

Poking is my middle name.

Em was a friend she'd made on the usenets, trading tech advice and buyer tips. She was pretty sure he didn't actually live in Los Angeles. For all she knew, he was right here in Missoula or in Maine, Milan, or Moscow, but he'd weathermanned his lines through L.A. for cover. He said he was wanted by the FBI. That was probably just geek posturing, but Em was good at what he did.

Julie typed up the two buildings' addresses and a run-down on Machovsky. Maybe her hacker buddy would draw some connections she couldn't.

He didn't test her patience. A mere twenty minutes passed. If she was worth her weight, she would've jumped Highsong or at least smooched a bit, but she wasn't nineteen anymore, she was thirty-four, and it had been a long day. They both napped. Other people came and went through the parking lot, shouting, banging doors, as Julie curled on the long bench seat with her head on Highsong's thigh. Then his laptop chimed.

You're neck-deep in slime, Em emailed. *A lot of DawnTech's records are sealed. FEDERALLY sealed. Ready for the good news?*

"Oh boy," Julie said. *There's good news?* she typed.

Em dumped a handful of files on her. *Enjoy*, he said. *I'm out. You don't know me.*

"Oh boy," Julie said again.

DawnTech was so familiar with termites because they'd been experimenting with the bugs as a clean energy source. Termites could produce as much as two liters of hydrogen from digesting a single piece of paper. The highly specialized microbes in their digestive tracts made each bug an efficient bioreactor, which was why Julie's TI guns worked so well.

It was also why Em thought gene-spliced termites could be used as living firebombs. A mating pair might infiltrate enemy territory — tiny, insignificant, organic, untraceable — then breed until they hit critical mass. Termites made love three times a day, Em noted, and some of DawnTech's funding came from DARPA, which meant the Pentagon. Top secret.

"Where did you say you knew this guy from?" Highsong asked, reading over Julie's shoulder.

"Okay, so some of it's nuts."

"Some of it?"

"Here's the good news. Next file. Look at this."

The first building where they'd met the saboteur held the national ordering center and sales offices of Holiday House, a billion dollar name in Christmas, Hanukkah, Kwanzaa, and Easter supplies. The embargo on Christmas trees had halved their earnings in past years. More interestingly, the same parent corporation that controlled Holiday House also owned the second building and more in Missoula. Em hadn't been able to draw a link between that corporate blind and DawnTech, but he suggested it was obvious. Who else could be supplying the saboteur with bugs? According to Em's numbers, the whole thing looked like an insurance scam. They were infesting their own business holdings and testing an insanely lucrative weapons program at the same time.

Highsong just shook his head. "How do we get into stuff like this?" he asked.

"Oh my god. You can say that again."

"You, uh, you want to tell Agent Leber?"

"No." Julie met his eyes and said, "No. This is our city."

THEY SLIPPED BACK into Missoula as dusk fell. Driving Highsong's truck through Army lines was easy enough. They had ID and their partly-completed chart and maps. "We're just trying to finish up," Julie told the lieutenant who inspected her DHS-issued pass, and it wasn't a lie. She wanted revenge.

Things got more complicated after dark. To start with, they worked without lights. Worse, there were only two of them, and Em had provided four addresses to stake out. Highsong suggested splitting up, but Julie said no. The city was quieting down, but there were still looters and Army patrols and God Knew Who Else poking around. It was better to stick together. If they got bored, maybe she'd get up the courage to offer him a key to her house. Too bad the first hour was anything but dull as they raced from site to site with his headlights off, rifling through the truckbed for their packs, TI guns, and other gear.

Once they crunched over an abandoned bike lying in the street. Another time they nearly flattened a stray dog. Julie wanted to go after it. She had soft spot for animals, but Highsong convinced her to stay on mission.

Then the waiting began. They'd hidden his truck alongside a bakery across the street from a mortgage brokers' offices, which seemed the most valuable of their four targets.

"What do you think the paperwork is worth if the machos eat it?" Julie asked, holding his hand.

"Everything's electronic now, isn't it?" Highsong said. "I think the insurance might pay them more for lost business and damaged real estate than paper files. Maybe they can also play loose with their taxes if a bunch of receipts disappear. I dunno. If they wipe out every place they own, it's gotta be worth bazillions."

"And meanwhile the bugs are chewing up other people's homes. What a bunch of—"

Beep! His radio lit up.

"That's channel two," Highsong said. "We're in the wrong place."

"Go!" Julie shouted, even as he hit the ignition. She figured they had five minutes, even ten, but she didn't want to miss the kill. In her excitement, she lifted her camcorder from the seat beside her and hugged it like a mad scientist. "Ha! Ha ha ha! We got the son of a bitch!"

Highsong careened through town with his lights on. They were sure their trap was foolproof and unconcerned with scaring their man off. Speed was only slightly less important than getting there alive.

"Whoa!" Julie screamed as Highsong swung around a corner only to find the road peppered with stand-still cars. The fender on her side banged against a white Buick, throwing sparks. The side mirror splintered. Then he pinballed through the other vehicles and slammed on his brakes, squashing Julie's chest against her seatbelt.

"Where is he?"

"I don't— There!" Julie flung her door open and dragged her pack onto her shoulders as she ran. Above her loomed one of Missoula's "skyscrapers," a six-story office complex with lower buildings on either side.

A dark Lexus hidden in one of the garage entrances must have belonged to their victim. He'd opened the driver door before it was too late. Their trap had attracted machos from all directions.

The frenzy enshrouding him looked like a nine-foot tornado. He shrieked and kicked inside it, creating brief, man-shaped holes in the gleaming yellow termite storm. One glimpse was enough for Julie to see that his clothes were coming away in shreds.

"Can he breathe!?" Highsong yelled behind her.

Who cares? Julie thought. "It'll be over in seconds!"

Half-blind, disoriented, and naked — and God save him if he was ticklish — the man flailed helplessly against his car as the machos ripped into its luxury interior. Wet masses of bugs surged against the glass.

Julie was jubilant. *Got you!* she thought, trying to point her camcorder at him as she dashed onto the sidewalk.

But it was too late for her, too.

A long spiral of termites swept away from the bad guy and

dimmed the corona of Highsong's headlights, enfolding Julie in the nasty fluttering swarm.

"Gaaaaaaa!" she shrieked.

They'd obviously hidden their beacons well enough for the man to set off the tripwire in the building's entrance, and no one but evil-doers should be entering this office complex tonight. The same electrical impulse that alerted Highsong via radio had also opened a handful of chem packets, covering the man with an invisible fog. The machos' sex pheromones were too subtle for a human nose, even laced with the molecular signature of pine rust, but the bad guy probably heard the beacons pop and then saw Julie's wiring and radio transceiver.

Unfortunately, neither Julie nor Highsong had noticed the leaking beacon they must have broken or triggered inside his truck. They were coated with sex juice, too, and the machos were in a confused, rapturous craze. The bugs tried to eat anything that was plant-based — like cotton.

Julie grabbed at her top as she dropped and thrashed on the sidewalk, hoping to crush the termites, but it was no good. She was grateful just to get enough air. Then her shirt came apart in her hands and her pants sagged away from her hips. Her bra went next and she staggered up, bewildered and choking.

The bad guy got clear of the swarm first. Maybe he'd lost his keys. Maybe jumping into the bug orgy inside his car was too horrible to contemplate. Either way, his pale white hiney broke into a sprint down the street, each cheek shining in Highsong's headlights.

"Don't move or I'll shoot!" Julie shouted, swimming through the machos after him. Highsong was on his feet, too, but tripped over the ragged fabric of his jeans. Julie was lucky her pants had separated completely — and her nylon shoes were intact. It was only by the grace of God that she'd worn her leather jacket, which survived. Otherwise she would have been wearing less than a stripper, and she wasn't a small girl. She felt herself bounce as she charged after the bad guy, armed only with her camcorder. What if he had a gun?

"Julie!" Highsong yelled.

The canisters left beside the bad guy's car were vital evidence — could they trace this equipment back to the people who'd packed more termite colonies into those steel tubes for him? — but she wanted this lunatic to pay personally for he'd done, so she didn't stop.

The naked chase was on.

They quickly left the headlights, but the bad guy wasn't getting enough sun. His back had some color, yet his buttocks were like round little ghosts churning in the night. He ran like he still had a few bugs where it counted.

Bouncing, Julie began to fall behind. Cold, she hollered in frustration: "Freeze! I said freeze!"

The world went supernova. In front of them, the street flared with two dazzling flood lamps and the 4th Infantry pinned the bad guy with fifteen rifles, several glue guns, and a bullhorn. "HALT! PUT YOUR HANDS UP! THIS IS THE UNITED STATES ARMY AND YOU ARE—" The voice turned away. "They're not wearing any clothes," it said before swinging back again at full volume. "YOU'RE UNDER ARREST!"

Julie caught up with the bad guy as he stood motionless in the brilliant light, casting a thin shadow like a rat with his hands crossed over his goodies. Behind her, Highsong's truck joined the scene, but stopped when the bullhorn shouted again.

"HALT!"

A dozen soldiers ran forward, their smooth helmets bobbing through the glare. Julie tried her best to pull her jacket down past her waist, but she was more interested in making sure the bad guy saw her grin.

It was the same brown-haired dude from before.

"Gotcha," she said.

THE SOLDIERS WERE a security detail assigned to two neighboring banks. They didn't have any blankets or tarps on hand, but one man gave Julie his pants, earning a round of hoots and commentary that doubled in volume when she thanked him with a chaste kiss.

Minutes later, DHS came down on their location like a ton of horse puckey. No less than twenty agents pushed in among the soldiers, taking the bad guy and isolating Julie and Highsong. That was okay. Julie had already passed her camcorder to the corporal without any pants and asked him to keep it safe for her — and to smuggle it to the CNN crews outside of town if she didn't return for it. The digital Sony not only contained the machos' assault of the bad guy and Julie's pursuit but also the interviews she'd taped earlier with Highsong and herself, explaining everything with detailed maps, Em's documentation, and property records. Highsong had already uploaded the same files to YouTube, though he'd kept the videos private and inactive for now.

The easy part was done. Agent Reaves brought them to the medical tents for their scrapes and bruises and then to the cafeteria for a hot meal, playing the good cop to the hilt — and Julie and Highsong were as sweet as butter, chatting him up like long-lost family. They'd violated a federal quarantine by reentering Missoula, but they'd also nabbed the villain. Depending on how Reaves decided to play it, they would sink or swim.

Finally the claws came out. Reaves wanted all the information they had, their sources, an oath of silence, and their voluntary resignation from the bug teams.

Julie grinned and made her counter-offer. Nah," she said. "I think DHS should give us a public commendation for our valor above and beyond the call of duty."

"We can press charges."

"We'll lawyer up and dump our videos on the net for the world to see how DHS is testing their bioweapons programs on innocent civilians."

"What?"

"You heard me. Organic firebombs. We know DawnTech is in bed with the Pentagon."

Reaves stared at her.

"We don't want to pee on your parade," Julie said. "We're good Americans. We'd prefer not to make noise about your bug programs, but we will to protect ourselves if we have to. Which we shouldn't. We're heroes."

Reaves slowly held out his hand. "You need a medal with that commendation?" he asked, and they shook on it.

Julie laughed.

But the next morning she and Highsong were covered in sweat and bugs again. The termite war continued. At least they seemed to be getting ahead of the machos with no one bringing new colonies into the city. She was more aggravated by the fact that four days passed before Reaves called to follow up.

Julie had to dig her phone out of her pack when it rang, setting aside her TI gun and an Army radio.

"Beauchain?" Reaves said, getting it right.

The bad guy was a low-level assistant in Machovsky's research facilities. He'd spilled like a leaky bag. Working from his confession, DHS uncovered ties between DawnTech's board of directors and the ownership of Holiday House. Apparently business was down. Way down. More and more Americans were secularizing Christmas and buying all sorts of inane junk — blow-up lawn dolls, roof displays, plastic trees — but competition for those spiking sales was brutal and Holiday House lost their price margin when their tree sales went down the toilet.

Someone had decided to cut corners, take advantage of the machos' outbreak, and kill the business and all of its subsidiary holdings. That was the extent of the scheme, Reaves said, no federal involvement, no *Men In Black* weapons programs, nobody but the usual suspects — a few inept corporate masters with their eyes on fat pay-offs instead of hard work. People were going to jail. Holiday House would be sued to the ground.

Julie was almost disappointed when she hung up the phone, standing beside a gluey patch of termites on a smoke-ridden Missoula street. "It's over," she told Highsong. "There's no conspiracy. Reaves has everything sewn up tight."

"Maybe next time," he said, smiling as he roughly embraced her.

END

Afterword

"Christmas Fire" was even more fun to write than "Gunfight," partly because it's larger in scope and mayhem, partly because I looked forward to spending more time with these characters.

What a pair. Nudity! Glue guns! Bug swarms! Hooray!

I love blowing things up. Missoula is a great town, and I apologize for visiting a plague of termites upon it.

Part of the inspiration for this story was a challenge by my German editor, who was assembling writers for a Christmas-themed anthology to be published early in December. A clever man, my German editor. He wanted to hook new readers for my novels, and the novels of all of the anthology's contributors.

His one request was our stories should have something to do with Christmas, so of course I set mine in July and burned every Christmas tree in sight. Then I handed the same story to *Asimov's* for their pre-holiday issue.

If I was always that smart, I'd be a millionaire.

As for the super bugs, they came from the Joint Genome Institute, where I was given an eye-popping tour while researching a different project. Naturally I took my termites a step farther than any modification programs currently underway... but a year from now... Who knows?

SNACK FOOD

NO ONE EVER caught me eating hair before — and this dude wasn't shy. He shouted, "What are you doing!"

I'd just begun styling a natural blonde, a wonderfully plump little thing whose body was all curves. She looked around and I nearly hacked open her jugular.

"Careful." I palmed my scissors and used both hands to size out her bangs, pretending I didn't realize the dude meant me, hoping he'd go away. But he was a Watch. I'd already spotted the pin-point cameras tucked behind his ears, as if his puffy wolfman curls, shaped to conceal, weren't indication enough.

The good news was that he probably wasn't live on-line. Not even tourist sites like 24Chicago or e-Seattle, notoriously desperate for footage, were so full of themselves as to believe that an audience would be interested in random points-of-view meandering through their ever-beautiful streets. I had a little time before this friggin' peeper could post his video.

"You're eating hair!" he boomed, marching from the tiny lobby toward our eight chair-and-mirror cubbies.

"Huh?" I play stupid with the best. Americans never expect a foreigner to be any sharper than a marble, anyway, a presumption that I often use to my advantage.

"Who's in charge here!"

Our assistant manager, Becky, was a sandy-haired darling who failed a new diet every other week but always summoned the courage to try another. I don't know why. She was perfect, stout and healthy.

I'd sampled her the day I was hired.

She left her customer to confront the Watch, speaking slowly. "Sir, can I help you?"

"You'd certainly better!" A shout seemed to be his normal tone of voice. He tossed his head to flip his mane back and reveal the pinpoint behind his left ear.

In Dante's Hell, the geeks responsible for this technology will only be able to see up their own rectums. I admire the work of a few directors who've seeded concert crowds or busy downtown areas with Watches and, from many perspectives, made an intriguing kaleidoscope — but most of the video-driven sites are crap, twitchy and neurotic, bouncing from camera to camera for no reason except that many channel surfers grow lazy or mesmerized enough to remain on the same channel if it appears to be surfing for them. That's great for ad revenue but awful for the world's children, who only learn what they are taught.

Literacy scores erode each year as sensation crimes are copy-catted from sea to shining sea, idiots and hooligans competing for the headlines. Possibly worse was that otherwise unemployable morons now found themselves in positions of imagined power. The cameras needed legs, after all.

Some of those legs belonged to genuine celebrities — I followed Alfonzo myself — but most were just blustering clowns or sneaks and snoops, given that popular sites like FootMouth.com and iImpact paid bonuses for embarrassing or shocking footage.

I wondered why this dude, with his unfashionable mop-top, had come into The Upper Cut. There were basically only two categories of Watches, revealed and concealed, and he definitely belonged to the latter group. A sneak. A hairy sweat-foul sneak with the smirk of a stunted ego now swollen with importance.

He thrust identification into Becky's face. The lettering was purple, all caps, hard to miss. *No Sparrow Shall Fall, Inc.*

I groaned.

The NSSF believed that through the ever-vigilant eyes of His disciples, God would now expose and expunge all muggers, cheats, speeders, shop-lifters... and perverts.

"This disgusting wacko right here was eating that woman's hair!" he said. "Disgusting!"

Some folks need to believe in that sort of authority. More enjoy seeing freaks get their come-uppance. Others still get off debating witch-hunts and civil liberty. Everyone likes to keep busy. I have hobbies of my own.

"That's ridiculous," I said.

"You were eating my hair?" My plump little blonde thing leaned away in her seat, pressing one hand down on her head.

The eyes of a dozen people lanced into me as the thumping hip-hop on the radio became the only sound. Becky frowned at me, at the Watch, then me again. She's a good woman, protective of her crew, but we were hardly old friends. I'd been in town only four weeks and had worked at The Upper Cut a few days less than that, and never socialized after hours with the girls.

They probably thought I was gay. Male hair-dressers are always gay, right? Especially those with funny accents and customized Italian shoes.

I didn't care what they thought as long as I was left alone in my work.

I enjoy using my hands. I enjoy touching people and talking. Most of it's just chit-chat but I've learned enough to earn a Ph.D in anthropology. Every city is different. I feel in tune with today's America and its mundane concerns of family, finances, fun and food, which to my thinking are more the essence of life than global economy or politics.

"It's here! I have it all in here!" The Watch banged a finger on one of his pin-points, practically bouncing. Maybe he was trying to be taller. I'm a big guy with a big chest and he obviously felt threatened.

I said, "Are you live on-line?"

"Ha! You're worried! You did do it!"

"I'm just thinking about our customer base and reputation." I turned to Becky. "And maybe a libel suit."

She nodded. "Turn it off."

"I'm protected by the Amended First Amendment!" His stiff posture would have made Superman proud. *Evil doers, beware!*

"Sir, turn it off."

"I'm only on storage up-link," he confessed, the one time I heard him use a regular speaking voice, and I relaxed without letting it show. Realistically I had at least an hour before he could get to his office, download, edit, then post his footage or come back with a tape.

He boomed again, using Moses-at-the-Red-Sea gestures. "Why would I make this up! He's some sort of disgusting wacko!"

"Becky, come on." I laughed.

But I must not have been entirely convincing. My little blonde was going to fall out of her chair if she kept leaning away, and Becky's brow knotted to match her pursed lips.

She had been glad to hire me. Turn-over was high, and my license was current, but I guess drifters are always suspect.

Their wariness made me sad and heavy. I've never hurt anyone. Never. I want to be friends with the special ladies whose hair I collect, since I can never truly have them. Where's the harm? I've even sent flowers and candy anonymously to my absolute favorites.

So I stretched my mouth open like a camel and snaked my tongue around, making an *ahhhh* noise.

My little blonde giggled and I said, "Who eats hair?"

"I can prove it!" The Watch kept bouncing like a boy with a bloated bladder.

What could he really have? Footage of me seeming to rub my mouth would be inconclusive. It had only been a single strand, after all, and pin-points were not high definition.

"I'm sorry," I said. "I just think it's homophobic."

"Homo!" He froze.

"You know some folks are like that, Becky. Men especially. And he was next in line for me."

Actually plenty of people are strange about having their hair cut. Back in the Dark Ages, Europeans meticulously burned their clippings to prevent witches from using these articles to cast hexes on them. It makes you wonder who was walking around back then that everyone was so badly scared.

We simply toss unidentifiably jumbled haystacks of the stuff into a dumpster out back. Every third customer asked. Could there be something in the hindbrain, some ancient survival paranoia that warns against leaving behind genetic samples? I think it's simpler than that. I think people's awkwardness with stylists stems from something far more mundane.

Lots of people fear being touched.

I find that fascinating, being so sensitive and eager myself. It's as if they'd prefer to have fewer senses, or at least duller ones. The voyeurism and passivity that made the convergence of television and the Internet so incredibly profitable seems ample proof of a widespread desire to become more insulated from the world. Maybe it's a failing of human evolution. Anything that's colorful and in motion tends to engage the eye and mind, the great irony being that most audiences are themselves immobile lumps.

I let my wrist flutter girlishly as I waved toward the lobby and said, "It's okay, I'll just take the next customer."

"You can't let this wacko keep working here!"

Becky had had enough. "Sir, you'll have to leave."

"I'll post the footage tonight!"

Tonight. That gave me more time than I'd hoped.

"Sir, get out."

He stomped through the open door and tried to slam it shut, but there was a wedge at its base and he nearly hurled himself to the ground. "Have a nice day," I called, and my little blonde giggled again.

Becky's decision to believe me instead of the Watch was likely based in part on her belief that I was gay, and so would snack on men rather than women if I was eating hair at all.

Actually I'm no more sexual than a mushroom, having been born without a complete set of genitals. Had my co-workers known, I'm sure they would have been empathetic and extra nice, at least at first — but I've always avoided undue attention.

I finished my blonde's styling with extra care, both to reward her and to savor the moment. She kept flashing me smiles in the mirror, which I loved.

Today would be my last day at The Upper Cut.

The damnable Watch would be back with his footage, whether he had anything conclusive or not, and I couldn't chance being exposed. I felt melancholy but excited. It would have been nice to settle in for a while. I'm so far away from home. But I do enjoy traveling and sampling different regions. That's what gives me distinction and purpose, after all.

My family, the reptile hive of a star system called Tau Ceti by human astronomers, created me in much the same way that they grow mindless clones from the DNA that I collect inside my throat pouch — and they prefer females, whose body fat content is far higher than that of males.

Good snack food needs that luxurious flavor.

END

Afterword

I hate getting my hair cut. First of all, it feels like a waste of time. You gotta drive to Super Cuts. You gotta sit and wait. Then there's the chitchat with a stranger who's got her hands in your hair, hey, how it's going, what a nice day, blah blah blah. There are too many other things I could be doing!

"Snack Food" is one of those ideas that came to me whole while I sat in the chair watching someone sweep up these amazing drifts of different people's hair. Black hair. Blond hair. Long hair. Curly hair.

It was all going in bags to their dumpster — off to the landfill again — and I realized there were vast piles of DNA being gathered every day all over the world.

Who would want it? And why? Witches and psychopaths and aliens, oh my.

INTERRUPT

WHATEVER HAPPENED TO the sun seems to be intensifying. This time I blacked out for at least five days — I haven't grown so much beard since I was seventeen. Jan would have been shocked. It's shaved now. I managed a quick sponge bath, too. Jan ridiculed me for being "an anal robot" but keeping clean might be the only way to mark the length of each interrupt. I can't trust myself not to lose this journal, or start a fire with its pages. I think we're still smart enough to use tools.

These notes can't be my first attempt to document the phenomenon, but none of the laptops will even boot up. Electromagnetic pulses strong enough to affect our brains might have fried every computer chip on the planet. Wolsinger's mini-D was on my desk with a fresh disc in it, half recorded, but the playback is badly garbled.

Have I already tried to build a shield? That was my first thought now. It was probably my first thought before. How else to explain the trash heap of metal in the cafeteria? Pots, pans, garbage cans, the hoods of the truck and the jeep.

How many times have I already failed? With only a limited ability to form short-term memories, I could waste my lucid periods attempting the same thing over and over and over.

NOT MUCH TO do now except write to stay awake. I don't know if I could sleep anyway, give up my conscious mind voluntarily. I'm dizzy, though. Blisters on my thumb. I'd like to wash again, get off the stink of hard labor and, yes, the reek of fear, but I'm still dehydrated from tramping around in the heat all day and the cafeteria tanks are nearly empty. The pumps aren't working, of course. And I have to conserve in case I'm trapped.

In a while I'll patrol the front again but I think they went away. It's a good thing the building's concrete or they might have tried to burn me out. The locals must think we're doing this to them, all those antennas and the dish array. No need to speak Spanish to understand. I've never seen such hatred, not even in Jan after our court battles. The people here were always suspicious, I guess, no matter if we paid well in hard American dollars or gave away our medical supplies. Most of them have tried all their lives to get out of here, tried for generations, yet in comes a pack of gringo Dr. Frankensteins like the jungle was a petting zoo, blabbering about new laser spectrometers and listening for people in the stars. And I am a gringo here, no matter that my skin is darker than theirs.

Why did they come up the hill this evening? Because they heard me tinkering and were afraid I'd unleash another interrupt? I wish I was a better shot — I only tried to wound that stupid loudmouth when he grabbed me.

The moon is quarter full and waxing. Last I remember it was August 16th but it may be September already. So near the equator there are no real seasons, and the constellations don't move half as much as when I was a boy much further north. The stars seem to say it's October but that can't be right.

My old friends look cold and ugly tonight, glittering wildly like polished flecks of bone. What pressure storms are surging through the upper atmosphere?

There's no way to build a shield. I wrote that on the wall in magic marker, just to be safe. Have to stop wasting time on the idea. If I had machining tools it would be different. If I wasn't alone. If I wasn't on this goddamn rock in the middle of nowhere. There's definitely enough metal to line the cafeteria walls and ceiling, armor it thick and deep, if I could dismantle the jeep and the truck and the panels of the main dish, make sheeting out of the fenders, cut and bend everything to fit, flatten every fuel drum and computer and appliance in this place.

If if if.

If this was one of those idiotic monster movies Blair insisted on playing every time it was his night to choose a DVD, we could probably wrap our heads in tinfoil and be safe. Metal umbrellas. The fence might have been easiest to mold into a shield, but the holes in the chain link are huge in comparison to most wavelengths in the solar spectrum — too much would pass. I considered a body suit or even just a spherical helmet made of interwoven layers of window screens, but this building has plastic filament instead of metal, rust-proof.

I have another plan. An EM cone. I should be able to pull Dish 4 off the tower, rewire it to transmit. If I can generate a broadcast of matching amplitude and frequencies, precisely out of phase, I can neutralize the interrupt phenomenon locally. But I'll need power and working electronics.

MORNING. IT'S STAYED quiet. If Wolsinger and Blair are still in the area, I hope they'll avoid the locals.

Scott McCay is dead. He has been for at least a week, by the look of him, though it's tough to judge given the condition of his body. There also are dead or feeble lizards and snakes everywhere. Something in their physiology. The birds are having a field day, feasting — but they're flying a bit unsteadily, I think. Maybe only deep-water life forms are completely unaffected. People in submarines and bomb shelters.

It's ironic that the next interrupt may actually help us. The locals might not decide we're at fault the next time they're lucid, if another flare hits soon enough. The brain requires days to fully absorb and organize new memories, and that process is being disrupted.

How?

Normal solar radiation can reach microscopic lengths on the nanometer scale and smaller, though the atmosphere typically deflects EM of these wavelengths — and the synaptic gap ranges between 30 and 40nm.

Extreme flares must be overriding our bioelectric processes, like white noise. But if it's interfering with our ability to think, why aren't we left twitching and drooling on the ground? Or maybe we are. Maybe at times we're completely incapacitated. Sudden collapses might explain the bruises on my hip and chest, the abrasion on my cheek.

Unless I got hurt fighting.

I found McCay near the wooden shack that we paid the locals to put up for a garage, his skull smashed. Something had been eating at his neck and belly but I left him there. Securing the generators took first priority. All eight were already topped off and someone had taken steps to reinforce the surrounding fence. Me? Someone unused to that kind of labor — a sloppy but effective job of stringing razor wire and chaining the downhill corner that always sagged. Extra fuel had been siphoned from the drums in the garage.

The garage. Was McCay trying to leave? I assumed at first that Wolsinger and Blair had wandered off in a delirium during the last interrupt. Where is there to escape to? Could we have had a plan, received a radio message?

No matter how long I concentrate, I can't summon more than a few random images of the past days, and it's all confused with my long-term memories of this place. Finding food must be our main focus. I remember hunger and base gratification. But there is also frustration and fear. Could I be aware, however faintly, of being mentally stunted? Do I search and search for what's been stolen from me? For months after Jan left I felt like every organ in my body was packed with gravel, but this is horror on another scale — decay, repeated death.

If it continues, I suppose we may begin to lose our established memories as well. The brain is a lot like a computer. These constant

shocks can't be healthy. I'm going to seal this journal in a waterproof CD-ROM container and chain it to my wrist.

EATING LUNCH IN the shade of the dish array, greasy canned stew. The roof is like a stove top. The heat started my head thumping an hour ago and it's not even noon. I feel like I've been working here forever. My time sense doesn't seem completely reliable anymore. At least my coordination's still good. I ripped the guts out of Dish 1. The spectrometers were designed to withstand the EM fields generated by our own equipment, and over-engineered like most of our toys. They should still work.

Had to stop and write down what's happened, in case there's another interrupt. I used two more bullets in the pistol this morning. The body of the loudmouth was gone, dragged away, and three people I vaguely recognized came out of the jungle — a scrawny old goat rancher flanked by his daughter and son. A year ago during the meet-and-greets, the same trio stood in the same formation, always in the very back, murmuring among themselves, the son too angry.

Today they were armed with gardening tools, and the rancher's hoe had gummy blood stains on it. That shouldn't have relieved me, but I was glad to know I wasn't the one who killed McCay. I fired over their heads and they ran. I've wasted every other minute since then looking behind me, listening, waiting for a rifle shot and sudden agony. Stupid bastards.

If I am the one who took care of the generators, that must be as far as I got last time. If I—

THERE WAS ANOTHER interrupt, a brief one. I'm sure it's the same day because the canned stew I was eating has drawn a knot of flies but isn't baked hard yet. And no beard. It was incredibly strange reading over this journal. I am a stranger to that earlier self. How many times have I felt orphaned, doomed? Now at least I have this signpost. This bible.

I became a thinking human again at the far edge of the roof, pacing, the sun dropped low enough to stare me right in the face. My teeth ached from chewing on the chain around my wrist, like a dog. What if the interrupt had lasted longer? Would I have jumped eventually, two stories or not? Starved? Or could I have figured out how to open the stairwell?

I sat there and cried for twenty minutes.

Pulling the spectrometers is only the beginning. I'll need a functioning computer to regulate my broadcast, and an auto switch to stop and start it in time with the flares. Otherwise I'll simply blast myself with an interrupt of my own making. And of course one dish won't be enough. I have to produce a second EM cone to protect the generators or else they'll fry while producing the current I need. I suppose I could live on top of them, under the same dish, but then I'd need to construct a shelter and run water from the building…

My safe zone will be small, no wider than the dish and maybe ten feet long, room for a few people and supplies.

Please let this work.

WOLSINGER'S GONE CRAZY. He got into the building without me noticing and I almost shot him. The sun had set and he was only a shadow, and he didn't answer when I shouted. He didn't even look up from his desk. I asked where he'd been, if he was okay. He just sat there holding his armrests like he was afraid he'd float away. When he did talk, his voice never rose above a mumble. I actually laughed at first. I thought he was saying that the villagers were doing this to us, until I realized he meant a different "they" altogether.

He said it was in our recordings, a carrier wave from somewhere in Epsilon Eridani. We didn't remember because the aliens didn't want us to. They were making the sun pulse in an abnormal pattern, blinding us, destroying us.

I spent an hour digging through our printouts to prove him wrong. There was no signal. There was nothing. Wolsinger didn't help, just sat there holding onto his chair and shaking his head. He said the computer records would show it if the aliens hadn't burned out our hard drives. He said he remembered.

I need his help, his hands. He said yes. Can I trust him?

His eyes are too large, red, always blinking. I made sure to keep the pistol out of his reach. Delusional paranoia. It has to be. Something in his brain. Even if he had seen an extraterrestrial message before the first interrupt, he couldn't know now. What's happening is a natural occurrence.

Humankind has always studied the sun, hoping to interpret the moods of the gods, and we know from ancient writings that our star has roiled and flared for millennia. An uncontained hydrogen reactor of such enormous scale could hardly be expected to do otherwise. Modern civilization with all its tools and sciences rapidly added to that knowledge, measuring random eruptions and recording a phenomenon known as solar maximum: extreme flares that occurred roughly every eleven years.

We assumed it had been happening like clockwork forever. But we only truly became aware of the phenomenon after we had power grids and communications to be disrupted — little more than a century. A hundred years is less than a blink in the life of the sun, and all of human history is hardly more.

It did seem as if each maximum came a bit sooner and did worse damage than the previous one, yet the few people who sounded an alarm were dismissed as nuts, Chicken Littles. Of course each max seemed worse — each decade we had more satellites and technology to be affected. No one worried much.

The maximums must have been a recent instability. Earth's magnetosphere and ionosphere are obviously being wildly compressed and distorted, allowing exceptional amounts of EM to strike the planet's surface. The sun may be older than we assumed. We are still only guessing about so much of astrophysics. And if it is pre-nova, the onslaught of particle radiation may continue until it ultimately explodes in ten thousand years. Or this could simply be a natural period of adjustment, "blowing steam," as the sun stabilizes itself. The lizards and snakes I've seen dead or crippled — cold-blooded life everywhere must be affected in the same way, except the amphibians capable of hiding underwater.

Maybe now we know what happened to the dinosaurs, and why only frogs and turtles still survive from those days. Crocodiles. Sharks and fish.

Maybe we're re-entering a phase of solar activity that kept complex brain function from arising for eons, which is why early humans appear to have been stuck in a series of long evolutionary ruts despite having a skull capacity equal to ours.

I've read enough anthropology to know it's the big question. Why did we take so long to become what we are today? For uncounted millennia we were brutes, with only the most simple tools and societies, and then in the space of four thousand years we built empires and cities and blanketed the entire planet with electricity and highways and super-agriculture. Maybe those few thousand years were an unusually quiet time for the sun. Maybe there were other bits of peace here and there, just enough for us to evolve as far as we did.

If so, my EM cone will be a very temporary solution, even if I had unlimited fuel. Maybe Wolsinger and I can rig a portable model on the jeep, locate more supplies, reach the caves in the mountains to the south. I can't see them but I know they're there, sixty or seventy miles by road. Central America is just one big spine of rock.

What's left of the human race will have to go underground, deep down, become moles and morlocks. Give up the stars, the sky, the rain and trees and everything we've ever known.

REMEMBER THIS. REMEMBER it always.

Your name is Roell Washington Carver Lloyd. You were born on July 21, 1969, just a day after a human being first walked on the face of the moon. Your mother, Marilyn, was forever proud of that. None of your professional accomplishments meant so much to her. Even as cancer ate out her bowels she still bragged to you, to her nurses, to other patients, that you had been a moon baby. She made you feel special. She wanted to name you Apollo or Armstrong or even Rocket but your father said those were white names. His name was Ed, which he hated. White as can be. He wasn't so proud of you for being book-smart. He wanted you tougher, better at sports, and made you waste a million afternoons throwing balls and bouncing balls and running with balls. But he raised you well enough, you and your sister Korba, in Richmond, California, which is very very far from here. Too far to walk. Too—

If I forget all of that I probably won't remember how to read, either, so what's the point?

I THINK EIGHT days have passed since I wrote anything. My beard growth fits that time and the moon is going on full now. I found the generators rigged to come on one after another as they run out of fuel, and the last two are equipped with big auxiliary tanks. A stranger that was me had calculated their running time in grease pencil on the side of the last tank — eight hundred hours, roughly thirty days, somewhat less depending on how much power I use drawing water from the well.

A heavy-duty power line was strung from the generators to the cafeteria, where the first dish was bolted to the wall and floor. I suppose mounting it on the ceiling was too much, and it doesn't matter. The EM cone can be pointed in any direction. But I still haven't cobbled together a working computer. I found several PCs pulled apart beside the crude shell of the jeep's hood. Looks like another interrupt caught me in mid-task, and probably burned out everything I'd salvaged. They're coming more often and lasting longer now.

I woke in a protected corner of the cafeteria near the water tanks, in a crude nest of blankets, surrounded by fruit and some of those meaty leaves the size of my head. And I had what must be a weapon. A metal table leg. The pistol is gone. I think I was dreaming of Jan.

Once upon a time I enjoyed solitude, the peace and clarity of my work, but even Wolsinger would be a happy sight now. Maybe he won't be crazy this time. I've never been this alone before. I talk just to hear a voice.

Obviously I don't fully understand yet what we may or may not be capable of during the interrupts. The memory was so vivid, I could almost smell her.

YOUR WIFE JANICE grew up an inner-city black, poor, exposed to gangs and drugs, but had more style than an egghead from Cal Tech could ever quantify. You made a great team. She was popular, graceful, and pretty, sometimes even stunning in the right dress. You gave her structure, paid the bills on time, remembered anniversaries. For a while that was enough.

It wasn't that you took her for granted — you were simply miserable at some of the things she needed, crowds, dancing, chitchat. And you were discovering new miracles every day that transported you twenty or fifty or a hundred and fifty light-years away. You made the safe choice, stuck with the things you understood, and eventually she left you for it.

Janice is probably dead. Things must be impossibly bad in urbanized areas.

Uncontrolled fires would barely be the beginning, entire cities roasting alive. Not enough food to go around. No water. And San Francisco already had its share of brutes and killers before people lost the ability to reason.

She might have been here with you and had some chance at survival if you'd been a better husband.

Survival. No one is going to live to a ripe old age if we're taking as much radiation as I suspect. We might have fifteen, twenty years, then slow and ugly deaths — and that also matches the fossil record. As far as we can tell, nobody grew old in the distant past. Some of us will also surely develop cataracts before then, and what kind of life will it be, fighting for safety, scratching for food?

Why do I bother? Jan would say because I'm a control freak, won't let even the sun tell me what to do.

I had to laugh at that but my voice sounded like a tortured ghost, screeching and echoing all through the building.

Wolsinger hung himself in the stairwell, triple-cinched a tough extension cord and then jumped. Maybe Blair did something, too. Mom ate a bottle of pills and I hated her for it. The doctors said she had a good chance but she didn't want to lose her hair, lose her dignity, suffer through the cure.

I hated Jan for quitting, too.

Hated my father. He also quit in his own way, quit before I was fifteen. It seemed like he put more energy into his stupid basketball games than he gave his own son, football, baseball. He could rattle off a million team statistics and scores but never remembered any of the things I cared about, things that were real and useful.

The EM cone will work, I'm sure of it. And if I do only have fifteen years, at least that's an eternity compared to a life span of days. Life spans. Just thinking about it makes me feel schizophrenic. I'm so tired.

MORE INTERRUPTS, TWO weeks' worth of beard but the moon's in the same phase as when I last recorded it, still waxing full. Madness. Clearly it's waxing again. It's been twenty-eight days and this time I'm going to write before shaving.

Self-awareness came back in jolts and stabs, blurred vision, some dizziness, as if my brain were a rusty engine. The burst of fear-adrenaline squeezing through my heart and limbs probably helped clear my head. I was sitting with a woman in the nest of blankets by the water tanks, a tangy flavor in my mouth and tough, half-eaten roots in my hand.

It was the rancher's daughter. I'll call her Bonita. Apparently about a month ago I shot at her as she threatened me with some kind of gardening tool, but I didn't know that as we sat there staring at each other. I recognized her from long-term memories but hadn't had a chance to read these notes yet. Bonita couldn't have remembered our confrontation either. Despite that and despite having no language in common, we immediately began to argue. She was understandably shocked, vulnerable. I was apologetic and kept my distance, kept my hands up, palms open, my voice low and comforting.

When she ran, I shouted after her like a puppy.

That desperation shouldn't surprise me. It's been several incarnations since I felt anything soft or good or sweet. Bonita was just as dirty as I was but her sweat smelled clean, like perfume synthesized from the pungent earth. She wore only a pair of shorts that were too big for her. I thought I recognized them as mine. It was an American brand. Her breasts were perfect, smooth and small, works of art. And there was the obvious evidence in our nest that we had made love, more than once.

I think we've been together before. I think that what I assumed was a dream of Jan after the previous interrupt was actually some trace of Bonita. Her or someone else. But why would any of the locals come to me? Because of my decorative coloring? I may be the only black man in a hundred miles.

It would be ironic if Bonita had been drawn to this hilltop by some vague memory of it being important, and that when we met we simply acted on our attraction. Enemies when able to think and speak, lovers when reduced to an animal state.

Enemies. Someone tore down the power line running from the cafeteria and sabotaged the generators. Number six is a total loss but I can salvage its auxiliary tank, though there may not be any point if I can't find more fuel. They crawled under the fence, I think, at the saggy corner. More fucking work.

If I save Bonita she'll love me. Jan did, for that same reason. Anyone would.

LOSING TOO MUCH time to interrupts, my hair's a great Afro cloud and the damn moon's not making sense, still waxing. Still! I have to write this down to keep from running in circles when I am lucid. Half insane even then, not sleeping. So close to beating it.

You've already patched together a computer, it's under the armor, stop tinkering with it.

You need to fine-tune your transmitter. The EM hitting us is bizarre, too short, 170 down to 25nm. Maybe Wolsinger was right.

THE CONE WORKS. I'm under it now. Day Three. I've been trying to build a portable version with the few scraps available. It will be very heavy. The generators sound like they're running OK but there's no way to walk out there and check. My biggest fear is that someone will get through the fence again and damage them, turn them off. The noise they make is a liability. I know we still possess curiosity in the animal state.

When the last interrupt stopped I was with Bonita again, making love, close to peaking. She shut her eyes as if to escape me and I paused, but her rhythm increased, maybe involuntarily. Then I slowed again to tease her. She turned to face me and murmured and groaned. We kissed like teenagers. It was wild and raw, far better than with Jan or anyone else ever. But climax was anticlimactic. Desire faded and awkwardness came over us. I tried to make her stay with words and gestures, tried to show her what I was working on, but she kept shaking her head. She ran.

DAY FIVE. I just don't have the gear necessary to build a smaller model, and I never had another power source anyway. I'm going to lower the strength of the broadcast, shrinking the safe area to conserve fuel. I think I can push most of my supplies outside the cone and hook them in as needed.

DAY NINE. I'M not alone. I can see a clearing and the edge of the lake from here and sometimes the locals come up the hill, but they won't enter the building even if I yell, or pretend to be hurt, or sing...

Bonita smiled at that, staring through the fence at my window and moving as close as possible, but she didn't seem to recognize the doors for what they were. Why not?

Our nest was here in this same room.

Maybe it was me she didn't recognize.

I've been studying them. No one talks but there is simple communication, hand gestures, squawks and grunts of impatience, pleasure, agreement. They cooperate. Fortunately, the previous civilization wiped out most of the predators, it's always warm here and the jungle seems to provide enough nourishment for all — and the trees and brush are also shelter from the worst of the ultraviolet.

I didn't mention that I'd lost weight. The desk belly is long gone, but I wasn't starved during the interrupts. In fact there's some evidence that I gorged myself. Obviously I was getting plenty of exercise. Hunting and gathering? And making love. Physically I may be at my best in ten years.

I'm so restless now.

Yesterday I saw Alex Blair playing a fetch-and-chase game with three others. They laughed like kids.

DAY SEVENTEEN. IT'S not ever going to end. Even if I had unlimited food and fuel, I can't stay in here forever. Now that I've finally had a chance to breathe, to think it though, I wonder what I'd hoped to accomplish. Escape to a cave and slowly starve there? Study the interrupt phenomenon and create a set of charts and graphs that nobody will ever see?

My biggest fear isn't that the generators will fail — it's that I'll improve my shelter, jury-rig a more permanent protected area, and sit alone in it as the sun flares forever.

I'd have my memories, but would there be any worth keeping?

If I quit now, I win as much as I lose. Bonita. Friends. I want to be a part of their Eden for as long as we have left.

I'll scar my forearm with a short message, in case there are moments of waking confusion and fear. Then I'm going to unchain this journal from my wrist and destroy the generators. I think Dad would be proud to see me pitch a Coke bottle full of gasoline all the way from here.

END

Afterword

Unlike "Pressure" and "Snack Food," the core concept behind "Interrupt" was something I purposely developed instead of having it spring whole into my imagination. Some stories are more work than others. I admit I enjoy it when my subconscious does most of the heavy lifting, but the stories that are the hardest work can also be the most satisfying.

I was between projects at the time. I'd been reading about our new solar observation satellites, and obviously I have a bent toward apocalyptic settings. But I didn't want to burn the world to a crisp. Larry Niven did that expertly in "Inconstant Moon." So I began to play around with different ways a solar storm might affect civilization.

Memory and time sense are all that separate us from animals. Yes, we have opposable thumbs and walk upright, but those advantages wouldn't mean much without our self-awareness. The mind is our greatest tool. Lose it, lose everything.

You can see my efforts to explore this idea all the way from my earliest story, "Exit," to later pieces such as "Long Eyes" and even "Monsters."

In part, I suppose that's because I suffered three major concussions as a boy. I was aggressive in sports. Before my fifteenth birthday, in addition to the head bangs, I'd broken four bones either stopping an opposing player on the soccer field, fighting at school, or skiing. Just be glad you weren't my parents!

I suffered the worst concussion playing ultimate frisbee in the gym. One of my teammates threw a low pass into the corner. No way was I going to let that frisbee go. Catching it, I slid beneath a table, then ricocheted my head off the table's edge into the hardwood floor.

Some people don't retain their short-term memories during severe concussions, but I remember being inhibited. One side of my face went slack, and I had limited control over that side of my body. This was back in the early 80's, so my gym teacher had me walk it off instead of calling an ambulance — nice work, buddy — and I burst into tears when it was time to take the bus home because I couldn't recall where I was supposed to get off. I knew the bus was right, but I'd lost my sense of the immediate future and any ability to plan even minutes ahead.

It was scary as hell.

How and what we think is who we are. That's the core idea behind "Interrupt." The rest is good, standard sci fi; the outpost of scientists confronted with a mysterious danger; the misunderstandings and violence between them and an uneducated mob; a spot of romance; and their efforts to overcome the threat.

Ultimately, that's impossible. The threat is too big. But I like to think there's a brave, lonely triumph in Lloyd's fight to escape.

The real question is why do I keep torturing my characters this way?

I wrote the following essay when Annalee Newitz at *io9* asked me why the heck I'm such an evil puppetmaster.

WRITING ABOUT
THE APOCALYPSE

I THINK WE'RE programmed for hardship. In my experience, human beings are happiest when they're working themselves to the bone. Call me crazy, but from what I've seen people are more likely to feel adrift and unsatisfied when they have too much leisure time. Purpose is the greatest gift. Obstacles are good.

Here's why. For hundreds of thousands of years, life was brutal. It still is for a good chunk of the planet. The technology and wealth we enjoy in North America is a very new development in history, and I think we miss the challenges of day-to-day survival in our comparatively easy modern lives. Some people will even create problems if they have none.

Everyone's had a psychotic girl- or boyfriend, right? Well, lots of 'em really are just nut-flavored bologna. They have a neurochemical imbalance or ate too many paint chips as a kid... but some people look for drama and emotional upheaval for reasons they can't explain themselves, reenacting the shortcomings, chaos, or abuse of their childhoods.

Surprise. These drama kings and queens might be exactly the kind of person you'd want at your back during the zombie apocalypse or the aftermath of a comet strike. Each of our nut-flavored friends is a sponge. They're ready to soak up as much as trauma as anybody can dish out. They have the stamina, heart and depth to keep on slogging through the radioactive bugs even long after the last shotgun shell is gone.

They're not the only ones. I like to think I'm the kind of guy you'd give the keys to the bomb shelter and I'm extremely boring and normal — wife, kids, mortgage, bleh — ha ha — except to say that I grew up fascinated with books like *Lucifer's Hammer* and *The Stand*.

We like to be scared because we have a huge capacity for fear. The most basic element of storytelling is conflict because we respond to it.

For me, writing post-apocalyptic novels isn't so much about exploding helicopters and fifty megaton doomsday bombs as it is about the pleasure of dealing with the best of everything that makes us human: cleverness, grit, loyalty, and self-sacrifice.

Sure, the hot-sex-with-our-last-breath and gunfights are fun, too, but ultimately my novels boil down to the ability of some people — the greatest of us — to overcome any hurdle. I back my heroes into corners just to watch them wiggle free.

We're evolved for less food; more exercise; less sleep; less security; more paranoia. The irony is that as a species we've been incredibly successful. We've made it normal to have more food; less exercise; more sleep; more security; less paranoia.

Look around. Humankind has remade the entire face of the planet, blanketing Earth with electrical grids, highways, super-agriculture, shipping lanes and aircraft, even wrapping the sky in satellites. It's easy to complain about your bills or morning traffic or the neighbor's neglected, ever-barking dogs (you know who you are), but these are fantastic problems to have.

The grocery stores are loaded, we have the industrial strength to roll off three cars per household, and every other family has enough money to spare to feed two dogs and a cat even though they don't have any inclination to walk Sparky and Spot every day and choose instead to leave their canines to noisily go insane, each set of dogs fenced off inside their own isolated little patch of suburbia.

Anyone with a computer to read this blog is richer than 99.99% of the human beings who've ever lived, and yet we can't help imagining what things would be like if we had to start over. Nuclear armageddon. Superflu. The living dead. Nanotech.

Give me a wild scenario and some smart good guys and I'm happy -- just so long as the lights stay on and there's iced tea in the fridge. I'd really rather not be sifting through the rubble for canned food and medicine while we keep one eye peeled for roving gangs of illiterate cannibals.

END

Afterword

This essay could have been a lot longer, but I'm a fiction writer, not a professor. What I'd like to add is that since the dawn of recorded history, there's an alarming pattern in the rise and fall of civilizations. Sometimes they're overrun by larger empires or armies with better technology. Sometimes they decay from within.

Luxury, complacency, and entitlement can be our worst enemies. It makes us lazy. Then we turn our deeper, unfulfilled needs on each other, inventing problems where they aren't any, an idea which leads nicely to this essay written for John DeNardo at *SF Signal...*

ROSE-COLORED DEMONS

FOR ME AND many writers, one of the most eye-opening changes since the e-revolution has been the rise and importance of book reviews on personal blogs and corporate sites like Goodreads, Amazon, and B&N.

To writers, strong word-of-mouth is catnip. Even bad reviews can be useful in honing your craft.

I spend a lot of time alone in a room with a laptop listening to the voices in my head. That sounds like a joke, but it's a large part of my job description. There's no one to hang out with at the water cooler in my office. Heck, there's no water cooler! That's why it's especially cool to get fan mail or to have my Google minions find reviews such as: "This novella was so fast paced and action packed from the very first line that I was sucked in like a two by four in a F5 twister!"

Reading that, I thought, *Fantastic. She gets it.*

Capturing you is exactly what I want — to connect, to entertain, to make you a 2x4 in my tornado.

When eight people say the ending is abrupt, that's useful, too. My brain says to me, *Okay, you thought you had every element in place, but you'd better add at least another paragraph to wrap things up.* Readers want to walk away with a feeling of completion. Sometimes I move too fast, so I'm learning to take it down a notch.

Even the people who hate a story are right. No writer reaches everybody, and it's perfectly fair for someone to leave a low-starred review if he doesn't feel like he got his money's worth. That's expected.

But in today's brave new world of e-media, my inbox is also peppered with a steady dose of diehard political outrage, accusations, and messages from weird alternate realities.

When I swap emails with my writer friends or when we meet up at cons, the new game is Who's Been Burned The Worst. It's almost funny.

We all view the world through the lenses of our personal life experiences. Sometimes the world is rose-colored. Sometimes we're not even aware of how thoroughly our own demons shape our perceptions, so let me share some of the over-the-top experiences I've had with folks from the fringe.

The Illinois Nazi

More than once I've received hate mail or nasty Amazon reviews for *Plague Year* because two of the main heroes are a Latino and a genius Jew. Worse, two of the villains are white guys. Obviously I've either turned on my own kind (I'm a white guy) or I've been so indoctrinated by the sinister liberal media that I don't even realize what I'm doing...

Here's the thing. The opening chapters of *Plague Year* are set in post-apocalyptic California. I don't know where our white supremacist friends live, but the West Coast is one of the most ethnically diverse areas on the planet. If everyone was forced into the mountains to escape a runaway nanotech plague, there's zero chance it would be only sparkly blond Caucasians who survived. More to the point, among my best friends growing up were Hispanic and Jewish families. I knew I could pull off those backgrounds competently, and a diverse cast added a bit of texture to what's ultimately just a rock-'em sock-'em sci fi thriller.

The One-Winger and the Classic Old Knee

As a writer, it's both frustrating and intriguing to have the same novel condemned as a subversive socialist pinko screed and as a right-wing manifesto. Yeah, it's nice to strike such a chord. Every writer wants their work to resonate. But reading is a subjective experience. People bring a lot of themselves to the experience... sometimes too much.

The One-Wingers are careful not to mention race like the Illinois Nazis, but they don't appreciate how the conservative remnants of the government are perceived by the heroes. By the same token, The Classic Old Knees are certain I must be a big fat Republican because the government is enforcing martial law and the tough Special Forces guys keep pushing the scientists around. It's crude symbolism, isn't it!?!?

Uh, no. In *Plague Year*, the new U.S. capital is a Colorado town that originally had a population of 3,000 people. Now it's been swamped by 600,000 refugees. There's no food, no shelter, and if I was in charge I'd darn well have the few remaining supplies surrounded by Army units. That doesn't mean I'm a liberal or a fascist or a purple polka dot Martian.

I think it's a very human phenomenon that individuals on far, opposite ends of the political spectrum are able to interpret the same story in different ways, seeing exactly what they want to see in order to support their beliefs.

Sometimes the smallest minds make the biggest noise. That's because feeling angry is pleasant. It makes you feel important. Condemning a book as dangerous and shouting your warnings from the rooftops... let's call that the Revere Complex. Each of our archetypes the Nazi, the Winger and the Knee fall into this same category, a truth which might outrage them all over again if they realized it.

The Nutcake.

Alas, these folks are even easier to explain. They're nutty. Three times I've received emails or comments insisting that *Plague Year* was penned by someone else, namely the person contacting me, and that I stole the book before he or she could publish it. Unfortunately, other writers tell me such accusations aren't uncommon, nor are personal threats. Welcome to my FBI file.

Slightly less bizarre but more fun, let me introduce you to the Owner Of Katie The Dog. Not long after my sequel *Plague War* hit stores, I received an email with two jpg attachments. Hmmm. All right. Let's read it...

A woman had felt compelled to say she liked the concept behind *Plague Year,* but (insert sneer), "it was written in a grocery-store thriller style."

Aha HA ha ha! First of all, the cover has an ominous red tagline that shouts *The Next Breath You Take Will Kill You.* Plus the title letters are on fire. If you're looking for a cozy literary novel, this ain't it. Second, having my books racked in grocery stores and big box outlets like Wal-Mart and CostCo is my goal! That's what I'm striving for!

Yet she was so offended she'd spent $7.99 on this trash, she added that she'd fed *Plague Year* to her dog and snapped pictures of Katie eating it.

Wow. That's wrong, isn't it? I mean, that takes *effort.*

I had no intention of opening her jpgs. Remember, I'd barely published my second novel. Being in stores still felt new and daunting. But my writer friends insisted I see what Katie had done. One accomplished old vet said, "You know you've arrived when you're making people that crazy."

Um... Thanks?

Conventional wisdom holds that authors and editors should remain above the fray. You're supposed to ignore bad reviews, especially those that are off-topic or smell like fruit. I know writers who engage their haters in the comment fields on Amazon, but the reason to avoid such arguments was best put to me like this: Never wrestle with a pig. The pig enjoys it, and you get covered in sh*t.

Which leads us to the most craven of them all.

The Dread Saboteur

In its first six months on Kindle and Nook, my novella "The Frozen Sky" sold 20,000 copies. That's not a huge number, but it's nothing to sneeze at. It's also gotten a lot of nice reviews, which is gratifying.

Unfortunately, "Sky" has also seen some attacks.

As the e-revolution evolves, the pages of successful books are experiencing not-so-subtle assaults by bitter would-be successes who post scathing low-starred reviews with as many dummy accounts as possible, then use the same dummy accounts to post five-star raves of their own novels in an attempt to draw traffic from the high-selling books.

Can the system be gamed so easily? My guess is no, not in the long run. Ultimately the Dread Saboteur's work needs to stand on its own. If it's garbage, it's garbage. Cardboard plots, wet dream characters, bad dialogue, and the inability to spell or use punctuation are common pitfalls.

Horse puckey reviews won't carry a flawed story beyond a few extra sales — and if those readers feel duped, well, let the bad karma begin! The fake five-star raves will be overwhelmed by genuinely unhappy reviews.

There are more archetypes and goofy anecdotes I could share, but we're out of time.

Here's a final thought. Things are changing fast in publishing, but I hope it will always be true that it's the fans who carry the day.

The loonies and the saboteurs want everyone to wear their demon-colored lenses. Don't let it happen. If you like a book, bang out a quick ranking-and-review. That positive feedback may be enough to see your favorite author through his next encounter with a Nutcake From The Eighth Dimension.

END

DAMNED WHEN YOU DO

IT WAS NOT a virgin birth, I can tell you that much. The boy never could fly or stop bullets with his teeth, and those people who say he was twenty feet tall are full of it. He didn't have God on the phone, either. I guess I'm not the one to say he wasn't Jesus come again, but if he was, the Book's got everything mixed.

There were signs before his birth. We had tremors, then record heat waves and drought and flood and drought again. Margie and me didn't think anything about it. The world was already going to hell in a hand basket. Every disaster was just business as usual — earthquakes in China, nukes in Iran, war, poverty, and hundreds of millions of people pumping carbon whatever into the sky, everybody knowing it was causing global warming but not changing their routines a bit.

I was one of them.

In the documentaries, they always show L.A. freeways and New York taxi jams. My neighbors had a great time complaining how the crops and grazing were hard hit by out-of-season storms and dry spells, which they blamed on pollution caused by the same city people who needed our farms, but no one can say Jack Shofield isn't honest. I accept my share of it. It doesn't matter that all of southern Oklahoma has less people in it than downtown Hollywood or that I typically saw no more than five or six other trucks on my way to the feed shop. Poison is poison. Like everyone, I just wanted to get about my business ASAP.

I'm no preacher and I think we've all heard all we need about sin, destruction, and salvation. I just want to set the record straight.

He was my son.

PEOPLE CALLED HIM everything from savior to satan in every language known to man. We named him Albert Timothy after his grandfathers. Margie and me are old-fashioned enough to believe in things like honor and respect, and we would have taught him so if we'd had the chance. But we only met him twice.

It's true in a literal sense that the world revolved around him. I think the real miracle lies in the fact that *people* revolved around him. From the news at the time, you wouldn't have thought there were twelve decent folk left anywhere, and yet he grew to be strong, caring and smart despite having every last one of six billion selfish apes as parents.

MARGIE'S A TOUGH girl. That's why I married her. She didn't scream until our baby was all the way out of her. The doctor yelled, too. I thought the boy must have three arms or something, so I shoved a nurse to get a look at him. He was already tumbling toward the door like a little pink log. Then the first quakes knocked the building down. I was thrown to the floor, and I never did catch up.

How did our infant son survive? Utter strangers fed and changed him as he passed. Folks kept him warm with the clothes off their backs. They emptied their wallets to get bottles and formula when store owners didn't put those things in their hands for free. After a few days, entire nations prepared for him even when his projected course was nowhere near, because the projections weren't worth much. He usually rolled east to west, opposite of Earth's natural rotation as if pushing the planet beneath him, but for the first few years he wobbled north and south seemingly at random — and when he learned to walk, he jaunted from pole to pole as he chose.

There's been a lot of talk from scientists, holy men and politicians. Believe what you want. The truth is nobody can explain him and nobody ever will. The proportion's all wrong. It's flat-out scary, in fact, like a flea spinning a ball the size and weight of Australia.

Clocks and calendars quickly became useless. One day would pass in twenty hours, the next in twenty-eight or seventeen. Seasons changed in a matter of weeks.

There was just no way to ignore him.

Wars stopped as he went by. Starving tribes in west Africa mashed their last handfuls of grain into mush for him.

Why didn't he bruise to death? Micro gravitational skins, they said. Angels, they said. Before he was old enough to control it, some instinct or higher power wove him around buildings and cliffs and trees. Later in life, he walked the globe like a man on a spherical treadmill. When he was just four months old he got stuck in a box canyon in Peru and the whole world shuddered for three hours until a brave rancher went in on hands and knees and shoved him in the right direction.

You'd think he would've had trouble keeping food down, rolling, always rolling, but eventually some big brain proved he was actually orbiting the sun as smooth as silk while it was the planet itself that did the shifting up and back and sideways beneath him.

And the oceans? Rivers and lakes? He walked on water. As a baby he returned to shore hungry and stinking, wailing because no one had fed or changed him. Later, as a child, he went hog-wild playing with dolphins and seals — and in the end, his only refuge was the sea.

Of course he had monstrous effects on the weather, tides, fault-lines and volcanoes. It's impossible to guess how many deaths he caused directly. Yesterday I heard a newsman say upward of twenty million. More than a few people tried to kill him right off the bat, but twice as many protected him. He took a razor in the shoulder somewhere in Burma. A man shot him in the guts outside Madrid. Five doctors across Spain saved his life that time, and dozens more around the world contributed to the treatment.

He had an obvious way of pulling people together.

FOR US, IT started badly. Albert broke Margie's heart before she even really saw him. Leaving his mother so fast, well, Margie never did recover.

She spent her days following him on the news. Pretty soon we had a TV and a computer in every room, not that she moved much off the couch. She kept saying she hurt even after Doc Hanley pronounced her fit.

People sent us things — money and things — mostly expecting us to keep these donations but plenty more of them looking for a blessing. We were easier to track down than our boy and easier to reach because the crowd around us was smaller.

Some ladies wanted me. I doubt I had much to do with what made Albert different, and that's a good thing. Can you imagine what the world would have done with two such boys?

Suddenly we were richer than we'd ever expected. I hated it — all the attention that came with it. We gave most of the money to charity, but that only seemed to brighten the media spotlight and triple the contributions coming in.

I had to quit my job at the feed shop. None of the reporters or those so-called holy pilgrims ever bought any feed or tack. They just got in the way and stole small items for souvenirs. By the end of the first week, you couldn't find a pen to save your life. They'd taken every one. We had to calculate weights and costs in our heads. It made the bookkeeper crazy, so I quit before my boss had to ask, which left me with nothing to do but hole up in our trailer with poor Margie as she talked to her TVs and computers. I don't mean she talked to them the way those things are like phones now. I mean she just laughed and chattered to herself as faces and maps flashed on the screens. Sometimes she cried, too, always when there was footage of mothers trying to touch their babies against him or when the Army lost track of him. None of those billion dollar satellites were much good in the beginning because the cloud cover got too thick.

Our boy never saw the sun or any real kind of sky until he was five. People say he backpeddled like crazy just so he could stare up at the clear patch for an instant.

Nothing else surprised him. He knew everything about the human condition before he took his first step, which didn't happen until he was three and a half. Some folks had the nerve to call him slow, but I'd like to see those full-grown fools stay on their feet if the world spun beneath them. He was fluent in more languages than you've got fingers and toes, comfortable in twice as many cultures and always learning. He personally witnessed more geology and biology and all the other ologies than a football stadium packed with teachers.

Margie and me learned with him on the TV. So did billions of others. And we all saw too much to be ashamed of.

No one could say hate, stupidity and greed were new. The effects of such things had been in the papers our whole lives, but everybody said this baby made it personal for them.

Hundreds of thousands of people tried to walk with him. Huge migrations rushed from the east side of every continent to the west end, then charged back again to wait for his next arrival. Knowing where he'd come ashore was a challenge in the early days, but crowds formed thirty-deep along hundreds of miles of coastline just hoping he'd land near them.

What else did they have to do while they were waiting except talk and make friends? Even during the migrations, most of them never got anywhere near the boy. In fact, sometimes ten thousand people got detached from the rest and paraded off on their own, never knowing and never worried that they were without their messiah. Just walking together was enough.

Maybe I should have been among them. It might have helped Albert and me. For years I puttered around our small trailer feeling like an empty sack because he was so far outside my reach. When he was two, he passed within a mile of our place, but that only hurt more. All of Lincoln county was buried in strangers, helicopters, hot dog vendors and the whole shebang. The dozens of times he touched through Oklahoma's borders felt almost as bad. I'd never been helpless before.

More than one corporation wanted to fly me into Albert's path, but they wanted me to dress up in logos for corn chips or vacuum cleaners. That didn't seem right. And I was afraid. Taking care of Margie helped fill the hollowness in me, but I was not a well man. Like millions of others, I had the nerve to envy him for being so powerful.

Somehow we all forgot he'd never use the lavish homes he'd been given by every government in the world. Roofs and walls were a danger to him. The elaborate playgrounds they built with train tracks and water slides, well, he would never play with any toy he couldn't carry. He never had any friends, either. I guess he had favorites everywhere and constantly tried to reach them, but more often than not he was blocked or distracted by new people with new problems. He was never alone, not even going to the bathroom. People actually fought over his leavings as keepsakes no matter how often he admonished them with a laugh and the promise to generate more.

Times like those, it was easy to remember Albert was just a kid. Eight-year-olds shouldn't rule the world.

That was how old he was when we first met him. We knew he was headed in our direction, of course. There were still some shows on the air that had nothing to do with Albert or the changes he was making, but all of them dedicated at least a small window to his progress so they could keep their viewers from surfing off. Margie was watching her dramas, silly romantic stuff I'd encouraged her to indulge in because it had nothing to do with our boy. I figured that was healthy.

Then she screamed and I burned myself rushing out of the kitchen. "What! What is it?"

She could only point at the TV.

"He's coming straight at us," I said, stupidly, but the thought was too big to keep in my head. "Straight at us."

It wasn't until then that the growing din outside made sense.

Margie and me didn't bother much with the outside anymore, and I'd figured the noise for another of the concerts or revivals always going on in town. When I pulled the drapes open, I yanked them shut again like a joker in one of her shows.

There was a stampede of people more than a mile wide bearing down on our trailer. At its head was our son — and the news vans. The dust cloud looked like a cape on a giant worm.

"Get up," I said.

Margie was trying to scream again but couldn't breath. She seemed like she was trying to look at me, too, but she couldn't pull her eyes away from the TV.

"Honey, please." I took her arm as gently as I could with all that adrenaline in my veins. "Get up. If you want to talk to your son, you'll have to get out there and move. Does this shirt match my good tie?"

THOSE SAME SMALL-MINDED people who'd tut-tutted about how slow he'd been to walk were also free with their opinions about a boy who never visited his parents, but you have to remember, he didn't know us and he wasn't used to thinking of any one place as being more special than the next. Also, the crowd was always in the way.

You couldn't have blamed Albert if Margie disappointed him. She slobbered and screamed and pawed. Embarrassment made my body so heavy I could barely keep up, but his smile was a mystery just like in that Lisa painting.

His smile was patient and knowing. He seemed to understand everything about Margie's pain and he was not afraid. We'd learned all about his empathy and genuine interest in people from the TV, but now that magic was real. It was hypnotizing.

"Walk with me," he said. We were already trudging alongside him, and his followers made sense of his invitation before we did. They backed off to give us some privacy.

Albert was much leaner than he appeared on TV. Up close, his robes couldn't hide the fact that he was all angles and elbows. He was beautiful. He had Margie's black hair and dark eyes. He also had a ridiculous walk like a kangaroo crossed with a drunk, bouncing, skipping, letting the earth zip by in between each step. Otherwise we never would have been able to keep up. Nobody understood yet what it meant that he'd developed this level of control.

"I love you," he said, and Margie screamed some more. His eyes locked with mine. "I'm sorry I haven't visited before."

"It's okay, son."

He smiled again, more of a grin this time like you'd expect on a boy. "I need some fatherly advice," he said.

"From me?"

He just grinned. I remember it perfectly; the gritty taste of the dust and rumbling crowd behind us; sunlight flashing on the camera lenses; his calm, strong words.

For whatever it's worth, so help me, I said his idea sounded mighty fine.

IT TOOK ALBERT most of a year because he started out careful, dodging back and forth across the equator, slowing the planet's rotation in unsteady spurts, foregoing meals and sleep to keep a schedule that only he knew. He riled up a storm unlike anyone had ever seen, a "strato"-something way at the top of the sky. Fortunately, during his first years every landmass in the world had shaken out at least a hundred years' worth of quakes. There were some small tidal waves and one big fault opened up in India, but all in all it wasn't bad.

The scientists lost a lot of weather balloons and robot planes trying to prove that he couldn't be doing what he was doing. For the next eighteen months, we had wicked beautiful sunsets in the States but not much sun. I was surprised at how little panic there was. He'd explained what he was doing and people believed him. People thanked him everywhere.

At that point we'd only had a taste of the future we'd created, damning our grandchildren, but one taste was plenty. For ten years we'd seen scorching summers and short, late winters. Fire ants had spread so far north they'd reached Idaho. New diseases were every-where. Most of Africa was baked sterile and other rainless hot spots had cropped up across Asia and California. Beach-side cities and in some places whole countries were seeping under the rising oceans...

Somehow he shook all the gases and carbon whatever out of the atmosphere.

At the same time, he was also talking up a storm. Albert was in a unique position to change things. People loved or feared him, but he always had everyone's attention.

Because he talked with everyone, he knew everything about those few who hid from him. He personally visited the fat cats who'd been sitting on clean technology because their fortunes came from dirty energy. He visited them again and again with the eyes of global television staring over his shoulder. "You've already got more money than you know what to do with," he said. It was practically that simple. Albert started things going and the new economies proved stronger than the old. Hydro-what's-it engines aren't any faster than oil-driven, but they don't pollute, which saved billions of dollars in health and clean-up costs. That didn't happen overnight, but the ben-efits were as obvious and dizzying as a stack of presents under a Christmas tree.

He visited warlords and dictators, too, especially the Chinese leaders, probably because they controlled so much land and so many people that he couldn't avoid their policies for more than a day at a time. Albert even brought several of these hard men with him around the globe, pushing them in heavy-duty wheelchairs he'd had designed for exactly this purpose. We don't know what they talked about, but he showed them a borderless world. He showed them their real size.

Meanwhile the weather in Oklahoma had become like I remem-bered it as a boy. It was steady and predictable. We sent our crop surpluses to places where they couldn't shake their trouble, countries where civil war or famine had held sway for generations.

There were some things he couldn't fix. Africa had reached the peak of its AIDS plague and something like seven out of every ten people were dying or seriously ill. Murderers and rapists still walked among us. Several endangered species had dwindled to such small numbers that they were doomed regardless of any new rescue effort, no matter how well funded or stocked with volunteers.

None of that ruined the sense of hope and cooperation sweeping the planet. Some people said he was an incarnation of Earth itself sent to scare us into taking responsibility before it was too late, but Albert didn't want to be worshipped. He just wanted to stop seeing so much pain.

He hadn't quite turned eleven yet when he took on that crazy bastard up north.

EMPATHY AND TRUST are not universal traits. Albert taught us that we were poorer because of it. He taught us to pity, but he also believed in taking action.

That madman in Korea had ruled his miserable half-frozen hunk of land for twenty years, building nukes, selling nukes, starving his own people so he could put more money into the walls and guns that kept them in and everyone else out.

Albert attempted to meet with this man for years but was rebuffed. He sent messages and was met with silence. At last he issued commands. More silence.

He stopped the world. Albert put that bastard's territory in eternal darkness even as he managed to bring sunshine to neighboring countries on a regular basis. It must have felt like God himself cursed them.

Weeks passed and our son exhausted himself, only catnapping, taking a bite or two when folks pleaded with him. It seemed to be working. The TV and the net were abuzz with praise from the leaders of the world, issuing the madman terms, promising relief to his beleaguered people. But that sick bastard had hunkered down in his luxurious shelters more than once before. He must have been used to the dark. I think it was pride that drove him to such extremes.

They call it ABC war: atomic, biological, chemical. The missiles were duds that got no further than Hawaii and often went wide or fell short into Japan, but the madman's agents had spread worldwide with three low-grade fission devices and more vials and test tubes than anyone could count.

Albert tried to keep the airborne diseases from spreading. He ran for days, stumbling, cutting his leg on the Himalayas, twisting an ankle in the Amazon delta.

It just wasn't enough.

Three days of massive retaliation from the U.S. and Britain demanded even more effort from our son or else another hundred million souls might have been killed by fallout.

Revenge was no consolation to Albert or to the billions of wounded survivors. He was stoned in the Philippines and shot at twice in New York, two areas that had taken the brunt of it. Albert renounced his political agenda and every good work he'd done in a terrified, sobbing message that was almost lost in the chorus of outrage.

He retreated to the oceans and the cold night-side of the planet. He denied himself sunshine and human companionship for two years, running whenever planes and ships came after him. There were sightings during this self-exile, some of which must have been real. Many more were surely hoaxes and lies like that woman in South Dakota and those German cults. He wouldn't have visited landlocked areas.

I still have nightmares for my son. The loneliness he must have experienced isn't something I can put into words.

Albert snuck across the narrowest stretches of Central America, picked his way through the densely laid islands of Malaysia and sprinted across Africa, but the chance of running into people on that broad continent was frequently too much for him. Most days the world shifted wildly as he ran south around Africa's horn.

What he ate, we don't know. Fish, I guess. Bugs and fruit. He needed fresh water, too, like any human being. Maybe he conjured it up from the sea somehow. I think too often he did without.

Hiding for seven hundred days would have been a sad existence for any boy, but it must have been a form of death for someone whose only home had been the crowd. Finally he tried to come back. He was smart enough to pull off the trick of resurrection, but I guess we were too dumb to let him.

MANY PEOPLE HAD yet to lose hold of their grieving. A hundred million lives was a heavy price to pay to get some sense knocked into us, but in a lot of ways the world was much improved. The big war had put a stop to border conflicts and most ethnic strife. Africa was still suffering its AIDS die-off, and China wasn't having a smooth time with its new Cultural Revolution, but we had clean industry and transportation. The global economy was roaring like crazy. There were also quite a few less people to share this wealth, although we were well into a worldwide baby boom.

Even Margie and me were trying. At least she thought we were. I'd had myself a vasectomy years before, paying thirty times the regular fee to buy the doctor's silence.

Margie was doing better. Her TVs and computers weren't exactly dusty but now she only spent an hour or two following her dramas. After the war, she'd found the chance to mother someone at last. We spent our fortune on an orphanage/soup kitchen and she became a part of more lives than I could count. Somehow she always knew their first names. She often came home humming.

I was doing better, too. I had a job again, good, hard, paying work at a dairy farm on top of helping out around the soup kitchen. The labor shortage was so bad there was even room for Albert's father. The cows didn't care who I was and I pulled overtime without complaining. It even got to point where my boss would offer me a beer at the end of the day and we'd talk some, no big questions or personal stuff, though he must have been tempted. I was an ordinary joe again and I liked that just fine.

Everything changed when Albert came ashore near Washington.

It's important to know why Margie acted the way she did. The reporters and the crazies ate up our small lives again. Having everything taken from her a second time, having her new life destroyed — they shoved her right off the fine edge she'd been walking. Suddenly we were right back in our cage. She couldn't call her friends because our lines were jammed. Even her TV shows were canceled for Albert Albert Albert. There was nothing to do but worry. A body can only sleep so many hours and it was impossible to go about any kind of business without fighting off fifty shouting maniacs. On the third day she tried baking pies but burst into tears when she spilled a cup of sugar. I put my arms around her and kissed her neck, but she pushed me away like she never wanted to be touched again. She retreated to her couch and stayed there playing old movies.

Albert was wicked pale on TV, taller and skinnier now. He was practically wasted away — but it wasn't food that brought him back.

He begged for an audience with the President as he was swarmed by passersby. A few hugged him, rejoicing that their messiah had returned. Others pelted him with soda bottles and hunks of asphalt. Amateur video shows him bleeding from his head but never using his awesome powers to knock down the people assaulting him.

He was small for a thirteen-year-old, stunted by malnutrition. He was obviously sick, too, with spots of fever burning through that fish-pale skin. How sick, nobody knew.

The President granted Albert's request. I don't suppose it matters that the boy's attitude was submissive or that he looked so fragile and lost. You can't say no to someone who's stopped the sun dead overhead.

Albert had an idea how he could make amends.

NOT EVERY DESERT can bloom. Albert explained it like this: Energy flows in patterns rather than existing as a blanket. Snow and sand, grassland and jungle, all of these things balance each other, but he thought he could improve on nature's work and turn every inch of the planet into a garden. The politicians agreed. No doubt they hoped to take credit for it.

He tried. Oh, how he tried, leaping valleys, fighting swamps, always running and running and running. He didn't have anything else, you see, and his spectacular plan did seem to be slowly coming true. Maintaining this delicate new balance would have become his life's work.

Unfortunately he'd picked up the HIV virus somewhere and he had scurvy and other vitamin deficiencies. Worse, people kicked at him or threw things as he passed. It was like some awful game of global whipping boy. He was a reminder of the war, an easy scapegoat, plus there were plenty of folks who'd always said he was evil for not fitting into their small religions.

Albert ran and bled and sweated and ran more until the pneumonia hit.

He was as ugly as a rabid stray when he came home for the last time. I've seen the replays now of Margie and me peeking out as he approached. I wish we hadn't looked so scared.

At first I didn't even think it was him because he'd stopped. I mean he was walking — stumbling, really — but other than that he was motionless. The world wasn't turning under his feet anymore. He was that far gone.

"Mother," he whispered and Margie screamed, a long high shriek like a horse would make if it broke all four legs. She ran back inside. After that, whatever bit of hope was left in him seemed to fade.

I did my best to say the right things, holding Albert as he died. It was important to him to share everything he'd seen and felt. His words weren't so much a confession as a confiding.

All he'd ever wanted was to be one of us.

If we're lucky, the world will never see anything like him again. We didn't deserve him. We never knew what to do with Albert, and some debts are so great you can only reject what's been given to you.

END

Afterword

"Damned" may be the only fantasy story I ever write. I enjoy a good sword-and-sorcery, but most of them are too long for me. That shouldn't surprise anyone. My own writing tends to be minimalist. I like it lean and mean, and I don't always have the patience for a 750-page doorstopper. Girth is intrinsic to the subgenre. The fans expect and even demand it, and that's fine, but I also have a problem with magic.

Magic is slippery. Most of the time, to me, it seems like the writer is simply imposing whatever powers or limitations work best at the moment, only to change the rules again. There's no consistency, and I'm too high-strung to go with that, man!

When I do read fantasy, I like fantasy-with-sf-guts such as Tim Power's *The Anubis Gates*, Ken Grimwood's *Replay*, or the classic series *The Gandalara Cycle* by Randall Garrett and Vicki Ann Heydron.

Like "Pressure," "Damned" originated from a dream. In my sleep, *I* was the one trotting around the globe, leaping tall buildings in a single bound, dodging through alleyways, ducking power lines and tree branches and freeways... and yet I wasn't only trying to keep up with Earth's revolution so I wasn't carried helplessly away. At the same time, I was also spinning the world beneath my feet.

Dream logic is illogical, but the image stayed with me. A speck-sized human being rolling the planet with each step? I knew I had to do something with it. And how could that person be anything but a messiah?

From there, it was easy to give Albert his blue-collar parents — my Joseph and Mary.

What wasn't so easy was watching him die.

MEME

THERE IS NO such thing as a part time job that is both meaningful and well paid. Most aren't either. Including his stints as a gas jockey during high school, Alan Lilly has held nineteen positions in at least seven separate fields, so his expectations are as low as mud. Driver, pressman, salesman, waiter, phone rep, cashier — he rarely stays more than twelve months and several times he's quit after one shift.

He is not a slacker, thief or trouble-maker. He's a musician. He has better things to do.

Processing overflow and night-drops at FastFoto offered neither purpose nor money. What it did provide was the opportunity to listen to his iPod and think, alone, while earning enough to cover his rent. He bought groceries and beer with the money he made off his music, all themes for corporate presentation videos and CD-ROMs so far, at no better than three hundred dollars a shot, but Alan believes that cream inevitably rises to the top and that he is cream. He's only thirty-two.

The 100 prints wouldn't normally have caught his eye. Most people who use cheap film take shots of their friends standing in a row and smiling. The rest snap pictures of their cats or cars.

These photographs are of a computer print-out marked only in one narrow vertical column.

Two days ago, Alan underbid an iGames.net spec assignment

and he's spent every spare moment since then reworking Mozart into heavy metal for their new Blammer sequel. Typical crap, not much of a challenge. But the IVS-550 photo processor is an incredibly diligent percussionist, and the endless four-four beat of its print stacker disrupts his concentration again and again. He's staring at the ceiling when the glare of white turns his head. Even black-and-white photos aren't typically so bleak. He strides over, drumming his pen against his leg, to make certain the 550 is operating correctly.

It is. The entire roll of thirty-six prints is close-up after close-up of the strange text.

Alan thinks it looks like music.

THE NUDIE PICTURES on the next roll do not distract him as he stands right there at the processor, wondering over handfuls of the unusual shots. For the first few nights on the job, he considered skin shots a perk, but it's a rare set of jugs that hold his attention now. Most people are too fat or pale or hairy, and everyone seems to use the same four poses.

Every job has its unique benefits and tortures, of course — often they are one and the same.

Working phones in the Classified Ads department, it was the idiots who wanted to complain about the delivery boy. *Why are you calling me?* Alan asked them, at first with a smile, at last with deadly boredom. Running a cash register at 7-Eleven and the bus station, it was the lonely folks who stayed to chat, sometimes even through a wall of security glass. At first he thought he found gems of wisdom in their late-night ramblings. At last he realized it was all desperate clichés.

Alan is not a people person. Human beings are mean and stupid and greedy too much of the time. He prefers the clean evocative world of music. All that Alan has ever wanted is to own and be owned by that beauty, to wield the magic.

Plus it would be nice to be neck deep in money and chicks.

Or even ankle deep. It wouldn't take much to free him from the crappy jobs that are wasting half of his life — one big break, one hit, one catchy original combination of sound.

THE BIZARRE TEXT in the photographs consists of just two spidery shapes, one stout, the other slim, but they're arranged in no less than seven angles as well as three left-middle-right positions. Like chords. Sharp, normal, flat.

But if the text is music, it's composed in two-five time as best he can tell, which is almost meaningless.

Is it an opera score? It's definitely the length of a mega-ballad, running thirty-plus pages, although at least two of those are repetitions. A chorus. The bass line is sporadic but Alan's starting to hear it in his head, which makes up for the lack.

Why is it in code? And given that it must be stored on a computer, why take pictures rather than printing out more copies?

The illogic of it is compelling and Alan shuts down the IVS-550 so its chatter won't distract him as he sketches out the beginnings of a translation. He knows he'll fall behind and hear about it from his boss if he leaves the processor off for more than a few minutes, but so what?

BY HIS COUNT, he's quit five times as often as he's been fired. When the hourly wage is just a buck or three over minimum, there's always something better.

His last girlfriend complained that he had the attention-span of a gerbil, and Alan agreed at least that each new job hunt was tedious and painful, but he's learned that it's important to stay positive in order to stay productive. When he starts worrying (when he's forced to borrow money from his folks), he finds that his music abandons him, which only deepens his depression — a wicked feedback cycle.

Alan tries to take pride in his checkered resume. It's proof that he's not just a cog in the nine-to-five machine, that he's using it rather than being used.

THE MUSIC INDUSTRY is crowded and vicious, perhaps worse than acting, writing, painting. Average ears are capable of perceiving no more than a dozen distinct musical notes or more than a handful of truly different styles — and in the few brief decades since recording technology began preserving every effort great and small, almost all of the pleasing combinations of sound have been done over and over. Most of the unpleasant ones have been done repeatedly as well.

At first the Internet offered new venues, buyers and stages, but it also quickly became a vast garbage dump into which every copycat and tin-ear poured their knock-offs.

Alan's not above borrowing concepts or inspiration from his favorites like Christ Butter or the Beatles, but he labors to make each composition fresh. He has fought for and earned each of his few professional credits, and puts only his best songs on the two web sites promoting his work... but it's nearly impossible for any single voice to rise above the global mob.

What it takes to stand out is a completely new style.

THE STRANGE TEXT in the photographs is definitely music, Alan decides. Strange music. He tries to give it voice, coughing through the unique tempo: "Dah dah wa. Wa dah."

Very strange. As if someone combined bagpipe marches with reggae, wind noise and dashes of punk.

Its clash and contrast are unspeakably lovely.

"DAH WA. DA dee..."

He finds himself roaming his one bedroom apartment like a slow-motion pinball, flopping down on the couch to continue his translation, rising to dig through the refrigerator, the whispering in his head escaping him in wet-dog shakes of his body and hands. "Dah dee. Dah dah."

He finds himself mumbling, always mumbling, water bubbling from his lips under the hot spray of the shower, flat echoes surrounding him as he paces in the short entry hall.

"Dah wa. Dah dah."

He finds himself in bed, lurching from a deep but restless sleep, the phone ringing. The answering machine speaks, his boss, furious. Apparently he left the FastFoto door unlocked.

Alan is exhausted, damp all over with sweat, his belly glued with semen. For the first time in twenty years he's had a wet dream. But it was a nightmare. He remembers thick conflicting emotion — anger, longing, joy — coupled with random sensations like hunger and heat as well as cascading memories of being a teenager, a child and, insanely, an old man heavy with arthritis.

He pushes out of the twisted sheets and hurries back to the shower. And, again, water bubbles from his lips as he begins to chant the magic sounds: "Wa dah. Wa dah."

For the first time he feels a touch of fear.

THE NAME ON the deposit envelope is Wendy Dannenbring.

Originally Alan had planned to observe her, meet her, at FastFoto when she came in for her film. But there isn't anything there for her anymore. The prints, the negatives and the deposit envelope all came home with him. And he can't wait.

Caught by the warm yellow dawn, sitting on a frigid bench for the cross-town bus, Alan examines the envelope again. Her address is not in an upscale neighborhood, so in that respect at least she is like him, still struggling. For the moment. Wendy Dannenbring is about to knock the world off its feet and he thinks he can help. He thinks he can improve her ballad by underscoring it with a more normal bass. Good reviews from the critics are wonderful, but if an audience doesn't understand what they're hearing, they won't come back for more.

"Dah dah, dah. Dah wa."

He imagines he's found his perfect match. She obviously under-stands the power of solitude, given that this creation must have required years of intense labor. Yet she's also passionate and starved for intimacy. It's all in the music.

Dreaming over her tight spiky cursive, he thinks of his few lovers — a teacher who earned his first crush, a favorite, untouchable cousin who mercilessly flaunted herself for years and once let him surprise her by the pool with her top off. He thinks of women he's only hoped for, daydreams, gentle nurturers.

The loud arrival of the bus shocks him like an alarm clock. So does discovering, as he rises, that he has an erection.

Fear spikes through his heart again.

A SAGGING OLD dumpling of a woman opens the door only as far as the security chain allows. Alan stares at her, then gives the apartment number a double-take. Her eyes, bright with anxiety, bruised by sleep-deprivation, sweep over him and past his shoulder as if expecting someone else.

He holds up the deposit envelope.

Her eyes widen, then slide to his face. Whatever she sees there does not seem to lessen her anxiety, but she raises one small hand to free the security chain.

WENDY DANNENBRING'S PLACE would have been cliché Grandma except that the frilly white doilies on the sofa and end tables are visible only where the massive drifts of paper have been organized into stacks. And it's unusual for people her age, the last of the pre-Boomer generation, to be high tech. She has three computers. Oddly, all are unplugged and two have been disassembled, the printers stacked upside down in a corner of the small room. Filthy crusted dishes sit among the paperwork.

Alan stands motionless while Wendy sits and fusses through the photos.

"Should've known," she mutters.

He waves at all the paper. "Why did you take pictures?" he says.

"To see if it would stay the same."

"What?" Disappointment is not uncommon in Alan's life, but this wacky old bat could not be farther from what he'd hoped for.

The shock of her temporarily quiets the song in his head.

"Should've known better," Wendy says again, still talking to the pictures or maybe the floor, rocking gently. "I thought it was all automated now." She stops and looks at him. "Do you know what this is? Can you understand it yet?"

"It's brilliant, beautiful, who wrote it?"

"It's extraordinarily dangerous."

Hope leaps through him like fire. "It wasn't you?"

Wendy's gaze lifts up, weary and scared — and determined. "I'm not sure," she says slowly.

"What the hell do—"

"Oh, I typed it. That much I'm sure of." Her eyes have not left his face. "Are you dreaming?"

He tries not to flush or look away.

"Me too," she says, her deliberate, measured tones infected now with a hint of panic. "Fantasies, real-life, sex, hope, death, everything mixed together non-stop."

"That's why this is so incredible! Good music should make you feel and think and remember."

"Music?"

"Of course, are you crazy?" Then Alan laughs. "What am I saying, obviously you're—"

"This is computer code. Binary."

He shakes his head and steps away from her.

"We're being read," she says. "We're being *learned*."

"You're crazy." Alan starts toward the door.

"Wait. Please." Wendy drags a revolver from between two of the sofa cushions and thrusts it at him. "Please."

THEY REMAIN LIKE that for several moments, Wendy's small hand steady despite the revolver's weight, Alan staring into its short dark barrel. His eyes flicker between it and her face as he tries to listen.

"My husband Richard was a neurologist who wanted to improve human intelligence by improving memory." Words fall out of her in a rush. "Three years ago he got sidetracked by the nature of dreams, which current science thinks are byproducts of the mind organizing each day's experiences. He thought maybe... He wanted to control the dream state and tried bio-feedback, drugs. Finally he created a universal program that would redirect the mind in organizing short-term memory more efficiently."

She pauses long enough that Alan considers running. But the mess will slow him down and make him a target.

Words spill from her again: "One of his test subjects went insane in her isolation tank and the other strangled on a contact wire. Intentionally. Two days later Richard jumped off a roof, I thought because of the disgrace, because they were going to ban him from..."

Wendy rocks and rocks on her cluttered sofa, covering both ears as if trying to drown out her own voice.

"Two months ago," she says, "when I had to move to this apartment, I found some of his programs in our PC. Artificial intelligence, maybe. Certainly it's self-replicating. Changing. I first noticed it when it piggybacked on an e-mail to my friends. It was trying to get out."

She stops rocking and glances up from the floor.

"We were all very lucky," she says. "The netserver software scrambled it into meaningless gibberish."

Alan tries to say something, anything, but his eyes are still locked on the revolver.

"It did get into me. And it's gestating." Wendy hugs herself with her free hand. Her voice is almost a whine. "It's using everything I know to evolve. Controlling me. I wipe magnets over the hard drive but catch myself rewriting it from memory. I burn stacks of notes and then find the most recent version still in my desk. The photos... Fortunately I'm not very educated. It hasn't benefited much. But it might not need to change a lot more to find a form that's easily communicable. If it does... if it reaches the world..." Her voice is genuinely sad. "I can't let it have whatever it might learn from y— "

Alan leaps across the coffee table, banging his knee into a stack of paper, slipping, clawing.

Wendy fires. She misses, barely, the muzzleflash scorching his cheek and deafening his left ear.

He slaps her hand aside as the revolver goes off again. This bullet scratches his right shoulder. The third punches a wet hole through her cheek as they struggle.

Alan barely remembers to grab the pictures and the deposit envelope before he escapes.

HOME AGAIN, HE composes for nineteen hours, burning, surging, stopping only to suck down half a gallon of water. The slapdash whirling collage inside him easily overpowers the aches of his damaged ear and bleeding shoulder — and eagerness mutes his fear. This is like nothing he's ever known: orgasm, pot dreams, the normal thrill of creation.

This is the unfettered confidence of a diving eagle.

He catches himself in the moment between finishing his long song and posting it on the Net, like a man at the edge of a building. Breathing hard, blinking, he recalls Wendy's wretched face, her dry voice. Can he stop himself?

It's too beautiful. He presses 'Enter.'

Adrenaline courses through his limbs, but fades as nothing happens... Then e-mail returns to him from all over the world, terribly fast. He double-clicks on several and his song pours from the computer speakers, altered, added to — accompanied by something more.

A fearsome storm explodes within Alan: other minds, other perspectives and personal histories, different languages, new bodies, a prism of humanity. Desire, energy, industriousness. Madness and perversion.

The darkness is just as strong as the light.

His physiology allows only a few instants of roaring input before he collapses onto the floor.

SEVENTY-ONE INDIVIDUALS ACROSS the planet died of cardiac arrest or cerebral events. Two hundred and thirty-nine more smothered, burned or were electrocuted as they lay unconscious. Another three thousand and four committed suicide in the minutes immediately following, unable to face what had been reflected back at them.

They all live on inside us now.

Millions of us experienced the merging. Millions of us everywhere were changed. The first crude version of the meme had been too much for isolated people to withstand, like Richard Dannenbring's test subjects and, later, his wife — yet it transformed into something truly majestic as it echoed back and forth through a sea of minds. It became an actual "collective unconscious," if only for several seconds.

Here and there a few delicate souls were deeply wounded, yet many more agitated ones were calmed. Together we found balance, empathy, the essence of peace.

But we didn't find as much of ourselves as we'd like. The wars in west Africa and eastern Europe continue, as do the politically-induced famines in central Africa and North Korea. Not enough minds were awakened in those places. Yet we know that our immortal union will be repeated and spread further in years to come as we study and recreate the phenomenon.

As instigator of the so-called Explosion, Alan Lilly finally discovered the fame and small fortune that he had long sought, but neither seem important to him now in comparison to our love of the human song.

END

Afterword

"Meme" is the brother story to "Pattern Masters." It originated from my obsession with the no-security photo drawers at the drug store.

It's also the only story I've written in present tense, and there's a good reason why. Reading in present tense is weird. Like our convention of three-acts-and-a-climax, we're trained to absorb stories in past tense. "This was what happened." But the unusual voice pays off in the ending, when the narration jumps from third person limited to plural omniscient. I also like the immediacy of the present tense voice in the opening section.

"Meme" holds a special place in my heart for two reasons.

First, Alan Lilly is me. I never worked in a photo department, and I'm not a musician, but everything else about his background came straight from an endless succession of lousy part-time jobs.

Second, this was my first story to sell to a magazine stocked in major chains like Barnes & Noble. DNA Publications' revival of *Fantastic Stories* had good distribution. Visibility made this sale more real to me than the check. I was in a real magazine! Early sales like "Meme" kept me on course through the long slog of mind-numbing jobs, and I still remember opening the acceptance letter. The editor, sneaky Ed McFadden, used letterhead as red as a stop sign, which at a glance I figured was another rejection. Then I read it and shouted to my bride, who'd married me just six weeks before.

Diana's patience and support have been exceptional. I think there's a hint of her in Wendy Dannenbring, the strong wife of "Meme"'s mad scientist.

ENTER SANDMAN

IN THE CLOSING moments of the game, smashball's greatest champion aimed for his opponent's head instead of a score zone. Jake Bolt led four-to-three, and rattling his challenger was easier and almost as good as extending his lead. It was also far more stylish. His fans loved it. No feints, no trick ricochets, just a hard "Bolt special" from one end of the box to the other. He took advantage of a weak volley, skipping the ball sideways off the nearest wall as he bounced himself off the ceiling and onto his upper platform — a spectacular move possible only in lunar gravity. Then he clubbed the ball downward.

Yet clearly Bolt had made too much a habit of kill shots. His opponent was ready and brought up both hands, fingers spread wide, pale blue fire sparking from each gloved palm.

The magnetized ball shot back at Bolt's lower platform, dead on the red score zone. Bolt dove, getting a pinky on it, but the ball still struck the zone's edge.

However, no points registered on the board.

"Rewind the last two seconds and play it slow. Somehow that genius son of a bitch is cheating." Gerold Sandifer stood with his back to a plush smart-chair that he couldn't seem to use for more than a few moments at a time.

He was a small man, made smaller by the partial crouch that put his weight on the balls of his feet. He unconsciously shifted from side to side exactly as the black-suited figures in the tape had done before each serve, gliding slightly above the floor.

"Don't be stupid." Sandifer's trainer, Anne Ramey, placed both hands on her hips as he glanced back. Ramey had seventeen centimeters and at least ten kilos on him — and sixteen years.

He knew she regretted the latter statistic but that she enjoyed having her breasts almost level with his face.

"There are hardly any *rules*," she said. "How could a smasher possibly cheat?"

Sandifer ignored her pose. "Just rewind it."

Ramey sighed and fussed with the old digital projector. "This thing's a pain in my ass. Let's feed the whole match into your NP and we can dissect it frame by frame, okay?"

"No. Nothing with a hard drive or Net connected."

"Well then hold your horses, my boy."

The wall of Sandifer's place had not been intended for use as a projection screen, and was dotted with adhesive buttons where he'd removed framed prints and proxy cards capturing the triumphs of old-time greats and his peers, including two shots from Jake Bolt's recent back-to-back Super Box wins. Sandifer's own trophies filled a closet upstairs — and decorated the front hall of Ramey's communal apartment across town.

They were watching an illegal bootleg, the left side of which was partially blocked by a woman's shaved head. Ramey had remarked more than once on that smooth, sexy scalp. Her jokes and comments had grown more frequent as her frustration increased, and Sandifer worried he might have to cut her loose. He didn't want that.

Each time she said, "Whew, love the close-up" or "Scan that skin," Sandifer replied that whoever she'd hired to smuggle in the camera must be an overpaid pervert.

In truth, he was pleased with the quality of the footage. A plastic micro-cam sewn into a shirt collar could hardly be expected to do better, and all the spectator's head concealed were the challenger's upper platform and mid-step. Sandifer was far more interested in what Bolt was doing across the box.

It was sheer paranoia to have burned the micro-cam chip after making a copy onto digital tape, rather than downloading the whole thing directly into his pricey NP wide-screen, but Sandifer wanted no traces left when he was done. Smashers were allowed to study publicly available broadcasts all they wanted, but the image and likeness of every player was strictly licensed by the Lunar Smashball League. And while the LSL unofficially encouraged extravagant behavior short of unprovoked homicide in its players — all the better to increase ratings and merchandise sales — bootlegging charges could get Sandifer suspended or even barred forever.

He might have considered it too sweet to risk if he hadn't found himself so close to the absolute pinnacle.

As the sixth-seeded player in the LSL, Sandifer should have come up short of next week's Finals, except the fourth seed disqualified herself by testing positive for Heavensent, and the fifth seed had broken several ribs when he charged his opponent's platforms and careened through the box in an uncontrolled fall that was still being replayed on the sports net. Numbers two and three would play each other — and Jake Bolt, top dog like always, had the privilege of facing the lowest seeded finalist.

Sandifer had never played Bolt before. He'd spent most of his brief career in the semi-pros. So when Ramey said she knew a guy who could get them actual video, Sandifer agreed to front the money, because publicly sold broadcasts consisted of just two mediums, flat-screen video tapes and ExoReal clips. The first were beautifully packaged, highly edited, useless — and ExoReal clips were even worse. Wearing Bolt's body wasn't the same as watching him objectively, and an opponent's point-of-view was maddening since Sandifer couldn't control where to look.

It was disorienting, too, to be constantly strobed by advertising and inundated with crowd noise, which was dubbed in. The game itself was played quietly — the constant drumming of the ball, the slap of repeller gloves. ER was too flashy to be a worthwhile study guide.

Now his paranoia felt justified. He would have rather discovered that Jake Bolt was a child molester than cheating in his games.

Finally Ramey muttered a happy curse at the projector. They watched Bolt attempt his kill-shot again.

"Hope he tries that on you!" Ramey practically shouted. "Look how he left himself open, he almost got scored on."

"I'm telling you he *was* scored on."

"He deflected it by a hair, my boy. It's just a micro-cam at a bad angle."

But the angle wasn't that bad. The man who'd worn the camera had sat second row, center box. Sandifer trusted his eyes and his instincts. He had to.

Once upon a time Ramey had played two seasons herself, before a horrific knee injury — but the sensors that saturated the box, the ball and the smashers' suits had improved a great deal since then. Everyone had total faith in LSL technology. There were no longer any referees or line judges, never time-outs or instant replays. There didn't need to be. The score zones centered in the upper and lower platforms automatically registered contact with the ball, no matter how slight.

Jake Bolt had not earned his latest win.

"You're crazy," Ramey insisted, and Sandifer imagined she was having a good time bickering. She obviously enjoyed leaning her head against his arm to sight down his finger. Lately she'd been touching him more than usual during work-outs, constantly correcting his posture with a rough hand or a poke.

But the evidence became incontrovertible half an hour later, after an OnStore courier arrived with a magnifying glass.

"Holy God," Ramey said. "God." Her usual gruff booming had been reduced to a whisper as intense as the fear crawling through Sandifer's vertebrae. They paced restlessly back and forth under the image of the golden ball touching the red mat of the score zone.

"This pisses me off," Sandifer said, bouncing high on his toes. "Doesn't this piss you off?"

"Holy Goddamn."

"If they can block points that should have counted against him, I bet they can give him scores, too, if he slaps the ball in close enough. Proximity triggers or something." Sandifer stepped aside when Ramey reached for him, as if seeking comfort. He said, "How long do you think this has been going on?"

"The LSL must know," Ramey babbled. "I mean, they're the ones who control the scoring computers, right? We are holding a bomb here, my boy, a big bomb, and I don't think we want credit for it. Let's stay anonymous when we blow him out of the water."

Sandifer smiled thinly. "We're not going public."

"What? Then why spend all this time—"

"We can use this in a much better way."

THE LUNAR SMASHBALL League made big, big money — as did everything extra-terrestrial — in what had become a careful, civilized era devoid of adventure aside from remote guerrilla wars and the legal squabbling of global mergers both political and corporate. There were Earth leagues, too, of course, but in comparison the action was lumbering and slow, despite the fact that they played in smaller boxes. No earthworm ever danced on the ceiling or pulled a "hurricane" defense in mid-air.

It was the very nature of the LSL's exotic environment that made the fraud so simple to perpetuate.

Box arenas were tiny. Even the Quartz in Armstrong City with its triple-deck seating fit no more than seven hundred people, which made ticket costs prohibitive — and shuttle-fare up from Earth wasn't exactly the price of lunch, either.

The majority of fans knew the game only through flat-screen broadcasts and ExoReality, both easily doctored given satellite transmission delays. Maybe the LSL even dubbed extraneous flash-static into the ER clips to cover the crucial edits. Maybe Sandifer had been subconsciously aware of the discrepancies, which was why he'd been so desperate to acquire a bootleg video.

As for the die-hards and fat cats who actually attended in person,

Sandifer wasn't shocked that none had noticed the deceit. Games were a social event. Those few who stayed sober were typically the most rabid fanatics, intent on their palm-tops, Exo helmets or, at a minimum, the cheap InfoGogs that came with each seat. Serve speeds, career statistics, injury reports, other scores, Vegas odds — so many peripherals bombarded the spectators, it was hardly surprising that no one ever realized they were being tricked.

Had the corporate backers decided long ago not to leave things to chance? Advertisers needed winners, good-looking winners at that, while the fans wanted heroes and rivalries and the occasional cinderella story.

That would be Sandifer, this year. Was his newfound success owed to cheating he wasn't even aware of? Could his destiny be fixed? It was too monstrous to consider.

And it was damned unlikely, he decided. A few techs and league officials might keep their mouths shut, but affecting even a small percentage of the games played would require an entire army of conspirators. Merely trying to keep Bolt on top would be more than enough of a risk.

The thieving bastard deserved what was coming to him.

"MY BOY, WE have to tell." Ramey sat down hard, shaking her head. "He'll forfeit and you'll—"

"No. That's no good. Think what they'll do. They might cancel the play-offs altogether." Sandifer knelt beside her, fighting down the urge to pace again and keeping his hands still. Ramey stared as he gently intertwined his fingers with hers.

Her skin was cool and calloused.

"Help me," he said. He kept his voice low. "We have an edge here. Bolt doesn't know we know."

Ramey started to shake her head again but Sandifer reached up with his other hand and cupped her jaw. Her lips parted slightly, involuntarily.

"Don't ruin this for me," he said. "For us."

THE TWO OF them first met when Ramey blocked Sandifer's path in the tunnels under the Gorbachev arena, a back-Box pass pinned to her tight jersey. "I can change your life," she declared.

Sandifer was smarting from a close loss and pushed past without a word, taking her for a groupie.

"Your style's all wrong," she said. "The power game's never going to work for you. But that fourth point, that was nice. You got out of that dumb set stance and used your natural dexterity."

Which was exactly what he'd been thinking.

He stopped and looked back. "Who the hell are you?"

"So long as we're trading names," she answered, grinning, "calling yourself the Darkside Destroyer is just stupid. It makes you sound like the super villain in some kid story. You've got to be more market savvy. If you ever want into the big leagues, you have to play that game, too."

Sandifer had dumped his first manager two weeks later, a man who'd been with him for three grueling years — a dedicated but unimaginative ape who'd pitched the same style of brute strength that, according to Ramey, eighty-five percent of all players used. Jake Bolt had been too successful, Ramey said, for the modern game to have evolved any differently. "Me, I could play that way," she claimed. "You, you're a spider. You're never going to overpower anybody. Let's sneak up on them instead."

And so the Sandman was born.

Gerold Sandifer's background wasn't half as melodramatic as his official LSL bio, and to say that he'd never wanted to be anything except a smasher was an outright lie. Like every other kid, he'd dreamed of being a Belt miner. He had a gift for math and spatial relations that served him well in the box.

The LSL didn't believe in complicated personas, of course. The public had a multitude of interlocking alliances and rivalries to keep track of, so most smashers were reduced to a caricature with one memorable trait.

Sandifer had been built up as an ambitious madman, a bad guy

— maybe because he was hardly a sexy blond giant, maybe because he'd been in the minors for years but, once he mastered his game, suddenly knocked off a number of regional favorites. The news nets had a great time with it: "Sandman puts out the lights for the Vector King" and "Sandman is a bad dream for Khashabi!"

It was true that he was an airlock orphan who'd learned to fight early on, for food, for toys, because older kids wanted to work off some anger on him. The media made a lot of that, the traumas he'd supposedly suffered, pointing to his miserly spending habits and the fact that he wasn't dating a model or an ER star like many successful smashers. They could just as easily have highlighted his need for real intimacy and the fact that he was building a nest-egg to share with the right person, but that was just too sappy.

And while it was also true that he'd become single-minded in his hunger for a Super Box ring, his idea of success was not to garner endorsement deals or ER cameos or to impress women. He wanted a permanent place on the list of champions, something that he could always point to and say *I was there.*

He wanted a victory that could never be taken away.

Anne Ramey shared his desire for immortality, although her ambition was hot and loud whereas his lurked deep within him like an iceberg, only sometimes peeking up. Sandifer thought her infatuation with him was really just a side-effect. That her own career had ended so suddenly, when she was still in her prime, had clearly made her crazy in some ways. Ramey had been calling him "my boy" for months before he realized the subtext: an older, childless woman pursuing sexual relations with her student.

Maybe he should have leapt into her arms. It would have been easier for them both.

TWO DAYS ZIPPED by like an opening serve clocked at one eighty-five. Every minute that he wasn't exercising or asleep, including meal times, Sandifer reviewed ExoReal clips of Jake Bolt's games, comparing Bolt's point-of-view to his opponent's, studying hard for glitches.

The second night he dreamed that he actually was Bolt, a thick, confused nightmare in which he gave his own decapitated skull punishing whacks.

Ramey diligently waded through a tall stack of recordings herself, but even after they knew what to look for, it wasn't obvious. Many ER clips had no edits, sometimes because Bolt wasn't looking directly at the ball as he reached and stretched to defend a score zone — so the game continued and either the score board changed or it didn't, and mostly it didn't. Running the opponent's point-of-view in simulcast was often no help. Smashers wasted little time celebrating a score, and at the crucial moments were almost always busy trying to recover their defensive stance before Bolt returned the shot.

In other games there just wasn't a need to cheat. Bolt was truly a dominant player.

Yet at least a third of the clips contained questionable moments, flash-static covering saves that probably weren't saves, blocks that weren't blocks. Bolt seemed to have an easy time of hitting his opponents' score zones as well. His secret edge was a small one, rarely worth more than an extra point or two, but that was all that Great Jake had needed to rule the field for six years.

And whether the man had cheated in one game or in one million was immaterial. They had all the evidence they needed if Sandifer's plan went bad and they found themselves backed into a corner. They had the power to put Bolt in jail along with whichever LSL officials could be held accountable.

"This isn't going to be easy," Sandifer said. "I don't know anything about software." He'd set his smart-chair on high massage but still couldn't get the knots in his shoulders to loosen. He'd even allowed himself a cup of rum, his first in three weeks since his loss in the Semi-Finals to Savage Reiko, but instead of melting his tension the alcohol only seemed to focus his thoughts into one tight stubborn block about the size and shape of a smashball.

Ramey shook her head mournfully. "Sounds damn impossible

to me. They don't just let people waltz into the computer rooms, my boy, and whatever Bolt's paying them, you can't top it."

Her voice hadn't been loud since their discovery, not even during Sandifer's work-outs. Her gaze rarely seemed to lift from the ground now — and when she did look directly at him, her eyes flickered with a new watchfulness, a new hopefulness.

Somehow that made Sandifer happy. He was very fond of her. He just wished she'd be more quiet.

"I don't want to pay them," he said.

Ramey peered into the cup of rum that he'd pushed on her. "What else can you do," she asked, "talk sweet?"

"You know anyone who owns a gun?"

"Nobody off-Earth has guns, you bonehead, except maybe some 'hance runners in the ER dramas."

"Knives, then. Someone who also has a brain."

Ramey glanced up with a trace of her old enthusiasm. "You gonna tell me exactly what your plan is?"

"AND NOW... THE challenger..."

The moment before entering the box was always what Sandifer remembered most clearly afterward. During a game he was all instinct and reflex — but standing in the tunnel, he often felt like a giant thick-skinned heart, his entire body surging with anticipation inside his rubbery suit. Today he imagined himself as an explosion captured in a human shape.

"...SANDMAN!"

He trotted through the gate, head down, not waving. The gate hit the floor with a resonant bang, becoming part of the wall, as he leapt onto his lower platform in one smooth glide. He always tried to time it so that the impact and vibration appeared to be caused by his landing.

Jake Bolt was already atop his own upper platform, one hand raised like Caesar to the crowds outside the glass.

Without ceremony, Sandifer opened with a slap-shot, which was bad etiquette but not against any rule. He wanted to show that he was here to play.

He flexed his right hand open quickly, the repeller field snapping into place with a rifle crack, then smashed the ball off of the floor in front of Bolt's platforms at an angle. It careened from high on the left wall, off the ceiling and down at Bolt's lower platform.

Bolt dodged under the ball and flicked it sideways, buying himself time, leaping back onto his upper platform to intercept his own ricochet. Could he be about to throw a "Bolt special" so early in the game?

He did, but it went wide. Surprised, Sandifer glanced around for the rebound and ducked low to protect himself— And got a face full of hard metal ball. Bolt had aimed at the corner and brought a complicated double-bounce right into him.

The ball crunched against Sandifer's cheekbone, the thin, flexible suit protecting him not at all. He toppled. In that moment of free-fall, he was aware only of his embarrassment.

Then he hit the floor and the breath went out of him and his body would not get up.

Bolt racked up three quick points before Sandifer could push himself onto his feet. Bolt might have scored more except that a bad bounce sent the ball careening laterally through the no-man's-land between them.

Sandifer had time to crawl back into a ready position before the ball returned to Bolt. Maybe Bolt had wanted it that way. He clubbed another "special" straight in to hit Sandifer again.

Sandifer's cheek was bloody raw but, strangely, his splintered cheekbone felt like it had been dipped in liquid hydrogen, flash-frozen and torn from the warm muscle.

The impact of repelling the ball was fantastic agony. But the sight of it careening dead-center off the score zone of Bolt's lower platform, Bolt chasing it futilely, made him feel like a human explosion again. The pain faded. And as the ball clattered from ceiling-to-floor-to-ceiling back toward him, Sandifer leapt from his upper platform to meet it, arcing high like a meteor. He wrenched his shoulder, putting everything he had into the shot.

Anticipating its angle, Bolt leapt back toward his own upper platform even as Sandifer swung. Sandifer was vaguely aware of the crowd rising to its feet all around them.

Bolt guessed badly and the ball bashed off his lower platform. Another point for Sandifer.

The ball came off of the back wall in a steep line, well over Bolt's attempt to collect it, giving Sandifer time to retreat back to his platforms in two springing hops. Then he sent another slap-shot off the left wall.

This one was all finesse. It careened high into the middle of the ceiling, low off the back wall, then lower still on the right wall. Bolt seemed off-balance now but nearly got under this shot as well, stretching out one hand.

The ball glanced off his fingers near the edge of the score zone. It could have gone either way.

Sandifer dared a glance at the display board as the ball bounced lazily over the prone champion. Three-three. The score had counted and it wasn't until then that he'd had any way of knowing if Ramey's people successfully forced their way into the control room, making the conspirators shut down the selective programs that gave Bolt his advantage. They hadn't dared to make their move until right before game time.

In that moment, something like love yammered through Sandifer's chest, pure and fiery. He was playing an honest game, which is all he'd ever wanted.

Bolt grabbed the ball — poor etiquette again but not against the rules, since the next serve was his. He also glanced at the score board. The cheating bastard was clearly shaken and trying to slow the pace of the game.

Sandifer never gave him a chance. He kept working the left wall and the ceiling, throwing in change-ups off the back corners, deliberately aiming for the borders of Bolt's score zones. By then Bolt must have known what had happened - he should have been ready for it — but the champ had gotten sloppy after having some his work done for him for so long.

Sandifer took two points that might have been erased if Bolt's programs were still working, and losing that advantage also seemed to cost Bolt a psychological edge. Sandifer gained another point toward the end when the champ gave up on chasing a multiple ricochet.

Bolt tried repeatedly to overpower him and caught him again in the ribs, a glancing blow, but Sandifer never returned the favor. He didn't want to hurt Bolt. He wanted the title.

They called it the Blackout because Ramey's people turned off more control programs than necessary and knocked out the ExoReal broadcast of what many later said was the greatest upset of all time. The final score was nine-four and even before the final seconds ticked off, Sandifer could imagine the bulletins screaming "Sandman to Bolt: Goodnight!"

Above and around him, people crowded against the glass, cheering and booing so loudly he actually heard a low grumble through the sound-proofing. For once, he waved back.

Bolt had already turned to leave and Sandifer jogged across the box, feeling no pain until he forced his jaw to move.

"Jake, wait."

Tomorrow he'd be swollen like a tube squash and the Super Box was just a week away — yet win or lose it, he would always have this moment.

Bolt paused at his gate, pushing his gogs up onto his forehead. His dark eyes were hard and angry.

"Listen to me," Sandifer whispered. You tell them to stop. If I ever see any cheating again, I'll go public. I will."

"This isn't the place to talk about—"

Sandifer interrupted with a bloody grin. "If you think you can rope me in, forget it. A win that's handed to you isn't any kind of win."

"You got lucky once."

"I kicked your ass fair and square."

"But you'll never get at the software again. And you'll just ruin the sport if you make any noise about it." Bolt's mouth curled into a smile, though his eyes stayed as emotionless as dirt. "We can make things sweet for you."

"Not interested. Do it my way. Try anything stupid and it's all ready to go, Net, vid, ER. You'll be shit forever."

Bolt turned away.

Across the box, Sandifer's gate snapped up with a resounding clang and Ramey bounded out, whooping, "You did it! You did it, my boy!" She was so happy she was pretty.

Bolt slapped at the controls of his own gate and dodged through. Sandifer almost went after him, thinking he'd better force a promise — but there would be time for that later. Ramey deserved his attention first.

He laughed as she smothered him in an embrace. And when she kissed him wetly, he kissed back.

The Sandman wanted always to be honest about his debts.

END

Afterword

I invented the Lunar Smashball League after playing "whack ball" for hours and hours with Diana and our friends on the beaches near San Luis Obispo.

The companies who sell the equipment for this sport call it "paddle ball" or "beach badminton." That was too tame for us. We called it whack ball because we liked to smack the guts out of the bright rubber ball. With effort, players can stand as far apart as fifty feet or, for a more violent and faster game, close to a circle only a few yards in diameter.

Good times.

We were young, fresh into dating each other, and thought nothing of disappearing for an entire day with a cooler full of sandwiches and iced tea. The bikinis were great, too.

The game can be played competitively or cooperatively, either trying to make your friends miss or trying to volley as long as possible. With pretty girls, cooperative is better. But crashing into the surf in competitive play was a different kind of fun.

At the time, *Artemis Magazine* had just hit stores, a new, glossy publication loaded with hard sf. I slanted my story for a high tech setting, borrowed some elements from TV wrestling, stole the title outright from Metallica, introduced my older lover from college (don't tell my wife), and the Sandman was born.

These stories were a lot of fun to write. Some were more challenging than others. Always the process was gratifying, and I hope this collection struck a chord.

I'll see you in the future.

Jeff Carlson

If you liked *Long Eyes...*

LOOK FOR THE
BEST-SELLING NOVELS
BY JEFF CARLSON

"I'm hooked."
—Larry Niven, *New York Times* bestselling author of *The Fate of Worlds*

Beneath The Ice

"A first-rate adventure set in one of our solar system's most fascinating places. Carlson is a fine storyteller, and this is his best book yet."

—Allen Steele, Hugo Award-winning author of the *Coyote* series

"Pulse pounding."

—*Publishers Weekly*

"Nothing short of amazing."

—David Marusek, Sturgeon Award-winning author of *The Wedding Album*

"Believable and compelling. This is the perfect eerie setting for Carlson to flex his creative muscle."

—*Bookworm Blues*

The Next Breath You Take Will Kill You

"An epic of apocalyptic fiction: Harrowing, heartfelt,
and rock-hard realistic."

—James Rollins, *New York Times*
bestselling author of *Bloodline*

"*Plague Year* is exactly the kind of no-holds-barred escapist
thriller you would hope any book with that title would be. Jeff
Carlson's gripping debut is kind of like *Blood Music* meets *The
Hot Zone*. It might also remind some readers of Stephen King's
The Stand. He keeps the action in fifth gear throughout."

—*SF Reviews.net*

"One of the best post-apocalyptic novels I've read. Part
Michael Crichton, a little Stephen King, and a lot of
good writing… Plausible and thrilling. This is a master
at work and I can't wait to read the sequel."

—*Quiet Earth* (www.quietearth.us)

About The Author

Jeff Carlson is the international bestselling author of *Plague Year* and *The Frozen Sky*. To date, his work has been translated into fifteen languages worldwide.

His next novel is apocalyptic thriller *Interrupt*, coming July 2013 from 47North.

Readers can find free fiction, videos, contests, and more on his website at www.jverse.com.

Jeff welcomes email at **jeff@jverse.com**.

He can also be found on Facebook and Twitter at **www.Facebook. com/PlagueYear** and **@authorjcarlson**.

Reader reviews on Amazon, Goodreads, and elsewhere are always appreciated.

About the Artists:

Jacob Charles Dietz (**www.jacobcharlesdietz.com**) is an art director, illustrator, and matte painter who specializes in science fiction and fantasy work for digital, film, and print. Working in both traditional and digital mediums, Jacob's work encompasses everything from future noir and science fiction to technology and the plight of man, making it very accessible to a broad audience. Bridging the gap between the now and the then, Jacob's work is constructed with layers upon layers of intricate detail and almost always includes elements of the 21st century in whatever time and place he is depicting, making the foreign seem strangely familiar.

His work has been published internationally on numerous book covers and magazines including Ballistic Publishing titles and MacWorld. Jacob's work can also be seen on limited edition tee's at Barney's New York and Fred Segal Los Angeles and can be counted as part of Steve Wozniak's personal art collection. He's done work for Virgin, Penguin Publishing, USAToday, Discovery Channel and more.

Born and raised in Seattle, Washington, Jacob now makes his home in the Sonoran desert with his wife, son, and two cats, far away from the gray skies and soggy ground of Seattle. Jacob studied visual communications at the University of Washington and has a ridiculous collection of Star Trek toys that he still manages to store at his parents' house. He dreads the day they send him a bill for years of back storage fees.

Margus Lokk is a professional artist living in Estonia. His illustrations appear frequently in publications from Fantaasia Press such as the *Täheaeg #7* anthology.

Karel Zeman lives in Jeviněves near Mělník in Central Bohemia. Trained as a mechanic of printing machinery, in the beginning he considered his artwork a hobby. At that time, he was better known as a soccer player. Today, his illustrations focus mainly on sci-fi and fantasy. He also creates caricatures of current affairs. He is an avid collector of comics. His love for ancient artifacts is reflected in his paintings and drawings in which he often depicts railways, trains and engines, especially from the era of steam power. He is interested in old books illustrated by well-known Czech artists such as Miloš Novák, Bohumil Konečný, Zdeněk Burian, and Gustav Krum. He is also interested in history, movies, and the work of Czech writer Jaroslav Foglar. He is fascinated by old Prague, especially on the paintings of Jaroslav Šetelík, Václav Jansa, and Jan Minařík. From the contemporary painters, illustrators, and cartoonists, he prefers Lubomír Kupčík, Pavel Čech, Jiří Grus, Tomáš Kučerovský and many others. Readers can find more of Zeman's work at **http://www. karelzem.cz/**